Murder
in a
Scottish
Shire

Murder
in a
Scottish
Shire

TRACI HALL

KENSINGTON BOOKS
www.kensingtonbooks.com

KENSINGTON BOOKS are published by

Kensington Publishing Corp.
119 West 40th Street
New York, NY 10018

All Kensington titles, imprints, and distributed lines are available at special quantity discounts for bulk purchases for sales promotion, premiums, fundraising, educational, or institutional use.

Special book excerpts or customized printings can also be created to fit specific needs. For details, write or phone the office of the Kensington Sales Manager: Kensington Publishing Corp., 119 West 40th Street, New York, NY 10018. Attn. Sales Department. Phone: 1-800-221-2647.

Kensington and the K logo Reg. U.S. Pat. & TM Off.

ISBN-13: 978-1-4967-2600-1 (ebook)
ISBN-10: 1-4967-2600-6 (ebook)

ISBN-13: 978-1-4967-2599-8
ISBN-10: 1-4967-2599-9
First Kensington Trade Paperback Printing: July 2020

10 9 8 7 6 5 4 3 2 1

Printed in the United States of America

To Christopher, for climbing the mountain with me.

And to Judi, Brighton, Destini, and Kennedi—can't say
enough how much I love my family.

Acknowledgments

Thank you to the McGavin family for acting out the ending of the original version to show me a better way. I wish I could have been a fly on the wall. ☺ You're lucky the neighbors didn't call the cops.

Thank you to Allan Thornton for all of your incredible assistance in adding local authenticity. Any mistakes are my own! Your generosity and time allowed this book to flourish.

Thank you also to my editor, John Scognamiglio, for this opportunity to tell my stories. And always to Evan Marshall, who transformed my career.

Chapter 1

Nairn, Scotland
United Kingdom

Paislee Shaw eyed the clock above the cooker as if Father Time were her mortal enemy. Half past eight *already*? She whirled to her son, just finishing breakfast at the round kitchen table, and caught him sneaking bits of sausage to the dog.

"Brody, if ye give Wallace one more bite it'll be oatmeal tomorrow!"

Their black Scottish terrier lowered his ears even as he licked his whiskers and plopped down on the braided rag rug beneath Brody's chair.

"Mum!"

Paislee wiped her hands on a cotton dishcloth and glared at her ten-year-old. "Tell me why I should take the time to make a special breakfast, then? Ye could have had a bowl of cereal and we'd both be happy." And not running late. Her own fault, because she couldn't leave the dishes until later like a sane single mother, short on time and long on responsibilities.

"Sairy," Brody mumbled, dark auburn hair falling over a pale forehead. He was growing again, all teeth and gangly limbs as he propped bony elbows on the worn-smooth wooden surface.

If Paislee knew one thing, it was that her son detested oatmeal. She'd added brown sugar, sweet cream, orange currants—nothing swayed him. Most mornings they had Weetabix and blueberries, but since it was Monday and neither wanted their Sunday to be over, she'd made eggs, Lorne sausage, and toast. And the minute she wasn't paying attention, the little imp fed Wallace on the sly.

Brody brought his empty plate to the sink, and she brushed off the crumbs, then dunked it in the soapy water. Modern appliances were what she dreamed about at night—there was nothing that sent her to a sweeter sleep than imagining a stainless-steel dishwasher and matching refrigerator. She rinsed the dish in the white double sink and put it in the dish rack on the laminated counter.

"Quick! Go brush your teeth and get your books for school. We have tae stop at the shop before I drop ye off."

She didn't wait to hear an argument as he stomped toward the downstairs bathroom but climbed the stairs to her bedroom for her cardigan. The third and fifth steps creaked, but such things were to be expected in a one-hundred-year-old house.

Two bedrooms upstairs, and a bathroom, for her and Brody. Gran's suite of two rooms, mostly storage since Gran had died, a kitchen, living room, and covered back porch that led to a long and narrow garden for Wallace to chase squirrels.

The old sweet chestnut and wild cherry trees provided nuts and berries for birds and squirrels alike—sometimes leaving enough for her to make jam. She told herself that if things got too tight, she could clean the bottom bedroom and rent it out during the three summer months when tourism in Nairn was at its peak.

Grabbing the sweater off the back of her dressing room chair, Paislee dared a peek into the mirror. She groaned, glanced at her watch, and knew she didn't have time for more than a slash of lip gloss. "Pale as moonlight," her da used to tease; her face had nary a freckle to add color. Sky-blue eyes with auburn lashes and auburn hair that was so thin she was happiest with it up in a messy bun for the illusion of body. She applied the gloss as she ran down the stairs, pocketing the tube.

"Ready, Brody?" Her yarn order was supposed to arrive at nine on the dot and she'd promised to unlock the back door for Jerry, in case he arrived while she was dropping her son off at school. Even in heavy traffic, the two miles round trip should be no more than ten minutes. She hoped Isla, a very part-time rehire, could start right away and mornings wouldn't be such a chore. They had an interview today at nine thirty.

Miracle of all miracles, her son had his jacket and runners on and was waiting by the door. "Have yer lunch?"

He smacked his forehead and ran to the kitchen for his cheese sandwich.

She expected a full morning of crafters at Cashmere Crush and had promised to help Mary Beth with the fancy soft pink hem around her blanket whose wool Paislee'd special ordered from Jerry. A christening gift for a wee baby girl. Aye, babies were adorable, but she was glad that her son was now able to brush his own hair, usually. Reaching for his head, she smoothed a defiant lock.

"I know, I know, ye cannae take one more thing." Brody stuck out his lower lip and shrugged away from her touch.

She hated getting her own words tossed back at her. "Bein' smart, are we?"

He grinned and she ushered him out the door and into the faded silver Nissan Juke. A carport protected her eight-year-old vehicle from the elements—usually rain, and lots of it, though compared to the rest of Scotland, Nairn had the driest weather with the most sunshine, something the Earl of Cawdor had been using in his slogans to repopulate the town and create prosperity for all.

They drove the mile to Cashmere Crush, her specialty sweaters and yarn shop on Market Street—hers was on the end of a long row of single-story brick businesses the length of a block. Market Street was a main thoroughfare in front, and the road was separated from the shops by a narrow, uneven sidewalk.

Seaside scents and gulls' caws rode the winds from the marina. In the back was a proper alley big enough for the delivery trucks, and across Market a row of two-story businesses in old stone. Behind the alley, she was back-to-back with a string of restaurants.

Her favorite restaurant across the alley was the Chinese one because she liked the fortune cookies. She and her granny used to make up funny fortunes that had them in stitches, and now she and Brody carried on the tradition—the sillier the better, like, *the fortune you seek is another cookie.*

"Brody, how do ye feel about chicken lo mein tonight for supper?"

"Aye! And orange beef?"

She nodded, her taste buds watering as she justified the expense with a full day ahead at the shop, which meant money in the register. Making a left on Hammond, she thought back to when she'd moved in with her granny, grateful for her insistence that Paislee could make it as a very young single parent—the belief that she owed nobody an explanation and had to hold her head high.

After her da had died, before her graduation from S6 at the age of seventeen—back when she'd still considered going to university—her mum had gone mental and married an American within the year just to get as far away from her grief as possible.

Paislee, grieving herself, had given up on ideas of college and moved in with her granny, who'd taught her to knit sweaters, sharing family patterns with pride. Somehow, ten years later,

Paislee had managed to keep her and Brody fed—not smoked salmon or Aberdeen Angus, but they didn't starve.

She'd been raised on stories of a big family, with aunts and uncles and cousins, but she'd grown up an only child and after her da's death and her mum's desertion—who fled the country, for mercy's sake?—Granny had taken her in without judgment, showing unconditional love as Paislee was forced to navigate adulthood.

With a sniff of sorrow for her granny, Paislee parked her Juke behind Cashmere Crush to unlock the back door for Jerry's delivery of local yarn, specifically, the light pink for Mary Beth's blanket. "I'll be right back," she said to Brody, who ignored her and jumped out of the passenger side.

"Ye always say so, but . . ." Brody followed behind her, his sneakers scuffing the rough pavement. "Somethin' happens. I can't be late again. Mrs. Martin doesnae like it."

"I'll hurry." After receiving Isla's email last Sunday asking for her job back, Paislee had crunched numbers. Things were tight, but she could just manage fifteen hours a week and prayed that Isla would accept, because tourist season started at the end of April.

They entered through the back door of the shop, and Paislee flipped up the light switch just inside the storage area. The bulb above flickered, flared, and then fizzled. Did she even have a spare?

Brody giggled nervously in the dim interior. The store was a long rectangular shape less than eight hundred square feet and any natural morning light was blocked by the buildings across Market.

She carefully maneuvered around the crates, armchair, oval table, and small television she'd set up for Brody when he had to be at work with her to the switch for the overhead lights but then stopped, her gaze drawn to the shadowy entrance. Her heart hammered in her chest and she reached for Brody as she made out two silhouettes peering through the frosted glass of her front window.

"What?" he said, sliding free to walk around her to the register where she kept a jar of candy.

"Stop—they'll see you."

He froze like a squirrel targeted by Wallace in the garden. "We don't have time tae open, Mum."

"I know!" But she hated to turn away business. Too late—they'd been spotted. A light tap sounded against the frosted pane.

And now she didn't feel comfortable leaving the back door open for Jerry, either. What if the strangers decided to find another way in?

Two of her ladies were due in this morning and they sometimes came early for tea and a blether. Could this be them? Not with those shoulders—not even Mary Beth at two hundred pounds.

Torn, Paislee slowly stepped to the door. Maybe if she explained that they didn't open until half past nine, the two would come back . . . but she had a wild feeling in the pit of her belly that warned against a warm welcome.

Granny's gift of premonitions hadn't been handed down with the knack for knitting—this was something else. Fight or flight. She rubbed the goose bumps on her nape.

One shadow straightened and, moving to the door, pounded a heavy fist. The brass knob shook.

"Open up!" a man called.

"Mum." Brody was suddenly at her side. "I don't think that's Jerry."

"No. He'd use the back door."

"Mibbe we should wait for him?"

Was she transferring her anxiety to her child? *Get ahold of yourself, Paislee Shaw.* With a heft of her chin, she smiled confidently. "I'm sure it's nothing."

Another firm knock sounded.

Taking a deep breath, she pulled the bolt and opened the door. A square-jawed gentleman with cool green eyes, shiny black shoes, and a Police Scotland rain jacket stood on the threshold next to an older man, seventy-ish, in a long tweed trench coat and with a dark green Tam-o'-shanter on his head.

The older man had dark glasses, a silver beard, and a brown suitcase.

Her breath caught. The last time a police officer had been at her door her da had died in a boating accident.

Brody stuck to her hip like a burr.

The officer smiled down at her son, then looked at her with mild reproof, as if reminding her of her manners. "May we come in?"

"Aye, of course." She widened the door and then sucked at her teeth as she studied the older man.

It couldn't be.

"I'm Detective Inspector Mack Zeffer," the officer said. "I found this gentleman down at the park, sleeping on a bench. He says ye're his only family." He escorted the man in by the elbow.

"Grandpa Angus?" She'd seen him at Granny's funeral five years ago. He lived with his son in Dairlee . . . or so she'd thought.

"You recognize him, lass?" The officer's tone held more than a hint of relief.

"Aye."

"Yer my grandpa?" Brody asked with a welcoming smile. Were they that starved for family that Brody had no reservations? The man hadn't bothered to come around for years.

"*Great*-grandfather," he corrected. The words were sharp and Brody lost his exuberance.

She pulled her son back to her side.

The clock tower chimed from the center of town, and she

bowed her head as Brody pulled her cardigan. Nine on the dot. They were late. Again. "I have to go. . . ."

"All right, then, I'll leave ye tae it," the detective said as he headed for the door.

Grandpa Angus stayed put. "Wait—what do you mean?" Panic rose.

Detective Inspector Zeffer halted by a chest-high work-table stacked with pattern books and looked from the suitcase at her grandfather's feet to Paislee. Zeffer's russet hair, groomed into place, didn't budge. "*You* are his only kin. He cannae go on sleeping in the park."

Paislee shook her head. "I don't understand."

"I have nowhere else tae go." Grandpa Shaw crossed his arms as if she were being purposefully dense.

A knock sounded on the back door and Jerry marched in. "Mornin', lass. I've a wee bit of bad news—the pink yarn isnae ready yet." Jerry McFadden joined them with a clomp of work boots and the scent of fresh spring air. He stopped at the counter separating the front of the shop from the supplies and nodded with chagrin at the police officer and her grandfather, then Brody. "Sairy—I thought ye'd be alone. Is everything all right?"

"Fine," Paislee said automatically. "When will it be in?"

Jerry scrubbed his hand along his jaw. "Tomorrow, first thing. The dyeing machine broke, but it's fixed now."

She inhaled, clenched her fingers, and counted to five for patience. Mary Beth needed the pink yarn to finish the chris-tening blanket—and to be billed. No yarn, no blanket, no money, no lo mein. Losing her temper was not an option. As a single mum, she had to set a proper example.

The front door swung open with a clatter, and in walked her landlord.

"Mr. Marcus?" The owner of the building was a man in his

mid-fifties who'd rarely made an appearance in the last year due to ill health. She and the others in their brick row had worried aloud what might happen to their prized leases and Paislee was not the only business owner to say prayers of gratitude when Mr. Marcus had miraculously rallied, as evidenced by his brown comb-over and plump cheeks.

"How're ye the day?" Glancing at her company, Mr. Marcus cleared his throat and handed her a letter with a green certification stamped on the front. "Ye can open it later, but it is time sensitive."

Paislee frowned at the nervous gentleman. His skin wasn't Scots pale but had an orange tint. A spray tan? Using her thumbnail, she lifted the adhesive and pulled out a sheet of paper on a solicitor's letterhead.

She reeled backward as the black type swam before her eyes. Her grandfather steadied her elbow. "What is it, lass?"

"An eviction notice? But my lease is good for another year!" And she'd hoped to keep renewing until she could buy her own shop.

"Which is void on point of sale." Mr. Marcus realized that Paislee was not taking the news well, and backed up, quickly wiping the smile from his face.

"How long?" Jerry asked in a threatening growl that made the detective look at him with warning.

"Thirty days," Paislee managed. Her stomach clenched and the shop tilted. Cashmere Crush was her livelihood. She'd poured her life into it to create something for her and Brody to survive.

"Now, Ms. Shaw, I'm sure ye'll find another place tae lease." Mr. Marcus took a step toward the door.

Her temper flared at the tone of his condescending words. She forced herself to sound calm. "Will the new owner be willing tae consider the previous tenants?"

Mr. Marcus waved his hand, the flash of a gold ring catching the light from the window. "Doubtful—they'll be tearing down these old bricks tae make a boutique hotel."

Paislee cursed aloud.

Brody handed her his toffee with a disappointed look on his sweet face. "Ah, Mum, that's fifty pence for the swear jar."

Chapter 2

Paislee stood in the middle of Cashmere Crush, reeling from all directions. She eyed the men around her and ground her teeth together. Shawn Marcus retreated two steps closer to the front door.

"Wait just a"—she glanced at her wide-eyed son—"a blasted minute. Have you talked tae the others yet?" She gestured to her left and the shared wall with her neighbor James, who owned the leather repair shop. She'd lined both long walls with shelves for vibrantly colored yarn and it brightened the interior, even without the overhead lights on.

"You were the last stop," Mr. Marcus said. "But the only one tae actually open yer letter." His mouth turned down in disapproval, as if by reading his notice she'd been impolite.

Detective Inspector Zeffer wore the slightest frown as he observed them, his hands folded before him.

Brody tugged on her sweater. "Mum! We have tae go."

"Where?" the detective asked.

"School." Brody crossed his arms. "We are *always* late."

"Not always," Paislee said, her face on fire as all four of the men looked to her with judgment. Really?

They had no idea what it was like to raise a son *and* run a business *and* a home.

And if she lost this location for Cashmere Crush? She'd lose the eight years she'd spent building up her clientele; the loyal group of crafters were now like family.

"If ye want, I can drop him off," Jerry offered from behind her. "I only have two more stops tae make."

"Naw, I can do it," Paislee said, feeling the pressure. "I'll need you all tae go now, though." She shooed the detective and her landlord toward the door.

Her grandpa adjusted his tam, but his brown boots didn't move. What on this green earth was she supposed to do about him?

Jerry made for the back door and called out his good-bye, apologizing about the yarn.

She lifted her hand, but the yarn had moved to the last worry on her list. "Tomorrow, then, Jerry. Cheers."

Mr. Marcus shuffled awkwardly before just ducking out. What could the man possibly have to say that she would want to hear? Thirty days to be gone?

Detective Inspector Zeffer hesitated, his hand on the tabletop. She could feel his need to fix whatever had just happened, but since no crime had been committed his services weren't needed. He squared his shoulders and followed her landlord out. Paislee didn't bother saying good-bye—she had no words for the havoc those two men had just created in her life.

No lease, and a new responsibility.

"You'll have tae come with us," she told Grandpa Angus.

He didn't argue but didn't agree; he just picked up his suitcase.

She locked the door and herded Brody and Grandpa Angus to where she'd parked the Juke behind the store.

Brody eyed her grandfather before offering the old stranger the front seat, which the man refused, to Brody's relief.

She gave her son a nod of approval at the show of good manners, and they drove the mile to Fordythe, a single-story brick building that was very long, with central double doors that had been painted blue. A fenced lawn was to the left for the bairns to play on. She followed the paved drive where parents could drop off their children in the morning and then pick them up again at three thirty—normally there were two attendants and the teachers took turns to supervise.

The last attendant was just going inside and Brody dashed out without so much as a see-you, his black backpack over his arm.

"He only has one more year of primary school," she shared, her voice thick.

Her grandfather played mute.

What was she supposed to do with him? She couldn't take Grandpa Angus back to her house; she didn't know him from Adam. Her home was dear to her, and while she didn't have an abundance of new things, she treasured what she had.

What if he took off with the telly?

"Could you please sit up here so I dinnae feel like a cabby?"

With a grunt, Grandpa Angus opened the rear passenger door and climbed into the front passenger side. He stared straight ahead, his jaw hidden behind a full silver beard.

He smelled of the sea and she was reminded sharply that while things for her had been tight, for him they'd been worse.

"Would ye like tae get a bite tae eat?" When was the last time he'd eaten?

He didn't reply.

The digital clock on the car radio read 9:15. "I have customers in this morning." *And Isla, drat.* "I'll pick up some breakfast sandwiches from the market, and coffee—it's a coffee kind of day; then we'll go tae Cashmere Crush."

He still said nothing.

"I cannae help, if you don't talk tae me." She wanted to keep him off the streets, aye, but what could she do?

"I dinnae want yer help. Just let me oot somewhere."

"And have the detective bring ye back?" Her voice pitched high. "He knows who ye belong tae now."

"Dinnae fesh yerself." He removed his tam and focused out the window at the passing businesses in stone or brick. Nairn had once been a popular fishing village.

"Don't worry? Really?" That would be impossible now that she was aware he was in trouble. "Where's Craigh?"

He said not a word.

Paislee drove the half mile to the small market near her shop. She could practically hear the wheels in his silver head churn. She had no time for more drama, but it seemed impossible to avoid today.

Paislee parked and faced her grandpa. Her memories of him were vague, and colored by Granny's refusal to discuss him. She'd never outright disparaged him—but the mutterings whenever his name arose were enough for Paislee to realize he was not a welcome subject.

The last time she'd seen him had been at Granny's funeral, and Paislee had been such a mess that she could hardly recall the proceedings. Granny had been sick for months before she'd passed. Father Dixon had managed things, thank heaven.

Paislee's grandmother had not once asked to see her husband before she'd died. And why was that?

In a final act of love, Gran had bequeathed her home to Paislee, saying that nobody should fear being without a roof over their head, not if she could help it.

This couldnae be what ye meant, Gran.

Grandpa Angus finally looked at her. Clear brown eyes behind black glasses, silver hair and beard, deep wrinkles of a hard life furrowed his cheeks and brow.

"You can come in with me, and choose for yourself, or wait here and I'll be right back with two bacon butties and coffee. Aye?"

He nodded his thanks and stayed in the car.

Paislee kept her keys and cardigan as she ran inside the small market. It had odds and ends that a tourist might need—travel-sized shampoo, toothbrush and toothpaste, razors. Would her grandfather need any of those things?

Where the devil was Craigh?

She stepped up to the register and smiled at Colleen, fresh faced at twenty. Paislee would kill for the girl's boundless energy.

"Mornin'. Two bacon butties, two coffees."

"Hiya, Paislee," Colleen said, bouncing behind the counter as she gathered and rang up Paislee's order. The smell of the bacon made her mouth water, despite already having had a bit of breakfast earlier with Brody.

Colleen handed her the bag and two coffees in a cardboard box.

"Thanks!"

Colleen grinned and greeted the next customer in the queue.

Paislee took the goodies back to the Juke, apprehensive that maybe her grandpa had made a dash for it while she was gone.

Where would he go?

It was obvious that if he was sleeping in the park in cool spring his options were limited.

She breathed a sigh of relief when she saw the outline of his hat now back on his head and the glint of silver at his beard.

He didn't offer a smile, though he did reach across the inside of the car to open her door for her.

She climbed in and handed him the coffees first, then the bag.

"I hope you're hungry. These are huge."

He gave a nod and swallowed hard, his fingers trembling on the cardboard tray for the hot coffee.

She averted her eyes before she said something to offend his pride.

There weren't many cars on the back roads and she made it in five minutes to Cashmere Crush, where she parked in the alley.

"Would you like tae keep your suitcase in the car?"

He shook his head and got out of the Juke, balancing the coffee and his suitcase as she grabbed the bag of food.

When faced with any dilemma, Granny would put the kettle on for hot water and Brodies Scottish-blend tea, then warm the scones. They'd had so many life discussions at the kitchen table, overlooking the back garden. The biggest was when Paislee had arrived on the doorstep with her own suitcase at eighteen, and pregnant.

"Mind the step," she said, holding the back door open for Grandpa Angus. "I *know* the ledge is there, and I still trip over it."

He peered down and lifted his foot.

Once they were inside, the interior of the shop was dark— she'd have to replace the bulb for the storage area—and she quickly flicked on the overhead lighting.

A rush of pleasure, something she never took for granted, washed through her as the lights showcased her shop.

Paislee had separated the interior with floor-to-ceiling shelves that acted as room dividers, leaving the majority of the room open. Shelves lined both long walls toward the street and were filled with a variety of yarn.

Sweaters and knit goods were kept on a display by the front window. She brought out foldable worktables as needed, depending on the group. Her weekly Thursday night Knit and Sip event was very popular. Her floor was polished cement.

Cashmere Crush had been her home away from home for eight years. How dare Shawn Marcus sell it from underneath her like this? She pressed her hand to her stomach to stop it from rolling.

Grandpa set the tray of coffee on the counter next to the register that also had a cup of odds and ends pens, pencils, and crochet hooks. She put the bag of food next to the store laptop and took a subtle sniff as he passed her. The old man had an outdoor scent—trees, grass, the Firth—but he was fairly clean. How long had he been without shelter?

He shuffled toward a chair and sank down. She'd found eight sturdy high-backed wooden seats at an estate sale and nabbed them, giving them a coat of varnish to make them seem new, and a half-dozen assorted stools for the chest-high worktables.

She glanced at her watch. "I have a girl coming in for an interview at half past." Ten minutes. What could possibly be decided in ten minutes? Nothing—he had bags under his eyes, which meant he probably needed rest, not twenty questions fired at him. "A few crafters will be in tae finish some projects."

"I'll stay oot of yer way," he said in a low voice. His gaze flicked to the bag, but he didn't reach for the food.

She imagined herself in his place and flashed a smile, doling out the bacon sandwiches. "Cheap but good—they pile the bacon on thick. Comes with brown sauce, though; you have tae ask for ketchup if that's your preference."

"Brown sauce and butter is how I make mine at home," he

said, unwrapping the sandwich from the foil and eyeing it with a nod. "Plain white bread. Tasty."

Paislee liked the simple version best, too. "I ordered one of these down at the harbor café and they served it on toasted artisan bread, and added fried bananas."

"Spoilt it, then." Grandpa removed his tam and set it on the floor, then bit into the sandwich. His eyes closed as he savored the food. She admired his self-restraint as he took his time, wiping his mouth and beard between bites. He must have been starved.

She took the top off his coffee and handed it over. "Cream? Sugar?"

"Aye, both—I'll do it."

She checked the time again, seeing it was twenty-five minutes past. With brutal clarity she realized that there was no way she could hire Isla now. Not only did she have to move, but her grandfather would need whatever extra money she could scrape up.

She would have to tell Isla that she couldn't offer her any work at all, and that wasn't something she was eager to do. "So, where has Craigh got off tae?"

He focused on the sugar packet. "Missing."

"What?"

"Aye. I've told the authorities. They're lookin' into it, but havenae helped."

Paislee shook her head. "I don't understand."

"He went two months ago tae work on the *Mona*, an oil rig far out in the North Sea." Grandpa poured sugar into his dark coffee. "I know from past jobs that they dinnae always have phone or internet access, but he got in touch when he could. It's lonely work. There was a bonus tae be paid for doing a four-month stretch before taking the helicopter home tae Aberdeen."

"Aberdeen?"

"Aye. This was a new company and the money was enough so Craigh could retire in two years. He planned tae rent a car tae drive tae our flat in Dairlee."

Dairlee was eight miles from Nairn, and Aberdeen less than two hours away.

His voice became hoarse. "I wasnae alarmed until I realized that no money had come in tae the account he'd set up fer the expenses of the flat rental. I called the *Mona*." His body trembled. "They said Craigh Shaw never worked on that rig."

"That cannae be possible. Perhaps ye made a mistake about the name, being as it was new?"

Her grandfather's face turned ruddy with anger. "Now ye sound like the authorities. I'm a dotty old man makin' things up. Not so." He used a wooden stick to stir his coffee while adding powdered creamer.

Paislee thought he seemed sane enough to her. She gestured toward his square brown suitcase, so old-fashioned it didn't have wheels. "What happened?"

"Booted from our flat two weeks ago, having used up our savings. Craigh's accounts were empty." His cheeks flushed as if ashamed. "I get a little pension from when I'd worked at the fishery before me back injury, but it isnae enough tae pay for me own place."

"Why didnae you come tae me straightaway?"

He peeked at her before sipping his coffee. "You dinnae know me. I doubt what ye've heard is anything tae convince ye tae help me."

He had a point.

"Let me try tae call what numbers you have for Craigh later today."

He scowled. "The answer willnae be any different, but yer welcome tae waste yer time."

The immediate problem so far as Paislee could tell was where Grandpa was going to rest his head for the night. Paislee didn't have the cash to set him up in a hotel somewhere.

"There has tae be an agency we can contact about finding you a place tae live, or benefits so that ye don't have tae sleep in the park. What was yer plan?"

"I'll buy a tent and camp, once the campground is open for summer. I've got tae find out what happened tae Craigh. The library will have internet and phone service. I showered at the park."

Brr. Two weeks of sleeping outdoors already? It couldn't have been comfortable, and whether she knew her grandfather or not, they were still family. "Spring nights are cold—June is three months off." Maybe the old man *was* a wee bit mental.

Nine thirty. Her shoulders bowed. Isla would be here any minute, thinking she'd have at least a part-time job, but with the eviction and Grandpa, Paislee couldn't hire her at all.

"I didnae ask yer opinion, lass."

She bit her tongue and looked at her phone, then the front door, expecting to see Isla's smiling face any second.

Now twenty-two, Isla had come from Edinburgh at twenty, a bonny blonde who'd fallen for the wrong guy. He'd brought her to Nairn for a romantic weekend and then they'd broken up after a big fight. Cheery-natured but brash, Isla had walked in and asked for a job—she'd take anything, she said, and do anything, but she couldn't go crawling back to Edinburgh after the bum. She'd averted her face, but Paislee had glimpsed the tremble of her lower lip.

In the flush of tourist season, Paislee had hired her on the spot. She'd seen herself in the young woman trying to make her way. Isla had worked at Cashmere Crush until a few months ago when she'd moved to Inverness to be with her new boyfriend, Billy, in a bigger city.

Paislee had written Isla a glowing recommendation, happy to help her protégée find happiness and full-time employment. It had been an adjustment doing everything herself again, but the winter months were slower, so Paislee had been able to handle the shop on her own.

And now Isla was back in Nairn, and asking for her old position back. What had happened? It would be good to see her and catch up, though she knew it would be a blow for Isla to not work with Paislee. But how could she justify the hours, especially now that she might have another mouth to feed?

Grandpa wadded up a paper napkin and kept it in his palm. "Why do you keep looking at yer phone?"

"I told you that I have an appointment at nine thirty—I was going tae hire someone part-time."

He shifted in his chair. "Yer hiring?"

"Isla used tae work here, so when I got her email saying that she was back in town, I thought it a blessing—with tourist season, the timing was right."

Grandpa scratched his full beard and peered at her over the top of his black frames. "Now?"

Paislee lifted her shoulders and let them drop. "Now, thanks tae that rotter Shawn Marcus, I'll lose Cashmere Crush, and cannae hire anybody."

"Can't ye move?"

"Aye—but with what cash? This location is key tae foot traffic"—she gestured to her left and the Moray Firth inlet— "being close tae the beach, and downtown."

"What of yer savings?"

Paislee rolled her eyes. "Wiped out by the water pipe bursting like a ripe watermelon, and getting new tires on the Juke."

"Ah." He tapped his short nails on the table. "Life kicks ye when ye're down, don't I know it. It's a sair fecht for half a loaf."

"Da said that sometimes." A hard fight for half of what you wanted. He must've heard it from her grandfather. Da, Grandpa, and Brody all shared brown eyes. Family. She exhaled and offered him her other half of the bacon butty. "I already ate breakfast." Eggs churned in her tummy. "Take it, if you like."

He only accepted after checking her face to see if she was feeling sorry for him. She stood, patted her stomach, and took the lid off her coffee. She added cream and stirred before taking a cautious drink. Though the brew was a nice treat every once in a while, she preferred tea.

She washed her hands in the small bathroom at the rear of the shop. "You can sit back here and watch the telly, so long as the sound is low. Let's put our heads together and see what we can come up with. Sleeping in the park isnae an option. Is this all ye have?" She pointed to his suitcase.

"I pay a wee bit for a storage unit where I put Craigh's things. I slept there a few nights, but it isnae big enough. And they have guards."

Paislee's brain circled round the ugly truth, accepting that there was really only one awful solution. "You can stay with me for a while, until we figure your situation out."

"I willnae be a charity case," he announced, emanating pride in his wrinkled chambray shirt and khakis.

"Oh, it willnae be charity," Paislee quickly assured him. She'd prayed for a miracle, but this was not the miracle she'd had in mind. She felt like the butt of a cosmic joke.

His long fingers gave his beard another scratch. "Eh?"

"I could use some help in the shop." She studied him closely, searching for the truth in a man she didn't know. "Can ye drive?"

"Aye." His bearded mouth turned down.

"Where's your car?"

"Didnae need one in Dairlee. I walked where I needed tae go."

Hmm. "I think we can come tae an agreement."

"I willnae be free labor, lassie."

Couldn't he see she was going to help him? "You'll be working for room and board." Paislee crossed her arms and dared him to argue. "We'll have tae clean out Granny's room downstairs, but we can make do."

Her sweet gran was probably rolling over in her grave.

Chapter 3

At quarter to ten, the door to Cashmere Crush swung open. Paislee had put in two calls to Isla, who hadn't answered. Grandpa was in the back with the television on low.

Instead of the blond Isla, Mary Beth Mulholland ambled in, somehow graceful despite her heavy weight. Forty, with twin daughters in primary school, Mary Beth had been coming to Paislee for her yarn supplies since her shop first opened eight years ago.

Dark brown hair, cornflower-blue eyes, and pink cheeks gave Mary Beth a natural prettiness. She smiled wide as she came into the shop and set her purse on the chest-high table. Stools were packed around the rectangle, yet she preferred one of the wider padded wooden chairs.

"Good morning, Paislee!" Mary Beth rubbed her plump hands together, the large diamond on her wedding ring a crystalline flash. "I ran oot of me pink yarn for the blanket Friday, and I've been waiting all weekend for more. I was so anxious that Arran practically pushed me oot the door this morning."

Paislee's shoulders slumped. "I'm so sairy, Mary Beth. Jerry was in first thing and said it will be here tomorrow. The dyeing machine broke."

Mary Beth gasped.

"But is fixed now." Paislee lifted her hands at her sides to calm her customer down.

"The christening is Sunday," Mary Beth said, her tone rising.

Paislee tapped the long calendar she kept on the wall behind the register. "I know it. I'll help if you fall behind."

Mary Beth sighed. "I changed the pattern and this is a continuous bubble stich that cannae be pieced together, but I appreciate yer offer."

Paislee couldn't feel worse.

Through the frosted window, the blurry image of a white Volvo pulled up in the front. She recognized Flora Robertson, who tended to dress in bright colors and long, gauzy skirts or dresses.

"Hang on, Mary Beth." Paislee hurried to open the door as Flora brought in a crate of gorgeous vibrant emerald yarn. "Morning, Flora. What a terrific surprise!" Paislee hadn't been expecting Flora, but it was a treat when yarn arrived.

"Morning!" Mary Beth seconded as she peered inside the open box on the counter by the register. "That's so pretty, Flora."

Grandpa Angus peeked from behind the divider but stayed out of sight. His pride in accepting a breakfast sarnie eased Paislee's worries that he'd steal from her. He was paying for a storage unit for his son's things yet sleeping in the park, and he'd been embarrassed about being evicted from their flat. She would give him a chance, but he'd have to get over any shyness if he was to be of help to her in the shop.

Ach, she'd think about it later.

"Thank ye," Flora said, pleased. "I was oot runnin' errands and thought I'd bring this by."

The craftswoman was in her late thirties and managed to use all-natural dyes to color her yarn, as opposed to synthetics. Paislee was thrilled to sell them in her shop. Flora usually had a flower of some sort tucked in her long light brown hair and would have fit right in during the olden days when Nairn was a shire.

"We sold out of this color," Paislee said to Mary Beth, who knew Flora from their Knit and Sip nights.

"I'm not surprised!" Mary Beth said. "It's bright as a shamrock."

"When will the yellow be ready, Flora?" Paislee asked. "I saw daisies in a pattern book I'd like tae try."

"This week sometime." Flora tucked her car keys into the pocket of her skirt, fidgety as if she'd had too much tea. "I'm just waiting for the chrome tae set."

"And the sage—I'd like another twenty-four skeins." Paislee hoped she wasn't making a mistake buying the yarn, but in order to stay in business she had to have supplies. Selling and using local goods was her trademark at Cashmere Crush.

"Thank ye, lass. I'm on it." Flora turned to Mary Beth, her long hem sweeping the floor. "How's the christening blanket comin' along?"

Paislee put the box of yarn behind the counter. She didn't have the heart to tell the ladies yet about being evicted. What if this was the last order she was able to make for Flora's yarn?

"Stalled," Paislee interjected before Mary Beth could say anything. "The machine broke—the yarn will be here tomorrow."

"Oh no!" Flora said. "You know, I'd be happy tae make ye that color, if you'd like? I'm sure I can match the pink, with a few tries."

"That's all right." Mary Beth pleaded with Paislee, "I can wait a day—but no more?"

Paislee held up her hand. "Jerry promised. He was verra sorry about it—he knows that ye need it for the christening party."

In the knitting industry there were folks who believed that all-natural dyeing was the way to go, and Flora could often be seen around the local countryside gathering mushrooms and wildflowers in her basket.

Mary Beth believed that the "all-natural" ingredients were just as dangerous to the land as the synthetic dyes, only the synthetic companies had to follow proper disposal laws while the naturalists could do what they pleased and contaminate the rivers and seas if they weren't careful.

There had been many a heated argument during their Thursday nights with good-natured Mary Beth losing her temper, not at Flora, who used proper sanitation, but those who refused to take care of the earth.

This was often brought on after a glass or two of whisky—so none of the ladies took offense. In Paislee's opinion, there was room in the knitting community for both synthetic and natural. She'd learned firsthand that it was difficult to hold a bright color with natural dyes without the right fixing agent, which could be dangerous. Some were just as poisonous as the natural ingredients. Flora's skill with the mordants had a lot to do with their online success.

"Thank ye, though," Mary Beth told Flora, regarding the pink yarn. "How's Donnan?"

Flora exhaled and, arms empty, pushed her hair back over her shoulder, baring the miniature blue blossom above her ear. "Every day a wee bit better," she said. "I hope tae bring him tae the street fair this Saturday tae help me mind the booth."

Her husband had suffered a stroke two months prior and Flora had been managing their online yarn business as well as his health. Marriage was for better or worse, and Paislee wasn't the only one to feel sorry for Flora, who had been dealt a harsh hand—Donnan wasn't even forty.

Mary Beth admired the emerald yarn. "I just cannae believe ye can make such striking colors. What did you use for this again, Flora?"

"Scots broom, mostly."

"For that weed tae create such a green boggles the mind. What would you use for my pretty pink?"

Flora narrowed her eyes and tapped her lower lip. "Pink rose petals, mixed with . . ." She thought for a moment, "Purple lavender?"

"Oh!" Mary Beth considered this. "It wouldnae fade?"

"Could be set with lemon juice, if that's what yer worried about. But it will lighten after a few washings," Flora admitted. "It's why I prefer the chrome, which I know ye don't like."

"Well, they are pretty, Flora. You have a braw talent for creating color." Mary Beth returned to her seat.

Flora grinned. "Thank ye. I'll tell Donnan that you like his recipe. Mine was the sage."

"It'll be good tae see him," Paislee said. She felt a pang of guilt for only visiting once when he'd been in the hospital. How did time pass so fast?

"Speaking of," Flora said, "I should get going. I hate tae leave him too long. See you Thursday, lasses!" She hustled out the door like a flower garden on the run.

Mary Beth left soon after, her step a bit heavier than when she'd arrived. Paislee didn't blame Jerry—things happened— but she would do her best to make sure that Mary Beth's blanket was completed on time.

The rest of the morning passed quickly with Paislee's mostly female client base in to buy yarn for projects from blankets to sweaters to socks—the "men" were usually under five and dragged in by their mums. She'd even sold a cardigan to a woman visiting from London. Grandpa had changed the light-bulb for her.

She poked her head behind the partition to see how her grandfather was doing only to find him sound asleep, stretched out on a long storage crate he'd piled with homemade blankets, emitting soft snores that pierced her defenses.

How would Brody get along with Angus?

Her son's well-being mattered above all else, so they would try for tonight and see how they managed.

The shop phone rang and she jumped to answer it. Not Isla finally returning her calls, but a woman with a question on a particular knitting needle size.

By one, the shop had emptied and Paislee'd worried herself sick over not speaking with Isla regarding a job. What had happened to the girl? What if the full-time position had been too much for Isla, who had shared with Paislee under oath that she never told a soul that she had a heart condition? Paislee wanted to see her in person and make sure the lass was fine.

Opening the email from Isla, Paislee reread the messages to make sure she hadn't misunderstood: *Hey, Paislee—it's Isla, back in town and staying at Harborside Flats. Have a new venture in discount yarn, if yer interested? I know ye can't hire me for many hours, but I'll take what ye have. I need the work. I miss you! Life has been off the rails. Number is the same; call me. Love, Isla.* And then Paislee had responded, setting up their interview for nine thirty Monday morning, to which Isla had sent an aye, see you then. Nothing else.

Hmm. She found Isla's new address online and asked her grandfather, who was now refreshed from his nap, "Care for some lunch? We just need tae make a quick stop first."

Grandpa Angus nodded, running a wetted comb through his silver hair. "Aye. I cannae believe how many ladies like yarn."

"It isnae just yarn, Grandpa—it's a community. And I sold a sweater." That boost added more than what Mary Beth would pay tomorrow for her specialty yarn, and was a much-appreciated addition to her bank account.

"Yer granny used tae knit all the time—it's wise of ye tae put that talent tae use. You any good?"

"What kind of question is that?" She pointed him to the shelf of soft sweaters in varying colors and sizes. Next to that was a stack of blankets, then gloves, caps, and socks. With a sniff she said, "Take a look for yourself."

"Later," he said, turning his back on her treasures. "Where're we stopping?"

"My almost new hire," she said through gritted teeth. "Her email made it sound like she was desperate for whatever hours I could give, so I'm worried that she didnae show up for her interview, or return my calls."

Paislee wondered if the discount on wool for sale was through Billy. Isla hadn't mentioned what her boyfriend did for work, only that she was in love.

Grandpa adjusted his dark green tam over his hair at a jaunty angle and shrugged into his tweed trench coat.

She locked up the shop and they left out the back door.

"What time is yer son off of school?"

"Your *great-grandson*, Brody, is out of class at three thirty."

"Do you always pick him up? Why can't he walk? It does-nae seem very far."

"Two miles is too far," Paislee pronounced. Would the old man have an opinion on everything? She was used to being in charge of her own life.

"Humph."

She plugged Isla's address into her GPS, and they drove to-ward the harbor. Destination, ten minutes. Her stomach grum-bled. She hoped Isla would understand—and maybe once she got her new situation sorted, if Isla was still looking for work, she could hire her on then.

"Oh, this is nice," Paislee said. The three-story wood build-ing was partially shielded by branches of a broad oak. Across the road was a small park, and a wooden pier speared out into the choppy Firth. Each flat had two spaces of parking before it, and there was a side lot for overflow. Barren trees were starting to bud in the spring and would be pretty in just another week or two.

Her grandfather's bushy brows lifted at the sight. "Ye say she was desperate for a job?"

This was much nicer than what Isla'd had before; that was for sure. "Maybe she's staying with a friend until she gets back on her feet." Before Isla had moved to Inverness with Billy, she'd shared a flat with her best friend, Tabitha.

If things were tight, why hadn't Isla gone back there?

They parked in front of number 10. The next spot over was 8, and a shiny new BMW, silver with silver rims, took a place of pride. The other spaces were empty and Paislee imagined that the owners were at work doing whatever paid well enough for a harbor view and a sports car.

"Stay here? I should just be a few minutes."

Her grandfather gave a curt nod.

A fan of the grunt, the old man wasn't big on talking. Maybe that was one of the reasons he and Granny hadn't suited. She had loved to talk and tell stories into the night—keeping Paislee and Brody captivated with Scottish legends or family tales of folks in the far past.

Eager to see her protégée, Paislee got out of the Juke and knocked on the door. It opened an inch. "Hello?"

She knocked again, expecting Isla to open it farther.

"Isla? It's Paislee. . . ."

Uneasy now, with the door ajar and nobody answering, Paislee nudged it a bit more and peeked into the foyer.

A white mongrel carrying what looked like a beige rabbit in his teeth darted out and around the building to a grassy area on the side.

Since when did Isla like dogs? "Pup!" Paislee called.

Her grandfather, no better at staying in the car than Brody, whistled after the wee white dog and clapped for good measure.

She would feel terrible if something happened to it. "Isla? I'm coming in, lass. Your dog got out."

Paislee pushed the door inward and peered inside, standing on the wooden threshold. To the right was a black leather sofa and low table with an open laptop, to the left a custom stainless-steel kitchen. "Brilliant," she whispered. The kitchen of her dreams.

A door directly across the living room was open and re-vealed a made bed. Cardboard boxes were stacked behind the couch. The flat wasn't large, and her gaze returned to the square black dining table in the kitchen. There was no separate dining room.

A flash of metal caught her eye and she looked down in alarm. Her pulse steadied as she realized that it wasn't a knife. A crochet hook? Isla had preferred crocheting to knitting. A pale hand, slender fingers curled in toward her palm, then a thin arm in a sage sweater—Isla's favorite color—and then Isla, pale and blue-lipped on the beechwood floor, her eyes fixed on something inward, her blond hair spread beneath her.

Horrified, Paislee brought her knuckles to her mouth to stop a shout. *Oh, no, oh no oh no.* What had happened to Isla?

"She's dead," Grandpa Angus said in Paislee's ear.

Paislee grabbed the doorframe and screamed.

Chapter 4

Paislee's entire body shook with fear and she tightened her cardigan around her waist. She stepped inside the modern kitchen, unable to take her eyes off of Isla, who lay so still, like a broken doll.

Bile rose from her stomach.

Her voice cracked and she stood over Isla, looking to the living room and bedroom. "Hello?"

Nobody answered.

Grandpa's narrow shoulders let in the daylight at the doorway before he entered the kitchen and knelt at Isla's side. He pressed his fingers to her wrist.

"The police," Paislee whispered. She studied Isla and gulped a sob. Pale lips with a tinge of blue, white skin, a fixed gaze.

"Aye. Ye have a phone?" Grandpa asked, rising unsteadily. "No pulse."

It was too late for CPR on Isla. With trembling fingers, Paislee pulled her mobile from the pocket of her cardigan and dialed her friend Amelia Henry, who answered the phones at Nairn Police Station.

She struggled to think clearly, her mind in a thick mist.

"Nairn Police Station."

Yanking her gaze from Isla's curled hand, the blue fingernails, she said, "Amelia, Isla is dead." Paislee swallowed a cry that hurt her chest. *Dead.*

"What? Slow down." Amelia's tone switched from cheerful to serious. "Where are ye? I'll send an ambulance right away—are ye all right?"

"Fine." She took a breath and closed her eyes, then opened them again, finding a center of calm in emotional turbulence. *Just the facts, and don't look at Isla. She isnae there anymore.*

"Where are you?" Amelia asked in a steady tone.

"Harborside Flats." Her belly tumbled and twisted. "Number ten. My car is parked out front. Isla isnae breathing, Amelia." Paislee wrapped her arms around herself for comfort, but it didn't work.

"I've dispatched an ambulance—help is on the way."

It was too late to save Isla. Tears for her slipped hotly from her eyes. "Now what do I do?" She couldn't help but peek at Isla's foot, clad in a crocheted sage-green slipper that Paislee remembered her working on at Cashmere Crush. Not moving. She gulped more tears down her throat.

"Just wait there," Amelia instructed. "Dinnae touch anything."

"I won't."

"Yer sure she's . . ."

She glanced quickly at the rigid body, grateful that her grandpa had checked for sure. "Aye."

"Five minutes, Paislee. Do ye need me tae stay on the line with you?"

"No, no. Thanks." Paislee hung up and pocketed her phone.

"They're on the way?" Grandpa accidentally bumped into the dining room table, knocking over an orange prescription bottle.

"Five minutes. Careful, now." Paislee scowled at him but read the label. "Digoxin. Isla Campbell." The container lay on its side, empty.

A mug of tea, the Lipton tea bag visible, and a plate of shortbread cookies—the plastic container with the popular red band on the kitchen counter as if the package had just been opened. The chair she must have been sitting in askew from when she'd fallen to the floor. The opposite seat had been tucked tidily against the table.

Paislee got the sense that Isla had lived alone, though there was another mug in the sink.

Grandpa gestured to the empty pill bottle. "Suicide?"

"Naw—that's her heart medication." Paislee shivered and rubbed her arms. "Let's go outside for the ambulance."

Paislee and Grandpa waited on the sidewalk. Lost in thought, she recalled how fervent Isla had been regarding living life to its fullest. Her fragile health had given her a strong will to survive and she hated to be thought of as weak.

Isla's mother and father had divorced, and Isla's mother had little time for her daughter. After her mother found another man, who also had no time for Isla, Isla had moved out during her last year of school with an older boyfriend.

Paislee wiped a tear. They'd shared a few quiet moments at the shop, Paislee knitting and Isla crocheting. Paislee had even told Isla about her own mum's desertion to America after Paislee's dad had been killed in a boating accident. She'd seen glimpses of herself in Isla, and if the girl had hard edges, well, she had reason.

Despite her hardships, most days Isla had been sunshine to the point of needing sunglasses.

A navy-blue SUV pulled into the parking lot, taking the number 12 spot, to Paislee's left.

To her dismay, Detective Inspector Zeffer got out of the vehicle. He wore a tailored blue suit with a white shirt and black tie and had lost the hat and coat in today's warm weather.

When his cool green eyes settled on her, she had to remind herself that she hadn't done anything wrong.

"Hello," she babbled. "Paislee Shaw. We met this morning, when you brought Angus tae my shop."

"I recall," he said, his voice deep, his expression letting her know that he wasn't pleased to see the Shaws twice in one day. "What happened?"

She pointed to the front door, which was now open behind them. "Isla Campbell is dead."

"Did you go inside?"

"Uh, a little bit . . ."

He hiked his russet brow.

"We were both in the kitchen; Grandpa checked for her pulse. We bumped the table. There was a dog."

The detective stepped around where she and Grandpa stood to see inside Isla's flat, though he was also on the cement walkway.

She slid her hands into the pockets of her cardigan. "I mean to say that I called for Isla. The door wasn't latched all the way. And when she didn't answer, I nudged it open a bit more, and then a dog ran out with a rabbit, stuffed, I think, and . . ."

He rubbed his clean-shaven chin with his thumb and forefinger, assessing her once again.

Grandpa Angus whistled low beside her—was that code for *haud yer weesht*?

The detective edged past her inside the flat. "What did you touch?"

"Nothing!" She stayed on the threshold peering in and Grandpa remained on the walkway.

The detective's gaze landed on the door handle and back at Paislee.

"Other than that. I just saw her, Isla"—Paislee's voice broke—"and we called you—well, not you, but the police. Grandpa felt for her pulse; it was obvious that she was dead. Isla was supposed tae be at my shop for an interview at nine thirty, but she didnae show."

Zeffer dropped to Isla's side much more fluidly than Grandpa had done, fingers pressed to Isla's wrist despite her rigid body and the blue lips.

The staring eyes, into nothing.

Paislee circled away to face the pier and breathed in deep of the fresh air.

Grandpa slid his arm around her shoulders. "It'll be awright, lass."

Suddenly the door to the right, number 8, opened and a movie-star handsome man in denims and a fitted polo shirt exited with the white mutt and the rabbit—which was no rabbit, but a skein of beige yarn that she could tell was quality wool. Merino, possibly. Was that what poor Isla had been working with when she died?

The young man startled at noticing her and Grandpa on the walkway; then he peeked inside Isla's apartment to where the detective was now standing and blocking the view of Isla's prone body. His friendly smile faded. "What's going on?"

The DI braced his shoulders. "And you are?"

"Oh—Gerald Sanford. I live next door." He lifted the yarn. "I was just going tae return this tae Isla." The dog whined from his place tucked in the crook of the guy's arm. "Is she all right?"

"There's been an accident," Detective Inspector Zeffer informed him. "When was the last time you saw your neighbor?"

"Yesterday," Gerald said. He had a thick chest and muscled biceps, as if he worked out daily at the gym. He shifted so that he was speaking over the detective's shoulder. "Though she and Baxter here were guid friends, we didnae socialize."

Paislee didn't believe him—he'd looked away like Brody did when trying to pull the wool over her eyes.

Why would he lie about how well he knew Isla?

He was very good-looking, as Isla was pretty. Paislee didn't believe for a second that he wouldn't want to "socialize" with her.

The detective pressed, "What was your relationship with Ms. Campbell?"

Gerald shuffled his feet and tightened his grip on the white dog, who panted, pink tongue out. "She'd moved in two weeks ago. Didnae really know her. She seemed hung up on her ex."

Oh, had Isla and Billy broken up? Paislee brought her hand to her heart. *They'd seemed so in love. Poor Isla.*

"Billy Connal," Paislee supplied. Another tear slid down her cheek, and she wiped it with the back of her hand.

"Yeah, that's the guy," Gerald confirmed. "Had an old pickup truck."

"You know him?" Zeffer asked Paislee.

"I never met him, but he was the reason Isla left Nairn three months ago and moved tae Inverness." Paislee buttoned her sweater against a cool breeze from the inlet.

"What do you do?" The detective checked his watch and made a point of noticing Gerald's shiny new BMW.

Was he wondering, as Paislee did, why the man wasn't at a nine-to-five job, with a car like that?

"Weel, I'm actually a law student." Gerald's grin had just enough boy in it for Paislee to place him around twenty-five. "I work weekends as a reenactment actor in Inverness."

He must come from money, she thought. Law school was expensive. Unless actors pretending to be Braveheart made a good deal more than she'd realized?

"Have ye been home all day?"

"Studying." Gerald scratched Baxter's ears, the yarn in his hand.

"Where were you last night?" the detective asked Gerald.

Gerald flushed red. "At the movies."

The man was a terrible liar, Paislee thought. Behind her, Grandpa Angus coughed into his fist to show his disbelief at the answer.

Detective Inspector Zeffer widened his stance on the walkway and stared Gerald down.

"Listen, I havenae seen Isla since yesterday," Gerald said, this time in a more normal tone. "She sometimes watched Baxter for me, so she must have let him in tae play."

Paislee had a hard time believing that.

"I'll need your phone number," the detective said, his leather notepad and black pen out as suddenly as a magic trick.

Gerald rattled it off and then handed over the yarn. The dog woofed. "I have tae go hit the books." He didn't say good-bye as he returned to his flat.

The detective, holding tight to the yarn and notebook, focused his attention on her. She took a half step back.

"You said she moved from Nairn tae be with her boyfriend?"

"Aye. I wrote a recommendation for her tae get a job there. I thought she was happy."

"Place of employment?"

The man was glacial with his questions, not letting an emotion slip free. Did he have no compassion that someone she cared for had died?

"Vierra's Merino Wool Distributor." Her chin hefted a notch.

The detective jotted something down.

Paislee touched the hollow at her throat and sniffed.

Dead.

It just didn't make sense.

The officer tapped pen to pad. "What else can ye tell me about her?"

"Isla had heart problems," Paislee said. "She took medicine

for it—but she was so careful about her health. We saw her prescription on the table. I hope . . . Will you tell me what ye find out?"

Detective Inspector Zeffer didn't move from his position before Isla's door. "I'll be in touch."

The ambulance arrived, sirens blaring and lights flashing.

"Can we go?" She no longer felt like eating. Or going back to her wonderful shop. She yearned to be at the beach with her toes in the sand and the wind in her face to dry her tears. *Not gonna happen. Chin up.*

"Aye." He kept the skein of yarn in his hand and poised his pen over the open page of his notebook. "What is the best number tae reach you at?"

"My mobile." She gave him the information and he gave her his business card. She and Grandpa got into the Juke. Tears burned her eyes.

In a gruff tone her grandpa said, "I'm sairy for yer loss, Paislee."

She sniffed and rummaged in her purse for a tissue, dabbing at her nose and cheeks. "Thank you. She was just so young . . . it doesnae make sense."

"Death?"

"*Her* death."

"It's never easy."

She wondered if he was thinking of his son, Craigh, missing.

Wiping her eyes, she started the car and backed out, avoiding the emergency personnel casually removing a stretcher from the back of the ambulance.

Her gaze moved from Isla's open door to Gerald's flat. He was peeking out the window at them. He hadn't seemed the least bit upset by his neighbor's death—then again, he'd been surprised to see her, Grandpa, and the detective, saying that he was returning the yarn Baxter had taken from Isla's. There had been an extra mug in Isla's sink. Had it been Gerald's? Was that what he'd been lying about?

The space inside had been tidy, which made her wonder what was in those boxes by the leather sofa. The girl probably hadn't had the chance to unpack, and here Paislee was, butting her nose in. She shook her head. "A strong cuppa tea is in order."

"With whisky," Grandpa Angus said.

"That's just what I need, tae pick up Brody from school smelling like Glenlivet fumes. I'd be the one sent tae the office, maybe jail, and I don't think the detective wants tae lay eyes on us again today."

He adjusted his tam and settled back in the cloth seat, his trench coat unbuttoned. "Then what's yer plan?"

"I dinnae have anything scheduled for the afternoon. Let's go home and get Granny's room sorted so you have a place tae sleep."

"Just for a few days," he insisted, glaring out the passenger window as she left the harbor.

They both knew *that* was wishful thinking.

Chapter 5

By three fifteen, Paislee had stacked enough of Granny's things to the side for Grandpa to reach the bed. Gran had been a high school English teacher in Nairn for thirty years and most of the boxes were books. Paislee gave him the vacuum, clean sheets, and a comforter. "I willnae be gone long," she told him. Her black Scottish terrier growled at the old man. Wallace had been a gift to Brody after Granny had died, and the pup didn't let Grandpa out of his sight.

"This is only temporary," groused the old man.

Raising her palm to keep the peace, she didn't argue or bother saying good-bye. She climbed into the Juke and called her best friend, Lydia, on the way to Brody's school. "Lydia!" The skies had changed from the blue earlier to gray and stormy, which was somehow appropriate.

"Paislee—what's up?"

Her dearest friend was the best estate agent in all of the Highlands. If anybody could help her find a new space, it would be Lydia. She sniffed back tears, her throat thick and scratchy. She rarely cried, but Isla's death was tragic.

"What's wrong, love?"

She found a tissue in the console and dabbed her nose.

"Isla's dead, I got an eviction notice, and my long-lost grandfather was dumped off at my shop after being picked up for sleeping in the park."

Lydia started laughing. "Ye have tae be kidding."

"I'm not." She tossed the tissue to the empty cupholder.

"Wait—*your* Isla?"

"Aye. I told you she'd emailed me about wanting her job back?" Tension bit behind her eyes.

"She was supposed tae be there today, I thought."

"She didnae show . . . so, I went tae her flat . . . and found her . . . dead. Well, me and Grandpa Angus." She tightened her grip on the steering wheel.

The call went silent. "Sairy for laughing. I cannae believe it. What will ye do?"

"About which part?"

"Ah, Paislee," Lydia said. "Only you."

She supposed her grandfather was the most immediate need. "Grandpa showed up at the shop this morning, escorted by a new detective in Nairn. Busted for snoozing on a park bench. His plan was tae buy a tent and camp. Can ye believe it? Completely mental."

She heard a swift intake of air and then, "Paislee Ann Shaw, do not tell me that ye've invited him tae live with you? You dinnae know him! What if he murders ye in yer bed?"

"Where else is he supposed tae go?" She slowed to round a traffic circle near the primary school. Because Fordythe was in a family neighborhood, controlling speeders mattered more than the annoyance, or so she reminded herself on a daily basis.

"Yer granny didnae care for the man," Lydia reminded her.

As if Paislee didn't know that? Her nerves shot up into a raging headache. "I don't think he's dangerous. Cantankerous, aye."

She neared the school and the queue of cars waiting to enter Fordythe. She was the last of the line, but at least she wasn't late.

"I dinnae think it's a good idea."

"She also preached compassion, Lyd." Paislee opened her purse to search for ibuprofen, but there was none. "Aren't I living proof?"

Lydia clicked her tongue, which sounded like nails on a computer keyboard. "But moving in? Let me poke around and see what I can find. . . . Where are old people supposed tae go? My grands are passed already, so I dinnae ken."

Paislee inched forward in the line of cars. "Dinnae forget, that's not my only problem. I need you tae find Cashmere Crush a new home—something in as good of a location as Market Street, and at a better than cheap price."

Lydia groaned. "I'd rather take on Social Services. You know ye got a good deal on that old place. What happened?"

"Shawn Marcus sold it right out from under us."

"Too bad—that probably voids the lease."

"That's what he said, the spray-tanned prig."

Brody waited on the curb as she pulled forward. "I have tae go, Lyd. Call me tomorrow if you find anything?"

She wasn't looking forward to telling Brody about Isla, or their new "temporary" roommate.

"Love ya!" Lydia said before ending the call.

Brody climbed in the front passenger side of their SUV with a hangdog expression that could give Wallace a run for his whiskers. "Hey, Mum."

She pulled out of the queue and onto the street. "How was school?"

"The teacher sent home a note, sayin' if I'm late one more time, I get detention." He kicked his backpack. "When it's your fault."

She winced. "I'm sairy, hon."

"I told Mrs. Martin about what happened with you getting kicked out and that mean old guy sayin' he was me great-grandpa, sleepin' in the park. She didnae believe me."

"It does sound like a whopper," she said softly. "But I was there." She touched his elbow, but he yanked it out of reach. "I'll email her tomorrow."

"Mrs. Martin seemed mad, Mum."

"I'll take care of it." She'd set the alarm a half hour earlier.

Instead of home, she drove to the beach and parked. She lowered the visor against the gray afternoon sky, which was still too bright for her headache.

"What?" Brody asked suspiciously. The oppressive air in the Juke reminded her of when they'd come here after Granny died, and then gone to the pet shop to make them both feel better.

She couldn't afford another dog. "How about an ice cream?"

"Mum." He crossed his arms and stared at her, his auburn bangs brushing his eyebrows. His skin was as pale as hers, only he had freckles. "Just tell me."

She blinked tears back. "Isla is dead, love. She won't be coming tae work for me after all."

His nose scrunched and he rubbed the rounded end. "What happened?"

"I dinnae ken. The detective said he would be in touch." Which was quite vague, come to think of it. "It was the same man as from this morning."

Brody frowned, his brown eyes serious as he processed this information.

Death wasn't something that happened all the time—his only experience had been with Granny, and Paislee'd done her best to shield the true measure of her grief from him. She'd bought him Wallace for the kind of unconditional love that her grandmother had so generously given them both.

"Does she have family?" he asked after thinking for a minute.

"A mum, in Edinburgh."

"Oh."

Paislee would do some digging for her address and send the woman a sympathy card. "And," she said, "Grandpa Angus will be staying with us for a while."

At this, Brody scowled. "Where will he stay? I'm not sharing me room. He was mean."

She recalled how sharply Grandpa had spoken, and how her son had recoiled. "I think he was embarrassed, about not having a place tae live."

Brody kicked at his backpack again and she prayed he'd eaten all his crisps or there'd be a mess to clean.

She shifted to see him better. "I said he could sleep in Granny's room, until we figure out a few things."

"That's Gran's!" He pinned her with his gaze. "Not forever?"

Nothing was forever. If she had her way, in eight more years her son would be off to college to live his best life. She hadn't made it to university—she'd planned on going, but then her da had died, and her mom had remarried and moved to America, and Paislee, acting rashly, had ended up pregnant. The guy was nice enough, but Paislee hadn't been in love, she hadn't wanted to steer him from his path as he'd joined the military, so she'd kept her mouth shut.

Brody belonged to her.

He stared at her with wide eyes. Oh yes, he wanted to know if Grandpa would live with them forever.

"No," she said, ruffling his hair.

He ducked away. "Mum!"

"Sorry." He hated it when she did that, but she couldn't stop herself.

"Do we still get Chinese for dinner?" He studied her face to see if things were truly going to be all right. Take-away meals were a treat compared to home cooked, and she'd suggested it this morning.

Paislee pointed to her purse. "Even though Jerry didnae bring the special yarn for Mary Beth, I sold a sweater, so aye."

"What if Grandpa doesnae like it?"

"I don't think he'll be that picky." She remembered Grandpa's enjoyment of his bacon butty and coffee earlier and her throat ached with emotion. She had to get herself under control or she'd be a weeping disaster, and she'd no time for that. At the pounding of her temple, she had an awful thought. What if she was coming down with something?

Mums didn't get sick days. There was laundry to do, and Brody always had a reading assignment, fifteen minutes. She made him read out loud so she could enjoy the story, too, while she did the dishes.

The toe of her son's runner made contact with the backpack again, and she could tell he was brooding—it didn't take her maternal senses to notice; his tight mouth and narrowed eyes painted the picture. Because he was an only child, he was mature for his years. Gran said he'd been born with a contemplative nature.

"Brody, Lydia will find another place for Cashmere Crush, so I don't want ye tae worry. That's my job." She patted her chest. "Your job is tae get good grades."

"My job sucks."

"Language."

He rolled his eyes. "You still owe fifty pence."

"I willnae forget," she promised. They had a swear jar on the kitchen counter and donated the occasional coins to the church.

After a few moments passed and the abuse to his backpack slowed, he glanced at her and she asked, "So, are ye all right, about Isla?"

The two had only met a few times since Isla had worked

for Paislee during Brody's school hours, part-time, but death was still . . . gone.

"Aye. Can I still have ice cream?"

"That *and* Chinese?" She gave an exaggerated pout. "Dinnae push it, laddie."

A smile made a brief appearance and then, "Do you think Grandpa will take me fishing?"

And the subject took a hard-right turn. "Why on earth would he do that?"

"I've seen other grandpas on the pier, that's all."

Just when she thought it was safe to let down her guard, Brody unintentionally struck her in the heart.

She'd chosen to raise Brody on her own, well, with Granny's help—she couldn't have done nearly as well without her grandmother's support. Nairn had old-fashioned values, mired in the past, and being a single mother wasn't something to brag on.

Father Dixon had been surprisingly supportive, but the ladies around Nairn muttered about loose behavior and Paislee Shaw being no better than she had to be.

Her grandmother had counseled her to keep her chin high and ignore the gossips, telling Paislee she had nothing to be ashamed of. She'd made her choice and would live by it.

Brody was worth every hardship.

"We can always ask," she said. And if the old man said no, well, Paislee would take Brody fishing herself. Not her idea of fun, but raising a boy meant getting her hands dirty. Hadn't she learned to toss the baseball overhand instead of underhand, like a girl?

After adjusting her throw last fall, they'd had a talk about equality of the sexes that had gone right over his young head. She prayed daily that she did right by him.

"Ice cream or dinner, ye can't have both."

"Orange chicken!" He smacked his lips.

Paislee started the engine. She'd told him early on that his dad wasn't around anymore, which was the truth, and so far that answer had been enough.

As she studied his stubborn chin and pert nose, her heart literally thumped. Her head pounded.

What on earth would she do when it no longer was?

Chapter 6

Paislee woke with a start the next morning from strange noises downstairs. She sat up, her feet on the floor as she reached for her robe, before settling back with a sigh.

Angus Shaw was, no doubt, awake.

Her ears strained to hear. Was he going into the kitchen?

She hoped to put the kettle on, as she would need a large mug of Scottish Breakfast to get her through the day. A cold compress against her eyes after dinner yesterday had eased her headache before she went to bed.

She'd feared that Brody wouldn't sleep well, so she'd been up half the night making sure he was okay—each time she peeked into his room down the hall from hers, he was sleeping on his side like an angel, auburn hair curled against the pillow and Wallace tucked in at the crook of his knees.

Isla's ghost had kept her up the rest of the night, memories of her laughing at something that tickled her, or the rare glimpse of vulnerability in the girl's eyes. She'd been the same age Paislee had been when she'd opened her specialty sweater and yarn shop. Thanks to Gran, she had a skill, unlike Isla, who hadn't finished secondary school.

Paislee had started by selling scarves and knit caps at the

church bazaar, and then she'd set up a website for Cashmere Crush. Selling sweaters to people all over the world brought in a wee bit more money than she'd make at the market.

She loved knitting, and could do it while minding the baby.

Granny challenged her to take an online business course, to think of having a brick-and-mortar place for community to gather, and support other businesses while making a decent living for her and Brody.

Paislee had started Cashmere Crush at twenty—the first year of the lease Granny had co-signed for her, but after that, the paperwork was in her name alone.

It was as if Gran had known she wouldn't be around much longer, and she'd encouraged Paislee to be self-sufficient. Scots were known for their pride, and Paislee supposed she was no different.

Despite some wagging tongues and dark looks, Paislee had never taken a cent from the poor box or received benefits from the government for being an unwed single mum. *Thank ye, Granny.*

Now get up, lazybones!

She quickly brought her clothes down the hall to the upstairs bathroom she and Brody shared and showered to start her day. Fifteen minutes later, after she woke a groggy Brody, Wallace clicked at her heels, wanting out and then fed.

Grandpa Angus sat at the kitchen table, a steaming mug before him, the Brodies tea tin in the center of the round table. She opened the back door to the porch, which led to the fenced narrow garden, and Wallace woofed as he dashed out. "Morning."

"Morning, lass. The bed was quite comfy, but I swear I heard yer gran's ghostie yellin' at me all night long. I might have tae sleep on the porch."

The back porch was screened and maybe six feet wide.

Brody's old bicycle, the tire deflated, was stored there, along with gardening supplies. Who had time to garden, but they were Granny's and she didn't have the heart to toss them. There were also two wicker chairs and a skinny wicker bench she liked to sit and knit on when she passed the time.

"Suit yourself, but she'll probably find you."

From what she'd pieced together over the years, Grandpa and Gran had been happily married and had two children—her father, now dead, and a daughter, who had married and moved away, to Japan or something. Aunt Mora hadn't even come home for Gran's funeral.

Grandpa and Gran had been happily married *until* Gran found out about Craigh, Grandpa's adult son with another woman. Paislee must have been fourteen at the time—everything was hushed up, but she remembered that her father had wanted to meet Craigh. She wondered now if her da had met his half brother before he'd died?

"Do you ever hear from Aunt Mora?" she asked.

He scratched at his thick silver beard. His brow furrowed, though it was hard to tell with the wrinkles. "She passed a few years back. Two of me children are gone, the other missin'. My wife—Agnes Shaw was me *only* wife, and the love of my bleak life—dead too. Makes you wonder why I'm still here," he said.

His shadowed gaze found her. It did her heart good to know that he'd loved her gran, through it all—but how sad, that they couldn't be together in the end.

"If you loved her, why'd ye cheat?"

"I didnae break me vows," he said in a harsh tone, "but I had too wild of a time the night before. Being sloshed is no guid excuse, but I dinnae remember it at'all."

Paislee would not point fingers about precaution. She knew all too well that youth and alcohol made you think yourself invincible.

Wallace barked to be let back in, so Paislee crossed the

kitchen and opened the back door, closing it once the dog was inside. She gave the pooch an absent pat on the head.

"Did you try tae tell her?"

"Aye, but I dinnae know meself what happened." Grandpa removed his glasses and positioned them next to his mug. "Mibbe I dinnae handle things as smoothly as I'd wished."

Had Granny loved her husband so much that she couldn't stand the pain of what she thought had happened? His intimacy with another woman had resulted in a child just months older than her firstborn.

Paislee had never loved like that and instead poured all of her devotion into raising Brody properly. Romance was not an option.

Grandpa slurped from his mug.

The idea of Grandpa "home" while she was gone didn't sit right. Though she'd softened at his confession, Paislee didn't trust him one hundred percent. She didn't feel like he was dangerous to her or Brody or she wouldn't have let him in— but this was her sanctuary.

"What are ye starin' at?" Grandpa barked.

Paislee didn't blink or back down. "I'd like your help in the shop today. I'll train ye on the cash register and pay you hourly, as I planned tae do for Isla." Fifteen hours. Her mind scrambled to form a plan that didn't break the bank but allowed her to get to know him better —she hadn't been serious about him working for room and board.

"I can handle a register," he declared, fidgeting in his chair. Was he uncomfortable because of the conversation?

"I'll show ye my way." She liked to have a copy of her receipts and she kept tally of what sold on a spreadsheet at her shop computer.

"Bossy women," he mumbled, crossing his arms over his thin stomach as he pushed back from the table. His flannel shirt had a frayed cuff, and he wore thick woolen socks.

"Get things done." She would not put up with his whinge-ing much longer. "We leave at quarter till nine, so please be ready."

She went to the pantry and pulled down a box of Weet-abix, then grabbed some berries from the fridge, along with milk.

"Ye dinnae make the boy a hot breakfast?"

Her shoulders rose defensively. "Not every day, no. We usu-ally save that for Sunday morning, which is our day off." Yesterday had been the exception because neither of them had wanted it to be Monday morning. Maybe she'd had a bit of a premonition after all, for the day had been a tough one.

She poured dry kibble into Wallace's dish and gave him fresh water.

"What hours do ye keep at the shop?" Grandpa Angus rose to add more hot water to his tea mug, then sat back down, his khakis faded at the knees.

"It depends on Brody's schedule in the afternoon, but half past nine tae quarter past three Monday through Saturday is a typical day, and I bring him back tae the shop if I have work tae catch up on, then Thursday evenings, for a social hour where the ladies gather and work on a project."

"Blether," he said. "Like a bunch of hens."

"Aye." Paislee didn't bother hiding her grin. "We gab about the most interesting things." Anything from Widower Mann and his ladies to local politics.

He stirred his tea.

Paislee reached for her favorite mug—a birthday gift from Brody. She made her tea, adding a spoonful of sugar, then yelled up the stairs to her son.

The bathroom door slammed. Wallace barked from his po-sition by her feet on the braided rug and then raced up the stairs, his short black terrier legs hidden behind a fringe of fur.

Half past eight—she sighed and went to make Brody's lunch. He liked cheddar cheese on white bread with two slices of pickle. He didn't care that the pickle made it soggy—and she didn't complain, so long as he was eating.

His lunch bag was insulated and had a picture of Cawdor Castle on it. She added an apple and a packet of crisps.

He said he ate the apple, but she doubted it. Last to go in was a chocolate biscuit, only to be had after the rest of his lunch. She had little illusion that it was not eaten first.

Grandpa Angus watched her with hooded eyes. "Ye know he tosses all but the chocolate biscuit."

"I cannae verra well sit with him each day and make sure he eats it all, now can I?" She challenged her grandfather to say more, annoyed because he was only voicing aloud what she thought in her head.

Grandpa buried his face in his tea mug.

"We see Doc Whyte for his physical tomorrow afternoon. If he's healthy, then . . ." Paislee shrugged and let the sentence trail off.

Gran had said to pick her battles, and this wasn't one she was willing to fight—at ten, Brody knew what a healthy meal was, and that he was lucky to get it. He preferred to bring his rather than eat the school lunch.

She checked the clock on the wall. Thirty five minutes past eight. Where was he?

Paislee walked to the end of the stairs prepared to bellow his name when he appeared at the top, his hair sticking straight up from washing his face.

She opted not to say a word about it. "Cereal's ready; lunch is packed. We have tae leave in ten minutes."

Brody skipped down the stairs before her, swinging his hand on the bottom post to swivel toward the kitchen.

She followed, taking stock. Clean denims, clean T-shirt,

runners. "I'll go upstairs and get your backpack. You eat, and dinnae feed Wallace from the table." Paislee looked to her grandfather. "That goes for you, too."

His silver brow rose. "I would never."

How many times had she heard that? She tapped her watch. "Ten minutes before we need tae be at this door, ready tae go."

She climbed the stairs, pulled her hair into a ponytail, and chose a lightweight cardigan sweater she'd knit with Gran—she loved the ice-blue yarn, which matched her eyes. Jamming her feet into her brown leather half boots, she grabbed her purse, Brody's backpack, and made it downstairs in five minutes.

"Hustle," she said, out of habit. It didn't actually create speed, but it felt proactive.

Brody eyed Grandpa warily across the table as he ate his cereal, pushing aside the blueberries to eat for last.

She settled Wallace out back for the day—with access to the screened porch if it rained—and tucked Brody's lunch into his backpack.

"It's a miracle, but I think we're going tae be on time." She crossed her fingers for luck.

"I dinnae want detention," Brody said. "They should give it tae you, anyway, not me. I'm only ten."

"You could walk," Grandpa suggested.

Brody turned his back on Grandpa and the stranger's unwanted opinion. "I'm ready, Mum."

"Coat?"

"I dinnae need it."

"Your sweatshirt, then. It's still cool for recess."

He grumbled but retrieved it from the hall closet.

Her grandfather shrugged into his trench coat, his hair neatly combed. He left his tam in his room.

She patted her pocket for her keys, then shook her purse, listening for the jingle. Nothing. In a panic, she dumped her bag upside down on the small table by the front door. Lip gloss, coffee receipt from yesterday. "Where are they?"

"Not again!" Brody dropped his backpack to the floor with a huff. Her keys fell from the side pocket of his bag and he looked at her with very round brown eyes. "Oops." The rule was her keys belonged in her purse, so that she always knew where they were.

Her hand landed on her hip like a magnet. "How did that happen?"

"I dunno." Brody smacked his forehead. "I forgot me reading assignment in the car and needed yer keys tae get it. I guess I didnae put them back."

It was things like this that created tardiness, and whose fault was it? She brought out her mum tone. "Brody!"

"Sairy." He slung his backpack over his shoulder and handed her the keys.

Her grandfather wisely kept his gob shut, waiting in the foyer.

Paislee herded them out the front door like errant lambs. "Hurry!"

They made it at nine on the dot with Headmaster McCall tapping his watch. He wore a dark brown suit jacket and a frown. Had he been waiting for her? Today was not starting off any better than yesterday, which didn't bode well.

Brody darted out of the Juke and into the brick building without a backward wave. The headmaster followed Brody inside, the blue door closing behind them.

"Mibbe we need tae leave a few minutes earlier tomorrow?" Grandpa Angus suggested.

She pulled out of the drive to the main road. "You saw for yourself—I have the best of intentions, but things just . . . happen. Missing keys, Wallace gets out, Brody forgets his home-work or, even worse, forgets tae *do* his homework—"

Grandpa made a harrumphing noise.

They arrived at Cashmere Crush, and she parked in the back. Jerry's truck pulled up next to her as she got out.

"I've got the pink yarn, lass!" Jerry called. "With an extra, at no charge, since we were late."

"Oh—thank you." Paislee could knit a pair of booties to go with the blanket as an apology to Mary Beth.

She unlocked the back door and her grandfather and Jerry followed her inside. The smell of wool was both welcome and familiar and she switched on the light, illuminating the back of her shop. What would she do without it? It was her creation, her proof that she could thrive in their community.

She wrote a check to Jerry for her wholesale cost of the yarn, accepting the extra skein on Mary Beth's behalf. She'd learned from Gran to charge fair retail prices and not discount for everyone or else she would be out of business. And who would take care of Brody then?

"Did yer day get any better after I left?" Jerry looked from her to her grandfather.

The two men hadn't actually met yesterday. "Sairy—Angus Shaw, this is Jerry McFadden. My grandfather has come tae live with us."

"For a time," Grandpa interjected. "Only until me son is found."

Jerry rocked back on the heels of his workman's boots. "He's missing?"

"Off an oil rig," her grandpa said.

"Ach." Jerry glanced at Paislee for confirmation.

She nodded. "We'll look into that this week, Grandpa."

"And then there was the dead girl," Grandpa shared with a

theatrical sigh as he removed his trench coat and slung it over the armchair by the small television.

"The dead girl?" Jerry tugged off his cap and twisted it as he looked from her to Grandpa.

She barely refrained from elbowing her grandfather as a reminder to keep his mouth closed. "Isla Campbell—she used tae work with me? Bonny blonde?"

Jerry settled the cap back on his head. "Sorry tae hear that. Didnae she move away tae Inverness?"

"Aye."

"What happened?"

"We don't know yet." She thought of the prescription bottle on the table and goose bumps pricked down her spine.

"Poor lass. She was so young." Jerry headed for the back door. "Well, I better finish the deliveries. Give me best tae Mary Beth?"

"Of course—thanks, Jerry."

Jerry left and she whirled on her grandfather, who was studying the yarn in the box, oblivious to her annoyance. "Grandpa, do ye mind not being the town gossip?"

"What's wrong with ye?" He shook his head.

She exhaled. "Isla was someone I cared about."

"Sairy." His mouth pursed and he paced to the front of the shop, suddenly interested in whatever was out her front window.

Paislee knelt down and opened the safe below the register, readying the till for the day. When she was through, Grandpa had returned.

"Can I help ye with the yarn?" He tapped the box that was still on the counter.

"Naw. Normally, I would price these at twelve pounds a skein, but because they're for Mary Beth, who will be here any minute, we don't have tae bother marking them with the label gun."

"Twelve pounds?" he repeated, sounding as if she were robbing her customers blind. "Is the fleece made of gold?"

Picking up the light pink yarn, she smoothed her thumb over the silken strands. "This is high-quality pre-shrunk merino wool, specially dyed for Mary Beth to match her niece's baby's room." She met his eyes. "It's meant tae last a lifetime."

"Waste of money, if ye ask me," he pronounced. "The babe will outgrow it long before then."

"I didnae ask you." Baby blankets weren't meant to grow with the bairn for heaven's sake. "Why don't ye go watch the news or something?" She made a motion of zipping her lips and looked up at the ceiling. *I don't blame ye for givin' him the boot, Gran.*

He huffed off behind the divider and switched on the telly. She scanned her incoming messages online but hadn't gotten too far when Elspeth Booth entered at ten. Tall, slender, with iron-gray hair and few wrinkles, she'd had her seventieth birthday last week and created exquisite needlepoint. She was followed by Mary Beth, who literally cooed when she saw the pink yarn on the counter. "Thank ye, Paislee—this is perfect."

"I'm glad, and Jerry was so sairy by the delay that he gave you another skein at no cost. I'd be happy tae knit a pair of booties."

"Or a wee headband? I'll do it. How wonderful." Mary Beth lumbered toward a chair by a regular-height table rather than the long rectangular high-top and sank down.

Paislee brought the yarn over. "It's lovely. Your niece will be thrilled."

Elspeth joined them, sitting across from Mary Beth, who brought out the portion of her blanket already completed from the knitting bag at her side.

"The bubble stitch pattern is so pretty . . . what size needle is that again?" Elspeth noted the design with interest, her thumb the same size as the individual yarn bubble.

"UK eight," Mary Beth replied, admiring the yarn. "It's too precious. I'll need tae finish it on Thursday night, during the Knit and Sip. Mibbe Arran can watch the bairns." Mary Beth's husband was mildly overbearing and treated time with his kids as if he were doing Mary Beth a favor. She rarely missed a Thursday but always acted as if she needed permission.

Thursdays mattered to each of Paislee's ladies for various reasons. Elspeth, until last year, had worked at the church office with Father Dixon, but she was now retired and cared for her blind younger sister. The two argued constantly and it wasn't an easy relationship. Cashmere Crush was Elspeth's respite.

Flora used to come in, back before Donnan's stroke, to escape his temper—which was worse after a few drinks. Flora refused to discuss it and had flat-out denied any wrongdoing, so they'd all learned to avoid the subject.

Amelia played computer games and drank her whisky neat. She had once shyly admitted she'd never had a boyfriend, and had discovered knitting when she'd given up smoking two years ago.

They were all very different, yet they had knitting in common.

Lydia, who *never* missed a Thursday, couldn't knot thread but dropped by for the camaraderie and wine.

For a while, Paislee had completely forgotten about Grandpa, who sauntered from the back room as if he had nothing better to do. "Did ye tell the lasses that yer being evicted?"

Elspeth and Mary Beth gaped at her in horror.

Paislee shook her finger at her grandfather. He'd done that on purpose, she'd bet. "I'll call ye when I need you."

"What's he talking aboot?" Mary Beth dropped the yarn to the box at her feet as if it had given her an electric shock.

"Who is that?" Elspeth asked.

"My grandfather." She and Grandpa would have a heart-to-heart. He was a worse instigator than old Mrs. Peets at the church, constantly stirring up trouble. "I received a letter yesterday from the landlord, that's all."

"What did it say?" Mary Beth's cheeks were the same shade of pink as the yarn. "Arran is a solicitor. He can read it for ye. He kens knitting keeps me sane."

"With all that happened yesterday, I havenae even looked at it yet." A large part of her didn't want to acknowledge the eviction notice, but Grandpa wasn't letting her forget. Paislee dragged her feet but took her purse from the shelf beneath the register. Inside was the letter.

"That doesnae seem verra responsible, Paislee, and not like ye at all," Elspeth said. The older woman perched on a stool to stay awhile, taking out a lace square to work on while they caught up.

"Tell them about the dead girl," Paislee's grandpa shared before ducking into the back and out of her reach.

"Dead girl? What is *happening* around here?" Mary Beth's chins jiggled with concern.

She couldn't have him upsetting her customers!

"Isla Campbell. I was going tae hire her back tae work part-time, but I found her, dead, yesterday at her flat, with my grandfather." He'd been mellower yesterday. Good food and a good night's sleep had emboldened the man. There was something to be said for bread and a cold night in the park.

"Oh—I'm sairy, Paislee," Mary Beth said, setting a skein of pink yarn in her lap. "I know how ye liked her."

"She was a sly one." Elspeth's judgmental tone was exactly why Paislee felt the need to protect the girl. Sometimes there were extenuating circumstances, like a neglectful mother or frail health, that gave a person a rougher edge.

Those reasons weren't hers to share, so Paislee bit her tongue, pulled out the paperwork from her landlord, and skimmed the legalese.

"Well?" Mary Beth dropped the yarn in the box and rose from her chair to join her at the counter.

The message hadn't changed since the day before. "I have thirty days tae vacate—Mr. Marcus said the building had sold. Every one of the businesses on this strip will have tae move. They're tearing all this down tae build a boutique hotel."

"No!" Elspeth said, her mouth tight. "I'll contact the historical society. This building is two hundred years old."

Paislee hadn't thought of that. "Can they help?"

"Mibbe." Elspeth rested the lacework on her lap. "I dinnae mind making a few phone calls—we have tae protect the integrity of Nairn, no matter what the Earl of Cawdor wants," she huffed, looking ready to take on all comers—lean and sharp as an iron blade.

The Earl of Cawdor had plans to bring Nairn back as a popular tourist destination, and had increased the population from nine thousand to twelve in the last few years. There were growing pains, as the seaside town had its heyday in the Victorian era a hundred years ago and now its residents were expected to make room for new roads and traffic circles.

How to embrace the modern, while respecting the old?

Paislee felt like that on a personal level in Nairn all the time but had learned to curb her too-modern ideas in order to fit in and make a home for herself and Brody.

Being a single mum meant that she needed to be able to trust her neighbor, and the idea of living in a big city, like Edinburgh, boggled her mind.

She would take growing pains any day over the hustle and bustle of city life.

Paislee faced her ladies, arms lifted at her sides. "We'll figure this out—and no matter where I end up, we *will* have our

Thursday nights, even if it's on my back porch until the right place turns up."

The ladies sighed with relief.

Her grandpa muttered something from the back room about moving out as soon as possible.

She completely agreed—the crotchety man kept stirring up trouble and sharing unwanted opinions. It was no wonder Granny couldn't speak his name without looking like she'd sucked a lemon.

Chapter 7

The ladies left by noon, and Paislee's stomach rumbled. She poked her head behind the divider to see her grandfather watching the news.

"Not a word about yer girl Isla," he informed her.

Between customers, she'd searched the online news, thinking she'd missed it earlier, but Isla's death hadn't warranted a snippet anywhere. "It breaks my heart. Can you watch the place for a few minutes?" She hated to be the bearer of bad tidings, but Tabitha deserved to know that her best friend was dead. She, Billy, and Tabitha were all that Isla'd had in the world.

Grandpa straightened in his armchair. "I thought I'd step out fer a bite—ye could take it against my pay."

Oh, he did, did he? So far he hadn't done more than learn how to ring up a skein of yarn and empty her candy dish. "There's a packet of crackers below the television. I'm off across the street tae speak with her best friend, who works at the florist's, in case Tabitha doesnae know that Isla is gone. Then we'll discuss lunch."

He waved her off.

Guilt pinched like an ant bite. The old man wasn't used to

working. What had he done with his time while living with Craigh? "You can go home after I get back for the afternoon, awright? I have a cupboard full of food."

"Take yer time."

"Can you turn the telly off and listen for customers?"

He grumbled something she couldn't hear but flipped off the switch. "I'm just supposed tae sit at the counter and count sheep?"

Paislee compromised with, "You can listen tae the sound on low, but yes, I'd like you tae sit at the register and look . . . busy. Or you can read the news online; the laptop is open."

Grandpa shuffled his boots but pulled a stool to the counter and sat, propping his elbow on the laminate like a surly silver-haired teenager. Was this what she had to look forward to? *Ach.*

"Thank you." She left her shop and breathed in deep of the salty sea air—it gave her a bit of clarity after the morning's drama, brought on strong and steady no thanks to her grandfather. She had to put finding her uncle Craigh at the top of her list.

Everybody would be happier.

Both feet on the crooked sidewalk, her gaze was drawn toward the beach, and the police department on the right side of Market Street. She couldn't see the Moray Firth from her corner, but she could smell the salt and brine. Her friend Amelia would know what was going on, since Paislee hadn't heard a word yet from the detective.

She crossed the street, reflecting that this two-story row of gray stone businesses wouldn't be affected by the sale of their building. Was there an open spot for lease? She could ask Tabitha.

Paislee entered the flower shop, assaulted at once by the scent of roses—the heady perfume was thick in the chilled air: air conditioning? That must have cost the owner a pretty penny, as most of the old buildings didn't have it.

Two designers stood at back tables, surrounded by buckets of pale pink roses and vases of pink arrangements, each in the midst of arranging flowers.

"Hello!" the man singsonged. Wisps of black hair fell over his broad, pale forehead and dramatic black brows. A silver hoop adorned each ear. Thin and short—Tabitha, at the other table, was taller than him by a hair despite his black cowboy boots with heels. Each designer had a red-handled knife with a silver blade they used to slice the ends of rose stems and slide them into vases as if racing the clock.

"Is this a bad time?" Paislee asked.

"Wedding," the man explained. "Can I help you?"

Tabitha's brown eyes were red rimmed and puffy, her blondish-brown hair in a halfhearted bun.

Paislee took a hesitant step forward.

Tabitha sniffed and lowered her knife to the table. She knew, then, that her friend was dead, poor lass, and still had to work. It was obvious that the shop was busy and understaffed.

Paislee nodded with empathy, glancing to the sage-green scarf around Tabitha's neck and then zeroing in on it.

Paislee had made that for Isla as a going-away present. She recognized the tassel and her signature crocheted flower. The scarf was crafted with Flora's perfected sage color. Why did Tabitha have it?

Maybe Isla had given it to her before she died—but that wasn't really like Isla to give away her things. Now that she thought about it, Isla'd had a platter of shortbread cookies on the dining room table of her flat when she didn't eat sweets ever, because of her heart health, and a cup of tea, Lipton, when she was careful with caffeine.

Had Tabitha been to see Isla before she'd died, sharing tea and cookies? Her *borrowing* the scarf?

"Tabitha, I'm so sairy," she said. "You must be devastated tae lose your best friend."

Tabitha burst into sobs, dropped her knife, and ran into the back office, where she slammed the door closed.

Paislee made a step to follow her. "Should I?" she asked the designer.

"No—and dinnae feel too bad," the designer quipped. "Those aren't tears of grief, love." He pursed his thin lips and sliced a diagonal cut off the bottom of the next stem, fast and precise as he placed the pale pink rose in the bouquet with some sort of fern and a pink bow. "Guilty conscience, more like."

"Guilt?"

"They fought like two cats in a bag before Isla moved tae Inverness, and never made up," he said in a dry tone.

"What did they fight about?"

He pushed the vase of roses aside to get a better view of Paislee. "Same thing at the bottom of most squabbles—a man."

The only man Isla had been seeing was Billy—who she'd moved away with and, according to Gerald, was still hung up on after moving back to Nairn.

"Did Tabitha like Billy?" She heard the rise of her voice and reminded herself to calm down; she didn't know the whole story.

"Maybe she still does," he said smugly.

And now Isla was dead. Would that bring on tears of guilt? Or shame?

Maybe both. "Would you have her call me, or drop by, when she's feeling better?" Paislee wanted answers about how Tabitha had come by Isla's scarf.

"Sure."

Paislee had thought the two girls were best friends, and Isla had never said otherwise—of course, Isla hadn't called Paislee, either, just emailed her asking for a job. "Did Isla stop here recently, like in the last two weeks?"

"Heavens no. The only drama I condone is my own." He waved a rose stem and winked at Paislee.

She peered toward the office door, but Tabitha didn't make an appearance. "I dinnae think we've met. I'm Paislee Shaw. I own Cashmere Crush, across the way?"

"Ritchie Gordon, overworked manager and lead designer around here." He leaned in close and whispered, "It means I get a pound more an hour. Some days it isnae worth it."

A smile tugged at her mouth. "The roses are beautiful."

"Aye, but after twenty dozen, I'm over it. Why can't a lassie marry her true love in yellow?"

Paislee laughingly agreed. "I don't suppose you know if there are any spaces for lease on this side of the street?"

"Planning a move?" Ritchie sliced another rose stem and placed it in the vase. "I heard from Theadora that yer building is up for sale."

"Sold." She tightened her cardigan around her waist against the chill.

"Too bad. It's a prime location." He set the finished bouquet on the floor next to five others just like it. "It'll be hard tae find something else that centrally located and affordable."

She didn't think she could feel worse, and yet Ritchie's outside observation had done just that.

"Good luck with the wedding," she said, lifting her hand in a good-bye wave. "Tell Tabitha that it's important we speak?"

"Ta!"

Paislee left the flower shop. Where could she move her business? She'd worked so hard to build up Cashmere Crush. Most of her clientele lived nearby. Though she'd been mainly joking about having their Thursday nights on her back porch, she couldn't actually run her business from her home. She required a lot more space for her yarn and specialty sweaters.

She stuffed her hands in her pockets. Ned, the dry cleaner

across the street, watered the begonias in his flower boxes. All six of the businesses on her brick row had them built in. James had put green fern in his, Margot at the lab pink petunias, Lourdes and Jimmy at the office supply shop had yellow and white daisies, while Theadora on the corner had white impatiens and blue bonnets.

Her gaze was naturally drawn from Theadora's to A96, and the police station to the right. There was room for twenty cars in the half-full lot. Gerald Sanford parked his silver BMW closest to the entrance, got out—gorgeous in jeans and a buttondown black Oxford—and raced up the four stairs to go inside.

Had Detective Inspector Zeffer discovered something more about Isla's death? Why hadn't he been in touch, as he'd said he would be?

Gorgeous, yes, but she stayed away from Gerald's type. She'd stayed away from all men since Brody's birth, living like a nun beneath the scrutiny of her small town. Lydia dared her on occasion to let loose for a weekend—stealing away to Edinburgh, or London—but Paislee refused. Brody was her everything until the day he'd turn eighteen. And she had a feeling it would last beyond even then.

Instead of crossing the street to Cashmere Crush, Paislee walked toward the police station. Maybe she could text her friend Amelia and suggest a quick ten-minute break, bribing her with a treat from the tea shop.

Had Gerald remembered something about Isla that he'd needed to share with the detective, or had he been called in?

How had Isla died? She hoped that Tabitha and Isla had made up after their argument; otherwise Tabitha's guilt was sure to last a very long time.

Her phone rang, jarring her out of her curious musings.

"Paislee speaking," she answered.

"This is Headmaster McCall," a masculine voice said.

Her heart leapt in her chest. She could hardly breathe. Was Brody okay? She imagined an accident on the playground, or . . .

"Aye?"

"I'd like for you tae come in this afternoon," his very controlled voice droned.

She glared at her phone. "Is Brody okay?"

An audible sigh, then the man said, "He is. Come see me in my office at four? Good day, Ms. Shaw."

The headmaster hung up without waiting for her to agree. Surely this couldn't be about her being late—she'd been right on time this morning.

How rude! But Paislee would grit her teeth and deal with the pompous headmaster for Brody's sake. She would do anything for her son.

Chapter 8

Paislee gave a last curious glance to the station, then did an about-face, crossing the street and striding back toward Cashmere Crush, her pride stinging at being called into the primary school. In all her years as a student she'd never had an occasion to visit the headmaster's office. She pushed hard against the door. Her grandfather better not be watching the telly!

Her sails deflated when she found him seated calmly at the counter, flipping through the pages of a spring gardening magazine one of the ladies had left behind.

Temper, temper, Granny's voice admonished in her head.

"You garden?" he asked, raising his head.

"No." She stuck her hands in her pockets. "Granny did."

"Agnes had a green thumb." Grandpa sounded wistful.

"Aye." She missed her grandmother every day. It seemed Grandpa Angus might have, too, in his own way. She shook off her anger, knowing it was at herself for not managing her time better. The headmaster wouldn't call if she hadn't been tardy, and that was on her—no matter her rational excuses.

"How'd it go?" Grandpa turned another page of the magazine and jerked his thumb to the front window.

Paislee shivered at the memory of the cold flower shop and overwhelming scent of roses. "Tabitha started crying as soon as she saw me—she already knew about Isla, I could tell, though she never said. I had tae leave, she was so upset. I couldnae even talk tae her."

He tugged his beard, which she realized he'd trimmed to a square edge. Last night? And she was just now noticing?

She had to get a handle on her life before things spiraled out of control.

"Ye tried, lass, and sometimes that's all you can do."

"Maybe." She shared what Ritchie had said about Tabitha, and the girls fighting over Billy. "And Tabitha was wearing the scarf I'd made for Isla."

Grandpa Angus scoffed dismissively. "A scarf?" He propped his elbow on the counter. "She probably borrowed it. Girls share clothes, aye?"

"When would that have happened? I gave it to Isla right before she left for Inverness, and they'd fought, Ritchie said. I highly doubt Isla would give her the scarf if she was mad at her." And in the time Paislee'd known Isla, she'd noticed that she kept what was hers.

"Well, scarves arenae unique. Yer probably mistaken."

"This one was done in sage, Isla's favorite color—I made it personally, with my signature tassel, from Flora's naturally dyed yarn. It was *verra* unique."

He chuckled and closed the magazine. "Ye have a signature tassel?"

"As a matter of fact, I do." She went around the counter to the back area where she kept her supplies and brought out a box of crocheted tasseled flowers. "We need tae attach these tae keychains by Saturday for the fair." So much to do, and so little time.

"I'll be long gone by Saturday," he said, pushing aside her

crafts. "My stomach is as hollow as an empty keg." He thumped it to prove his point.

"Leave, then." She gestured toward the front door. "If you'd like tae walk home, you're welcome tae do so. There's a key under the flowerpot in the back garden."

"Isnae yer mongrel out there?"

Wallace hadn't cared for Grandpa Angus taking Gran's room and had growled at the old man since his arrival. "Wallace has a pedigree as long as your arm."

"Ha!" He stood and brushed his hands together. "Can I borrow a can of soup?"

"You can *have* a can of soup." Paislee joined him at the register. "But clean up after yourself, if ye please. There's bread in the cupboard, too, if you want tae make a sandwich. Payday is every other Friday."

She thought about the mile walk to her house, which was a relatively straight shot from the shop. Could he make it all that way? It wasn't a hard trek, but he had to be close to eighty.

He folded his coat over his arm.

"I can close up and drive ye if you'd like." She was not going tae give him the keys tae her Juke—she barely knew the man, as Lydia had said.

His response to that suggestion went over like a basket without a bottom. "I can walk, lassie. I bet I'm in better shape than you."

Paislee immediately thought of the ten pounds she'd like to lose. Who had time for exercise with a child and a business? Grandpa was lean—probably from lack of food, and no place to stay and worry over his son. She bit her tongue rather than banter back.

And he left, edging out and closing the front door firmly behind him.

The only thing saving her from owing another coin to the

swear jar was that neither Shaw was around to hear her curse beneath her breath.

Stuck behind the counter with Grandpa gone, Paislee immediately reached for her shop phone to call Amelia and ask about Isla, and Gerald. Paislee was dying to know why the law student had been at the station.

She dialed, waiting for Amelia's cheery voice to answer at the reception desk. Instead, a gruff older woman picked up the line. "Nairn Police Station."

"Is Amelia in?"

"She's out sick."

Now what? Paislee leaned her elbow on the counter.

"Is this an emergency?" the older lady asked.

"No—no, thank you."

"This is Norma. Would you like tae leave a message?"

"No, thanks anyway." Paislee quickly hung up the phone. She dug deep into her mind for an image of Norma—plump and shy was all she conjured.

She wished she had a reason for asking Detective Inspector Zeffer about Isla—would it be out of line for her to want to know, just because Isla'd been an employee? Friend? She'd discovered her poor body?

His cool green eyes left little room for empathy. Still?

The front door opened and in strutted Lydia. Lydia Barron was a twenty on a scale of one to ten. She left grown men lying in her wake. The fact that she was a genuinely kind person with a wicked sense of humor made her even more of a gem.

Lydia changed her hair color and style every six weeks when the previous style would grow out. Today she wore her hair black, in a sleek chin-level bob. Dramatic smoky shadow amplified the gray of her eyes. Tall—five ten—and slim, Paislee's dearest friend rocked a fitted gray pantsuit and black stilettos.

Paislee's shoulders lifted at Lydia's smile. They'd gotten through many hard times together and Lydia was sure to help her now.

"Paislee!" Lydia brought her purse—large, black leather, and designer—to the counter and dropped it to give Paislee a hug. "I've come tae rescue you like a knight in shining armor."

"You found me a new place tae lease for Cashmere Crush?"

"Don't be ridiculous."

"Then what?" She pulled back.

"Coffee?" Lydia preferred dark roast espresso to tea most days. "I have twenty minutes left of me lunch break."

Paislee shook her head. "I cannae shut up the shop. I'll be done early today as it is—I've been called in tae see the headmaster at Brody's school."

"Is my godson all right?" Lydia touched Paislee's wrist.

"Yes," Paislee assured her. "I have a feeling *I'm* the one in trouble."

She tsk-tsked. "Dinnae let the cranky old headmaster intimidate you. You are Paislee Ann Shaw, business proprietor—and ye own your home. You're not even thirty. That's pretty impressive."

"Gran gave me her house—it isnae the same."

"Nobody needs the details." Lydia leaned her elbow back on the counter, showing off the intricate black piping of her gray suit jacket. "About that . . ."

"What?"

"Would ye be willing tae take a loan against the property?"

Her house? She plunked down on a stool, feeling the blood drain from her face. "Absolutely not."

"But Paislee, you could have so much more freedom with working capital." Lydia peered into her eyes like a mesmerist. "You could be on the harbor, closer tae the golf course and the high-spending tourists."

"No." The idea of risking what little they had brought itchy hives along her skin. "Can't do it." She scratched her arms.

"Give me one good reason?"

"It's Brody's inheritance." She raised both hands against Lydia's intense gaze until her friend laughingly retreated.

But she had other ammunition. "Your granny would want you tae succeed."

Gran had wanted that, but she'd also wanted Paislee to be secure. "I've another mouth tae feed, thank ye, with Grandpa Angus making himself soup in my kitchen this moment. I cannae be that foolhardy."

"Not foolhardy, a calculated risk. This is not the Paislee I know and love. Didnae your grandma co-sign for ye when you first leased this place?"

"You are an evil woman, Lydia Barron."

"I want you tae reach for the stars." Her slender hand reached upward, then gestured to the interior of Cashmere Crush. "You have a beautiful shop filled with quality local yarn and yer sweaters are exquisite."

She warmed at the compliment, which she knew Lydia meant sincerely. Paislee's best friend had an eye for fine things and fashion. "I am not putting my home on the line. There has tae be another way."

"Let's make a plan then. I brought properties for you tae look at, but there is nothing in your price range—currently. Dinnae be afraid tae expand." Lydia set a packet of papers held together with a shiny black clip on the counter.

Paislee often found herself torn between fear and bravado. She usually managed to hide her anxiety from everyone but two. Gran was gone now, which left Lydia.

Fear equaled weak, and Paislee couldn't allow that emotion in—to her customers she was smart and savvy, to her son she was Mum, who handled everything, and from her community she'd earned a reputation as fair, hardworking, and honest. Nobody ever mentioned Brody's illegitimacy, which she considered a win.

God help the person who ever disparaged him about his lack of a father.

She lifted her chin and narrowed her eyes.

"Whoa, calm down," Lydia said. "What were you just thinking? You went from sweet American actress Emma Stone tae Rose Leslie in *Game of Thrones*."

She exhaled and blew back her bangs. "And why shouldnae I be Rose Leslie? She's Scottish, like me."

"You have a different kind of strong, Paislee, one that people tend tae overlook, because you arenae ragin' on about things. You just quietly get things done, until bam—you have a business, a healthy son, and *a house*."

She knew Lydia would somehow bring it back around to what she wanted. Paislee held fast. "Let's look at properties within my budget."

"Did I say strong? I meant stubborn." Lydia tapped the stack of papers with a glossy black nail. "Losing this prime location will affect your sales. I dinnae want tae be rude, but we need tae be on the same page. I say let's find something even better for Cashmere Crush."

The idea made her stomach twist. "I need some time tae think about it."

Lydia rolled her beautiful smoky eyes. "Fine." She switched gears. "Just out of curiosity, I checked tae see who had bought this property. It hasnae come up on the public record yet."

"What does that mean?"

"There should be something online somewhere. Maybe Mr. Marcus is still working out financing. I cannae imagine this place is cheap."

"It's historical, Elspeth said, so maybe there's a hang-up and he won't be able tae finalize the sale?" Hope filled her.

Lydia flipped her perfect hair behind her perfect ear. "Have you talked tae the other business owners yet?"

"No, but the florist across the street mentioned that Theadora from the tea shop had already talked tae him, asking about available space—there isnae any."

Lydia's long fingernail found her full lower lip. "Hmm. I might ask around, if you dinnae mind?"

"I'd love it if you could find out what's going on!"

She gave a nod. "Oh, my boss's sister knows somebody in the Elder Care department in Inverness."

"You're like a human internet search. I tell you one thing and you've got all the answers. Better than Siri."

"I want you tae be okay. Besties forever." Lydia's phone alarm *ding*ed and she checked the screen. "Time's up—have tae get back tae the lair."

Lydia, being the best estate agent around, had a prime office with a view of the Firth instead of a dragon's den, but she used her power for good, going stiletto to Italian loafer on behalf of her client. Not that Paislee could afford to pay full price, but she made a fabulous praline scone that Lydia loved, and kept her in bespoke cashmere, from chic winter caps to the finest of stockings.

Brody was her godchild, which didn't hurt.

"What about the Elder Care?" There was no sense in all of them being miserable if there was an alternate solution. And she needed to call the oil rig, *Mona*, that Craigh had supposedly been on.

"I'll email you the information," Lydia said. "I don't have time tae take it on, but we could use some serious reform for our retirees. Maybe the Earl of Cawdor should tackle that while he's making Nairn all shiny again. I saw him at a fundraiser last month, and he's verra approachable."

Paislee raised her eyes to the ceiling. Lydia was a social butterfly, hobnobbing at swanky dinners, while Paislee preferred smaller gatherings in the store. Hence, Lydia knew things going on in the world, while Paislee knew what Mrs. Williams was doing with her lawn boy while the mister was out of town.

"Since you have your ear tae the ground, what have ye heard about Isla's death? I cannae find anything on the news."

"Nothing," Lydia said. "She'd moved away though, and just returned, so maybe there isnae anything tae hear?"

"Isla is *dead*, Lydia."

"I know you cared, and I'm sairy. I'll see what's what," Lydia assured her. "I have tae go."

"Thanks. Wish me luck. I keep reminding myself that the headmaster cannae actually punish me."

"Is he old? Flirt a little."

What *did* the headmaster look like? She drew a blank. "I think . . . well, I dinnae ken. He's usually scowling at me, so I don't get past the overall disapproval part."

"A little smile, a little wink." Lydia shifted the strap of her designer bag over her arm and headed toward the door and her red Mercedes parked on the curb out front. "You can take this guy—you are an amazing woman with an amazing son." She looked over her slender shoulder before leaving. "Mibbe yer worrying over nothing because he wants to discuss Brody being a prodigy?"

Paislee burst out laughing.

Chapter 9

The thought of her son being a prodigy kept Paislee in good spirits for the rest of the afternoon, and she drove to Fordythe with high hopes, arriving at four on the nose.

Of course, she'd planned to leave earlier, but a customer visiting Nairn from Wales had fallen in love with all the colors of yarn, as well as Paislee's support of local goods and crafters. It had taken just a few minutes to ring up five skeins of Flora's emerald green—how could she turn down a sale?

She parked in the school lot, next to the large fenced grassy field where Brody was playing football with his friends as he liked to do a few days per week until four thirty. Mr. Mallory, who taught P3, was out supervising, bundled up in a jacket beneath the gray sky. It smelled like it could rain.

She waved to her son, who saw her but didn't wave back. That wasn't like Brody. Embarrassed, was he? Or mad? What in blue blazes had happened?

Once inside the school lobby, Paislee was hit by the scent of craft paint from a recent project that lingered near the receptionist's desk. No sign of Mrs. Jimenez.

Headmaster McCall, however, waited for her as soon as she

walked in. He glanced at the square clock above the reception desk. Two minutes after four.

Ach. She stopped herself from apologizing for being late, but just barely.

He stiffly gestured her inside his office. He still wore his brown suit jacket, buttoned in the center. File cabinets took up an entire wall, and a large school calendar was on another. A single window looked out to the parking lot, which was what he viewed when he sat at his desk. There was her Juke.

Not a single personal picture anywhere. His diploma and certificates were framed on the wall behind him. He sat in a brown leather chair with a serious expression, his elbows on the desktop.

"Thank you for coming on such short notice."

Paislee bristled as she perched on the edge of the hard-wood seat opposite his desk as she recalled his directive. "You didnae leave me much choice."

The headmaster was not old at all. A full head of thick blackish-brown hair—like dark cocoa, if she had to be precise—and kempt brows across a broad forehead. Brown eyes. His hair swooped to the side in a popular style, shorter in the back. His suit was brown, his shirt white, his tie a lighter brown. The man was thirty if he was a day and because of his youth seemed like he was ready to do his job to the letter.

"At Fordythe we consider the students' allover well-being crucial to their development."

His tone suggested that she was somehow lacking in his joint vision. "Aye?" Brody was, and always had been, her number one priority.

"I can see that you've been having some issues with time management. Even today you were late." His gaze sharpened on her as if she'd earned a demerit.

Two minutes? She crossed her ankles below the chair and set her purse in her lap. "I run a business."

"Selling yarn?" He steepled his hands before him, a smattering of dark hair on the knuckles, his nails short.

Could he be more condescending? She clenched her hands over the strap of her purse. "In addition tae specialty sweaters."

"From home?"

She rattled off her premiere business address on Market. "I have a storefront."

He sat back and rubbed his chin. "Employees?"

"Part-time," she hedged. Grandpa counted, and Isla—

"So you *could* make arrangements tae be here on time?" His question was smug, as if he'd won a point.

Paislee's temper flared and her chin hiked. She would not be intimidated—she did the best she could. "We have never been more than five minutes past—except when it was thirty because I had a flat tire on the Juke and Brody and I walked here, together. I personally explained his tardiness."

"We have rules for a reason," the headmaster said, bringing a school handbook from a drawer to lay before her on the desk. "Every parent signs it at the beginning of the school year. I have your copy here."

Embarrassed, Paislee was tempted to leap across the desk and stuff the handbook down his righteous throat.

He flipped to the page with her signature, and her face flamed.

"You have, on record, six incidents of being tardy since the school year began. Brody has just missed"—he squeezed his thumb and finger together—"being given detention due tae the fact that the maximum for tardiness is three days per grading period. He is again at that threshold."

Some of her fight deflated as she acknowledged the headmaster had a valid point.

Headmaster McCall used his pointer finger to tap next to the handbook. "When I brought him in to discuss this, your son explained something about a long-lost grandfather sleeping on a park bench and an eviction notice?"

Paislee's grip was so tight on her purse strap she feared tearing it off entirely. Anger and humiliation warred within her.

His expression suggested that something was not on the up-and-up and he was on the hunt to find out what. "Naturally, I felt compelled tae reach out tae you, as this seems unlikely."

She exhaled and counted to ten, calming herself down as she tried to rehearse a proper response in her mind.

Headmaster McCall stared at her across the desk, his brown eyes laser sharp. "Is your son in the habit of lying, Ms. Shaw?"

She reeled back on the chair. "Naw. He did *not* make that up."

He nudged the book aside and shook his head. Paislee could tell that he didn't believe her. "Rules are meant tae create safe boundaries. When rules are not enforced at home, we find that spills over tae a student's schoolwork."

She glared at the man across from her. He was so correct in his manner that she suspected he had everything in his life smooth and controlled. "How would you know? Do you have children of your own?"

"N-no," he sputtered.

"A wife?"

They both looked at his naked ring finger.

He tilted his head, his dark hair falling to one side. "*I* am not the one we've arranged this meeting for today."

What was his issue with her? Was she not measuring up to some parental standard he thought she should reach?

"I find your attitude toward me and Brody tae be judgmental. Maybe in your fancy university they missed the part about compassion and understanding?"

His jaw tightened and he straightened in his seat. "I beg your pardon?"

"For the record, my grandfather *was* brought tae my place of business, as he had been sleeping in the park. He is now living with us until we locate his son. I *did* receive a notice that the building I lease my business through was sold without my knowledge, and I have thirty days tae relocate."

He smoothed his tie, his nostrils slightly flared.

Paislee channeled Gran and managed a reasonable tone, finding strength in the truth. "My son knows better than tae lie; it's good you called me in so that we could get this matter cleared up." She rose, wishing she were taller than five foot three. "If he tells you that someone we know just died, well, that happened, too. I apologize for being two minutes tardy. We will not be late again."

Paislee sailed out of his office, her vision blurry, but she did not cry—she *would* not. They would all be getting up thirty minutes earlier for the rest of the school year. It was only three blasted months. She could do it.

Brody saw her in the parking lot and took his time saying good-bye to his mates before getting in the Juke.

He buckled up, still not speaking to her. She didn't look at the school window, not wanting to give Headmaster McCall the satisfaction of knowing she was upset.

"Why are *you* mad at *me*?" If anything, she should be the one having words with her son, telling all of their personal business to the judgmental headmaster.

"No one believed me!" Brody shouted. "Mrs. Martin didnae believe me, and sent me tae the headmaster—he asked if I was making up stories tae get out of trouble!"

She could well imagine how awful that must have been— she was still stung by it.

"I'm sairy, Brody." No matter what else had happened, it was her responsibility to make sure they were at school on time—even better would be ten minutes early. It was easy to get caught up in the rush of doing one last thing, like the dishes, or a load of laundry that could wait until the weekend.

He looked at her to see if she meant it, so she nodded.

"I dinnae want detention."

She flushed as she recalled the handbook of rules and her signature scrawled on the page. "I don't blame ye. Tell you what, if we are late, for any reason, and you get detention, I will serve it with you. Fair?"

Brody's eyes widened and then he grinned. "Aye."

Her son knew that she meant every word—overwhelmed she might be, but they didn't lie to each other—they'd made a pact to be honest, even if it hurt, back when he'd first asked about Santa Claus and the Tooth Fairy.

Gran had said to let him be a child, but at six Brody was wicked smart and when he'd looked at Paislee, demanding the truth, well, she went with her gut and explained that they were stories to make you feel good—but he wasn't to share this truth with any of his schoolmates.

To her knowledge, he hadn't.

Paislee had one job to do on this earth, and raising Brody was more important than her business, or some headmaster judging her decisions.

She would stand by her choices.

When they arrived home, Brody sprinted out back and threw a ball to play with Wallace. Her son's laughter was better medicine than a cup of tea. Her grandfather sat on the porch with a newspaper and what smelled like Earl Grey with whisky. Specifically, Glenlivet.

Had he gotten into her stash behind the oatmeal?

"Hiya," she said in greeting. "I see you found more than the soup?"

He tugged his beard, his eyes twinkling behind his black frames. "I didnae think ye'd begrudge your grandad a nip."

"So long as you left me some." Paislee rarely imbibed, but there were times when even Gran had claimed a dram of whisky to be what the doctor ordered.

His silver brows slammed together. "A gentleman never drains the last of the bottle. I'll replace it when I get me check."

Paislee sat and sipped from his mug, her eyes watering at the strong spirits. "I think we should have a heart-tae-heart."

He stiffened but then met her eyes. "Aboot?"

"I had a meeting with the headmaster today at school, and I cannae let Brody be one second late for the rest of the year."

"How long?"

"Three months." She held up her palm as she considered just how her grandpa might best be of assistance. "We havenae had a chance tae really discuss your living situation."

"Craigh is missing," he said defensively.

"I will call the *Mona*. You can help me out, too." She sat on the edge of the wicker chair to make eye contact—no games.

"How is that, lass?"

"Lydia is going tae email me a contact at Elder Care services in Inverness, in case there is some financial aid you can receive, or even housing?"

"Charity." His body went rigid. "I'm not movin' into a home—I'd rather take me chances camping, like I told ye."

"No camping!" She tilted her head back in frustration before looking at him again. "And it isnae charity. Ye worked all yer life and paid into the system. It's time the system paid ye

back, that's all. And I dinnae know if this will help. We just
need tae make a few phone calls tae see if you can have your
own place."

He drained his tea. "No."

She recognized his pride and gently clasped his wrist.
"Grandpa Angus, please make the calls. Get information. You
are welcome tae stay here—"

"Just until we find Craigh. I have a bit of money every
month, and I was a commercial fisherman before me back gave
out. I can fetch us Sunday dinner, so we willnae be starvin'."

Her Sundays were her day to sort socks and catch up with
household chores as she spent time with Brody and, if Craigh
didn't turn up, her grandfather. "I don't fish, but Brody mentioned he'd like tae give it a try." She glanced out at Brody,
who was chasing Wallace around the clothesline pole.

"I'm no babysitter, or free labor."

Why did he have to be so darn prickly? Scottish pride
combined with old age. *Ach.* "I think we can work out an arrangement that suits us both." He opened his mouth and she
raised her hand. "I know, I know, just until we find Craigh."

Brody and Wallace raced up the steps of the porch and
back down again. Paislee rose and held her hand out for
Grandpa's mug.

"What are ye doin'?"

"Making us each a mug of 'tea,' is that awright?" She had no
plans to leave for the night, and it had been one heck of a day.

Grandpa grinned but then pushed her gently down to the
wicker chair. "I'll get it, lass. Why don't ye put yer feet up?"

He shuffled inside and Paislee rested her feet on an old
milk crate. All she needed was her knitting. There were a million things she could be doing, but at this moment watching
Brody and Wallace chase a yellow ball around her back garden
was what she wanted to do most of all.

Grandpa bumped out the back with a tray of fortified tea and crackers with hard cheese. "Here ye are, lass."

He creaked down, his bones popping like the wicker chair. With a smack of his lips he clinked his mug to hers.

"Slainte," she said.

"Do dheagh shlàinte!"

They drank.

Chapter 10

As promised, Paislee dropped Brody off at school Wednesday morning at quarter till nine and tried not to take offense when Headmaster McCall politely clapped his hands. Arrogant man.

She could own up to her mistakes—but would he? Judging her on who knows what merit, and wrong about it besides.

Biting back a colorful complaint, she drove with her grandfather to Cashmere Crush. The idea of losing this place, so close to the bandstand and free parking, and downtown festivals like the one this Saturday, physically hurt her heart.

She entered the shop with Grandpa on her heels, his brown work boots clomping against her polished cement floor. "Get the light?" she asked.

He did, and she relaxed in the familiar space. The interior was cozy and bright with rows and rows of color-coordinated skeins of yarn. Granny's voice was at the back of her head— change, she'd say, was inevitable.

How could she manage this situation best? She would have to talk with Flora, whose natural-dyed-yarn website business was thriving, about ways to increase her online sweater sales.

She'd started out her business that way but had changed her focus to the storefront.

"I hear ye sighin'," Grandpa complained. "What now?"

"Nothing new—but I think I have plenty tae worry about, don't you?"

"Your choice, but it's a waste a time."

"You know, I used tae have a few minutes of quiet in the morning?"

"I'm happy tae go home."

They both bit their tongues at the fact that he didn't have one.

His home with her was temporary—as he kept saying.

"Sairy," Paislee said, putting her purse beneath the register. "I didnae sleep well last night. I kept dreaming of Isla." The girl had been crying and asking for help.

He crossed his arms, the elbows of his blue chambray shirt a lighter blue but clean. "It's a shame we havenae heard what happened tae her, and odd that it's been out of the news."

"I'm going tae call my friend Amelia again today—she was out sick yesterday; otherwise we might know something already."

He whistled dismissively. "If ye want tae know what's happening, call the detective."

"On what grounds?" She opened the safe and brought out the money for the till. "Curiosity?"

He snorted and tapped his nose. "Mibbe too . . . ?"

Paislee loaded the change drawer and checked the receipt tape, then switched the radio on with the sound low. The door opened and in walked the detective, minus his rain jacket as the morning was bright, the skies clear. For now. Weather in Nairn could change in an instant.

"Speak of the devil," Grandpa Angus said, taking a seat on the stool by the register.

"The devil?" Detective Inspector Zeffer asked. His blue suit looked Italian and very stylish for a man of the law. His black shoes had a shine as if polished. Did anybody polish their shoes these days?

"Never mind," Paislee said, blowing her bangs back. She was immediately self-conscious in her denims and loose bohemian-style blouse in light blue. Her hair was straight at her shoulders. Casual for work, but compared to the detective, she felt too casual in her own shop.

If he weren't married already, he'd be a handsome match for Lydia, who was always looking for her next love. Then again, the detective might give her frostbite, so Paislee wouldn't suggest it.

"I had a few more questions about Isla Campbell." The detective pulled a skein of yarn from a plastic bag and set it on the counter—no rings on any of his fingers.

She recognized the skein as the one Gerald's dog, Baxter, had been running around with, and realized it must have come from inside Isla's flat. "Is that the same . . ." she trailed off.

Detective Inspector Zeffer's pale green eyes seemed to bore into her for the truth before he'd even asked a question. "Aye."

"How did she die?" Paislee blurted. Though less than forty-eight hours had passed, it felt as if she'd been waiting for days for some piece of news.

He stepped back and tucked his hands in his trouser pockets. "Her death is under investigation."

"What does that mean?" Grandpa Angus asked.

Detective Inspector Zeffer cleared his throat. "I cannae say."

"For how long?" asked Paislee.

"Until we locate her next of kin. Isla used tae work for you. Do you have an emergency contact number for her?" The detective pulled his slim black leather notebook from his suit jacket pocket.

Cheeks flushed, her personal redhead curse, she said, "Naw, Isla never filled out an application. I have Isla's mobile number, but that willnae help."

"Do you happen tae have her mother's?"

"I dinnae. Don't even know her name. They didnae get along well. I think she lives in Edinburgh."

"The number we have has been disconnected. It's possible she's moved."

"Is that why ye've kept it out of the news?" Grandpa held up yesterday's paper. "I've been looking for a notice in the obituary."

"It's policy," the detective said. His no-frills tone reminded her of Headmaster McCall. Maybe arrogance bred success at a young age? She would teach Brody a different way.

"It's *sad*," Paislee countered, taking her place behind the counter next to the register. "I spoke with Tabitha, her best friend. They used tae share a flat on Dartmouth Street."

Detective Inspector Zeffer's eyes narrowed. "What did you talk about?"

"Well, nothing exactly. Tabitha burst into tears and hid in the office," she said. "Her co-worker mentioned the two had fought before Isla had moved."

He winced. "Tabitha . . ."

"Drake," she supplied. "She works at the flower shop across the street." Paislee hoped that if she helped him, then maybe the detective wouldn't be so closemouthed.

"I see."

She poked the yarn with a knitting needle that had been lying by her register. One end had been knotted, as if Isla had been ready to start a project. "You know that Isla took heart medication?"

Detective Inspector Zeffer gave a slight nod. "You said that before. Digoxin."

"Did she die of heart failure?" The prescription bottle had

been out on the table when she usually kept it in her purse. She hated for anyone to know she needed medication. Then again, it was her home, and Paislee was probably reading too much into it. She wanted to tell the detective about the short-bread cookies, too—Isla didn't eat sweets of any kind, and didn't like dogs.

"I cannae tell you that," he said, folding his arms. "This is an open investigation, which means that I get tae ask the questions and *you* get tae answer them."

Grandpa Angus chortled and turned away.

Paislee straightened. "Well then." She would keep her observations to herself.

"I also wanted tae ask you about this wool? Amelia Henry said you might be able tae help, since you have a yarn shop." He sounded doubtful.

On the verge of saying she knew absolutely nothing, she restrained herself on Isla's behalf.

She ran her finger over the grayish-beige skein. "This is merino wool, untreated, undyed, but excellent quality."

"Where can you buy it?"

"There are many sheep farms around Scotland that sell their wool for commercial yarn."

"I've noticed." His sarcasm was unmistakable. His accent was Scottish but had a unique cadence that meant he wasn't from around here. Not Edinburgh, either. Isla had been from there, and she hadn't sounded like the detective. It was a subtle difference in how the words were spoken.

"More sheep than people," Grandpa said.

The land was dotted with them, part of the countryside's charm. "Local crafters, such as myself, pride themselves on using local wool. It's what makes us unique tae the area, and tae those who visit."

"Have ye seen this before?" Detective Inspector Zeffer

held up the wool and glanced to the thousands of skeins on her shelves along the walls.

"I can't be certain. It helps tae have a label from the farm."

"It'll be like finding a needle in a haystack without one." The detective quickly closed his notebook and zipped the skein back in his plastic bag.

"Is it important? I can ask around. I know some distributors in Inverness and Edinburgh."

"There are close tae a hundred," he said. "I have an officer checking them out."

"That many?" Grandpa Angus asked in surprise.

Wool was a big business in Scotland, and while not as much a moneymaker as the oil and gas industries, sheep were still important for not only textiles but food. She enjoyed a leg of lamb as much as the next lass. "Isla worked for Vierra's Merino Wool Distributor, but what you have there was never treated, which they usually do before selling it. Vierra's is a large upscale operation near Inverness."

He shrugged. "I've spoken with her former boss."

"Maybe he has her mother's number?"

"It wasnae on Isla's application." Zeffer patted his suit pocket. "I'm new and you don't know me, but rest assured I willnae stop until I find answers." He firmed his lips and left, the sun glinting through her frosted front window to shine on his russet hair, turning the brown and auburn to burnt gold.

"He willnae get folks tae open up tae him like that," Paislee remarked. "In Nairn, people help each other out."

Grandpa pulled a worn fishing magazine from his back pocket and placed it on the counter, then helped himself to a wrapped candy—only five were left in the bowl. "I bet he's from Glasgow. I fished with a mate from there—crazy times."

"I'll ask Amelia. Poor dear, having tae work with him all day." She dropped her knitting needle in the cup holding her pens and pencils. "Can ye believe that Isla's mum might not know about her own daughter yet?" What pain and sorrow the woman had in store. "I wonder if Billy would have her phone number or address. . . ."

"Billy?" Grandpa popped the toffee into his mouth and balled up the foil wrapper.

"Isla's boyfriend, or ex, if her neighbor is correct and they broke up. Tabitha would have his number for sure. I'd like tae ask him if he has Isla's mum's number, and let him know that I cared for her, too."

"If they broke up, I have me doubts he cares at all."

She ignored that. "Isla had such high hopes when they left together, tae start a new life. She mentioned marriage."

Grandpa snorted. "Men and women have different ideas about that all the time."

Paislee walked to the front window and peered out to the flower shop. Ritchie was carrying a large bouquet of assorted flowers, which he placed in the back of the floral delivery van, and then sped off.

Tabitha would be alone, and maybe more talkative.

"I'll be right back, Grandpa."

He grunted something but read his magazine.

She quickly crossed the street to the flower shop, the scent of gardenia more potent than the roses had been the day before.

"Morning," she said cheerfully.

Tabitha was at the same back table as yesterday, only this time she worked on a bouquet of gladiolas and irises, perfect for spring. Low dishes of snow-white gardenia blossoms around the shop created a distinct perfume. "Hello." Tabitha's greeting was laden with reluctance. Her hair was in a tight bun, and Isla's scarf was absent.

"Feeling better?" Paislee kept her tone light and had even

decided to let her questions about the scarf go in order to help find Isla's mum. "I'd hoped tae speak tae you. . . ."

"Ritchie told me." Tabitha peered between the tall floral stems. "Now's not a good time."

Paislee took a step forward. "Tabitha, I'm sairy about Isla. I dinnae want tae bother you, but I'd hoped ye could give me Billy's phone number?"

"Why?" Her knife clattered to the table.

"Tae help the police locate Isla's mother."

"Isla hated her." The florist glared at Paislee, her brown eyes dull. With regret? Sadness? "Ye know she did nothin' but complain aboot her."

"Still, she deserves tae know her daughter's dead, don't you think?"

Tabitha picked up her knife and trimmed a purple gladiola. "I dinnae even ken the woman's name."

"Me either. But Billy might. They lived together." Paislee watched Tabitha closely to see if the girl would give anything of her cheating nature away. If Ritchie was right, then Tabitha had been no friend to Isla, and it was all Paislee could do to be polite.

Tabitha chose another flower.

"Do you have it?" Paislee asked again.

Tabitha's gaze veered to the purse on a shelf below the tall worktable, and probably her mobile. What was that red package next to it? Biscuits? "Naw."

What a liar and cool as ye please. "What about the name of where he works? It's important, Tabitha." She wasn't leaving until she got an answer.

Another minute passed. "He's shearing sheep at Lowe Farm." Tabitha broke the stem of a dark purple iris.

"Thanks." Just to give the girl a push back for being difficult, Paislee shrugged and said, "I might run up tae see him."

Tabitha flinched. Why wouldn't Tabitha want her to talk with Billy? The girl was hiding something, or jealous maybe of her unfaithful boyfriend? Paislee wanted to tell her that any man she couldn't trust wasn't worth having.

Paislee couldn't force Tabitha to give her Billy's number—it was childish when Paislee just wanted to help. As a mum, she couldn't imagine not knowing her child was . . . gone.

She decided to try kindness one more time. "I'm sairy that you and Isla argued before she moved." Paislee squinted at the shelf, Tabitha's purse, and the red packet. Those were short-bread cookies, the same brand as had been at Isla's. "Were you able tae patch things up when she returned?"

"I never spoke to her after she left for Inverness." Tabitha's eyes glittered with tears. "If ye don't mind? I have work tae do."

"Cheers."

Paislee hurried out of the flower shop with a sour taste at the back of her throat. Tabitha was a liar—and not any better at it than Gerald had been about telling the detective he'd been at the movies the night Isla had died.

Chapter 11

Paislee stood on the sidewalk outside the flower shop, rubbing her arms and wishing she'd snagged her sweater before visiting Tabitha. She waited for traffic on the two-way street to slow before darting across Market toward Cashmere Crush. It was imperative that she talk to Billy about how to track down Isla's mother. It was the last thing she could do to help the poor lass.

What if Isla had been so upset by Billy and Tabitha that her poor weak heart just gave out? *Naw. Isla had more spunk than that.*

Paislee made it five feet from her door when the owner of the neighboring leather repair shop, James Young, accosted her. At seventy-seven, he looked a wee bit like Mick Jagger, complete with impish glint in his eye.

"Paislee, love, come here." He tugged her inside his shop with strong, arthritic fingers.

The scent of leather and oil surrounded her and she found it more comforting than the heavy perfume of gardenia from the floral shop.

The company was a great sight better, too. "Aye, James? What is it?"

"What are we tae do about that rascal Shawn Marcus, up and sellin' the building beneath us?" He leaned a bony hip against his worktable located at the front window so that he could watch passerby as he worked, and entice them in as well.

"I dunno, James, but I have my friend Lydia looking into other spaces. If ye like, I can ask her for you, too."

"Sweet ye are, but where am I going tae find somethin' as big as this, for the price? Foot traffic during tourist season pays me bills in the winter months."

Paislee knew firsthand the value of having a low overhead for her business. "I get it." She scanned his shop with familiarity. Loops of leather hung on the back wall; metal buckets of brass snaps and buckles sat on either side of the table. A large calendar of the clock tower kept track of the days behind his register. Knives and hammers in varying sizes were arrayed on a shelf among framed photos of his family.

"We're having a meeting Sunday at the tea shop—Theadora's hosting. You should come."

Sundays were her days with Brody. Gran had taught her to have one day a week that was not work. "I dinnae ken. . . ."

" 'Tis important. We're going tae see if there's anything tae be done tae stop the sale of the building."

That would be the best solution, and far preferable to moving. "One of my knitters promised she'd contact the historical society, because the building is two hundred years old."

James rubbed his hands together like an ancient leprechaun standing over a pot of gold. "That's just the thing ye need tae share with the others, lass."

"I don't know anything just yet. What have *you* found out?"

"Ned"—he jerked his thumb to the left and the wall he shared with the dry cleaner—"said he'll do all right, everybody needs their washin' done, but he'll have tae raise prices.

Margot from the lab feels the same—she thinks she might even be able tae find cheaper space if she moves out of town center. Folks needin' bloodwork done arenae usually tourists, aye?"

"True."

"Lourdes isn't wed to the office supply biz and plans tae close shop completely tae do adult day care."

"What's that?" She imagined Grandpa Angus with a bowl of porridge, playing with plastic trucks, and cringed.

James screwed his wrinkled face up even more. "Droppin' the old folks off, instead of the kiddies. What a world we live in. Not the kind of diapers I'd be wantin' tae change. No matter the excellent money." He rubbed his fingers together.

She grinned. "Sounds like she'll be earning every penny."

"That she will, that she will. So, will we see ye Sunday?"

"I cannae promise, but I'll let you know what I find out from Elspeth either way. Sundays are family days."

"Right, right. Theadora will be disappointed, but I understand. The kids grow up so fast! And I heard yer grandfather is stayin' with ye?"

Small towns meant everybody knew everybody else's business; in addition to looking out for one another, they showed they cared by asking questions—which prodded her to track down Billy.

James cleared his throat, and she blinked back to attention. "Aye, for a while. He's helping out at the shop during tourist season."

"Yer a good lass, Paislee Shaw."

"Thanks. Is Theadora in, ye think? I'll go tell her myself about Sunday." Her mouth watered as she thought of raspberry scones, warm from the oven. Maybe she'd bring some back to Grandpa to keep him happy while she took a drive to see Billy.

"Aye. Cheers."

Paislee left with a wave and walked right, toward Theadora's Tea Shoppe. The jewel of a bakery on the corner of their block was painted turquoise blue. The flower boxes with the impatiens and bluebonnets added spring cheer. A blue-green awning provided shade over half a dozen turquoise tables and matching chairs.

The outside tables were full of locals and tourists taking advantage of the sunny day. If Paislee squinted, she could see the bandstand, and beyond that, the Firth.

She entered the bakery and breathed in deep—what she loved most was Theadora's raspberry scones, fresh from the oven. She could smell the sweet raspberry as she waited in a queue of six.

If business was this booming before the start of tourist season it was no wonder Theadora wanted to devise a plan to block the sale. She would see what Elspeth had to say regarding the historical society.

Theadora was behind the register, her white and turquoise hair a walking advertisement for the bakery. She was popular in town and supported local businesses and schools, though she didn't have bairns of her own.

"Paislee?"

She pivoted on her heel toward her name and smiled at Amelia behind her. Her friend was the receptionist at the police station across the street to the right. Her poor nose was red and her lips chapped. "Amelia! Are you feeling better?"

"Aye—how'd ye know I was sick?" Amelia's short brunette hair was cut close to her head in a wispy shag that suited her pixie face and blue eyes. She was not required to wear a uniform, though she often chose navy-blue slacks and a blue polo.

"Norma—I called you yesterday."

Her mouth pinched together. "A cold is a miserable thing."

They moved up in line together until Paislee was next.

Theadora greeted them with a smile. "And what will ye have today?"

Paislee nudged Amelia forward in the queue. "Go ahead of me."

Amelia nodded. "Ta. Hot green tea with lemon and honey, please, and a croissant."

Theadora reached into the glass case next to the register for the croissant, and then filled an insulated paper cup with hot water. Amelia asked Paislee, "Why did ye call?"

"I'd hoped you knew what had happened tae Isla? I have-nae heard a thing since we found her on Monday."

"I feel so bad for the lass, even though I didnae care for her in life; nobody should be unclaimed."

Unclaimed? What did that mean?

Theadora returned with Amelia's order, and Amelia paid, putting the change in a plastic jar with a photo of kids playing golf. It was for Theadora to support the local kiddies' golf club.

"What can I get for you, Paislee?" Theadora's hand was poised over the register.

"Two raspberry scones, please, and two coffees to go."

"Ah, that's right. Ned said that yer tending tae yer grandfather?"

"Aye. James told me about the meeting Sunday, but I can-nae commit—it's my day with Brody."

Though in her thirties, Theadora clucked her tongue like an old woman. "We have tae band together, Paislee."

"I will and you know it. I have a lady reaching out tae the historical society tae see if there is something that can be done."

Theadora nodded and relaxed the slightest bit. "Just try."

"Aye."

"What's going on?" Amelia asked. "Where did you suddenly get a grandfather?"

Paislee paid Theodora, who'd packed the scones and drinks in a bag, thanked her, and walked with Amelia toward the exit. "We have got tae catch up, my friend."

"I was out sick *one* day," said Amelia, pushing the door open with her shoulder.

They went to a corner table that had just been vacated. Amelia set down her bag with the croissant.

Paislee, impatient for answers, bumped her arm into Amelia's. "So, do you know how Isla died?"

Amelia lifted the top off her tea and inhaled the lemon scent. "The coroner's report concluded that she overdosed on her heart medication."

Isla had been so careful with her diet and her medicine that Paislee had a hard time imagining she'd be thoughtless. "Accidental?"

"He thinks suicide."

Paislee flinched and sucked in a breath. "Suicide?" Maybe Isla had been so broken up over Billy that she couldn't go on. . . . Paislee berated herself for not calling Isla right away. Fresh tears burned her eyes and stung her nose. She felt as if she'd let Isla down. "I cannae believe it."

Amelia put the lid back on and lowered her voice. "Detective Inspector Zeffer hasnae signed off on the findings, and that hasnae gone over well in the department. Everyone's walkin' on eggshells at the station this morning."

"What does that mean?" Did he not think it was a suicide? She would almost rather believe it had been accidental. She crumpled a napkin in her palm, overcome with grief.

"He wanted more tests. Some of the officers think he's trying tae throw his weight around, ye know? Tae prove he can fill Inspector Shinner's shoes."

She recalled the detective saying that he might be new to Nairn, but he would find the truth. "Do you agree?"

"I dinnae ken. He's only been in Nairn a week, and that doesnae seem long enough to judge whether or not a man can do his job."

Amelia's fair-mindedness was something Paislee admired.

A robin landed on the sidewalk next to them. Amelia reached into her bag and tossed a croissant crumb to the bird, who gobbled it back. "Norma told me that the coroner was overheard shouting at the detective at the hospital morgue, calling him an upstart with no experience." Amelia tossed another crumb. "She's normally chatty as ye please, but today she kept looking over her shoulder the whole time." Amelia blinked. "I miss Inspector Shinner."

"I didnae know him like you, but I'm sairy, love." She rested her bag on the table. "Zeffer stopped by the shop tae ask about that skein of wool in Isla's apartment, and also about Isla's mum. He wasnae very friendly." She put the wadded-up napkin in her pocket. "That's not how we do things around Nairn, is it?"

"Naw." Amelia checked her watch. "Got to go. See you tomorrow night?"

Knit and Sip. "I'm glad you're feeling better, Amelia."

Paislee lifted her bag of goodies and walked back to Cashmere Crush deep in thought.

Her grandfather looked quite pleased with himself when she entered. "I just sold some yarn. No trouble at all with the register, being as they paid in cash. Correct change."

Paislee offered him a coffee and scone, still very sad about Isla and the news that she may have taken her own life. "Glad to hear it, Grandpa. I have an errand tae run, but I should be back in less than two hours, and then ye can have the rest of the day free."

His demeanor brightened even more. "How did ye manage without me?"

"It's a wonder." She grabbed her coffee and scone to go. Folks cared in Nairn, and that meant asking questions. Paislee had quite a few for Billy Connal.

Chapter 12

Paislee, inside her Juke, plugged in the address to Lowe Farm. Even though Billy was now with Tabitha, he'd once cared for Isla. What had gone wrong in their relationship to lead to Isla's return, and possible suicide?

She kept hearing Amelia say that Isla's body remained "unclaimed" and it chilled her.

Nobody should be alone in death like that.

She'd sat with Granny until her last breath, and there was peace in knowing she had died a happy, loved woman.

Why hadn't Isla reached out to her, if she was hurting like that? Paislee just couldn't allow herself to believe the coroner's ruling. She preferred to think the death an accident, though even that didn't sit well on her conscience.

The GPS informed her that she had twenty minutes to her destination.

Drinking her coffee and eating her scone, Paislee switched on the radio to sing along with Belle and Sebastian. The road to the farm forked off into a large field from the main highway. Acres and acres of green as far as her eye could see, sheep and cows, mostly sheep, sporadically dotted the view, with none of the stop-and-go traffic that had increased in Nairn with the recent rise in population.

Paislee spotted a wooden sign that read: Lowe Farm at the same time the GPS directed her to turn to her right.

Paislee slowed and followed the dirt road to a large wooden barn and sheep in various stages of being shorn. Woolly beasts were in one pen, and shorn in another, the dear things shivering without their wool coats. The farm butted up against a stream.

She got out, wishing she could bring Brody to see the sweet naked lambs, but she knew she had to walk a fine line with Headmaster McCall throughout the rest of the P6 school year.

A farmer in coveralls and a straw hat left the barn and ambled toward her. "Can I help you?"

"Hi! I was wondering if Billy Connal is here? I'd like tae speak with him."

The farmer muttered something under his breath. "Billy just left after getting a call—claimed tae be sick, all the sudden. If I didnae need experienced shearers so bad, I'd fire him on the spot. If he doesnae show up tomorrow, I'll do it anyway."

A phone call?

The man stomped mud and raw wool from his boot heel. "What do you want with Billy?"

"I own Cashmere Crush, a sweater and yarn shop in Nairn."

He didn't look like he gave a sheep's behind. "Why are you here? Chasin' him? A lass like you can do better."

"No!" She shook her head. "A friend of Billy's and mine has passed away, and I wanted tae speak with him."

The farmer adjusted the straw hat on his head, his expression unchanging. "Sairy tae hear that."

She glanced around the farm. "Where do you sell your yarn?"

"Vierra's, mostly. Some tae local crafters."

"Oh?" Vierra's was where she'd helped Isla get her job. "We support our sheep farmers—McFadden's as well as JoJo's?"

His shoulders eased on his wiry frame. "Good luck tracking down Billy—he's in the process of movin', he said. I'll let him know ye stopped by?"

She had a feeling that someone already had let him know she was looking for him, which was why he'd suddenly gotten sick. *Tabitha*. Why wouldn't he want to talk to her? Guilt over leaving Isla?

She handed over a Cashmere Crush business card. "Please have him call. You have a wonderful farm here."

"Thanks." Farmer Lowe touched the brim of his straw hat, turned on a boot heel, and strode back to the barn.

Paislee got into the Juke. Now what?

Since she was out this way—how far was Vierra's? She plugged in the address and discovered it was only five minutes down the road.

Thinking about her options for all of thirty seconds, Paislee knew she had to stop at Vierra's—what had happened to Isla? This was supposed to be her new start in life and yet she'd ended up alone in Nairn. Dead. Maybe her boss could share what her last days had been like so that Paislee could understand.

Leaving the farm with disappointment, Paislee drove to Vierra's Merino Wool Distributor and parked in the busy lot, snagging a front-row spot. The stone building had been painted white, with black trim around the windows and black doors.

She went inside the modern lobby. This business seemed to be from a completely different century than Lowe Farm.

Waiting for the receptionist at a long black desk, Paislee noticed chrome and steel sculptures that she supposed were meant to be art. They left her confused.

The receptionist cleared her throat.

Paislee righted her posture wishing she'd worn something other than jeans. "May I speak with Mr. Vierra?"

"Aye," the young woman said. Wild brown curls had been pulled back from her face into a ponytail. "Which one? Roderick just got back from lunch and he handles all the hiring and firing. His brother Roger manages the wool."

"Roderick. About someone who used tae work here." That was who she'd written the letter to, anyway. Paislee followed the speedy receptionist down a tiled hall.

The young woman knocked on a partially open door, and a masculine voice called for them to enter.

"Roderick, this lady, oh, I didnae get your name, would like tae talk tae you about—?" The phone at the reception desk rang again and the woman hustled back to the front lobby, leaving Paislee to make her own introductions.

"Hello." Paislee stayed in the doorway and scanned the man's black and chrome office. He lounged behind a black desk, and she guessed him to be forty, with glossy dark brown hair, deep brown eyes, and a goatee. A chrome nameplate read: Roderick Vierra. *Ohhhh.* He and his brother Roger must own Vierra's.

Next to the nameplate was a picture of Roderick with a pretty brunette wife and two brown-haired daughters, and a bundle of sample cards of merino wool.

"Have a seat, Ms. . . ."

"Paislee Shaw." They shook hands and she sat in a black chair in front of his shiny desk. She preferred her walls of colored yarn. "I own Cashmere Crush."

The man put his hands on his desk, eyeing her quizzically. "How can I help you?"

"I'm here with some sad news, actually—Isla Campbell has passed away."

Grief filled his face and he tugged at his goatee. "Yes, I

know. I've spoken tae the police about it already. Do they know how . . . ?"

Paislee was glad that he seemed to care. "The officers are still investigating. I was hoping you could tell me what happened? I wrote her recommendation letter tae you on her behalf." Her eyes smarted with unshed tears, and she pulled a tissue from her bag.

He absentmindedly shuffled the sample cards of wool. "I still cannae believe she's dead."

That made two of them. "Did you know Billy? Her boyfriend?"

Roderick's mouth turned down in anger and he dropped the cards with a thwack to the desktop. "He was sweet on a girl back in Nairn. Isla was verra upset about it. . . ."

"What happened?"

"I don't have the details, but it wasnae an easy time for her." He twisted his wedding ring as he held her gaze. "I had to let her go, unfortunately. Her work suffered."

Isla had floated for weeks before moving to Inverness with Billy—what had gone wrong for the lovebirds?

Paislee studied the cards of samples. Wool had a particular oil from the sheep, and the untreated strand reminded her of the skein in Isla's flat. "May I?"

Paislee pointed to the wool pieces attached to the cards.

He opened his desk drawer and scooped them inside. "Sairy—these are from last year. If you're interested in carrying the wool in your shop, I'd be happy tae set up an appointment with Roger. We have a minimum purchase requirement, as we sell in bulk."

Paislee sat back. Why didn't he want her to see that wool?

"That's all right." She shifted on the hard chair. "Isla worked with me for over a year and she normally had a smile on her face." The only time Isla had been sad had to do with doctor's visits warning her to be careful, or not hearing from her mother.

"That wasnae the Isla we knew." Roderick stroked his goatee, his mouth in a thin line. "Love does strange things tae people. She seemed brokenhearted."

So he'd fired her? What a jerk.

"When did you let her go?"

"Two weeks ago."

He didn't even look at the computer or a file to know when she'd left his employ. "You're sure?"

Roderick raked a manicured hand through his dark hair. "We have hundreds of employees, but little turnover—most people stay with us for years. It's how I met my lovely wife." He glanced at the photo on his desk.

Paislee remembered that a hundred or more workers could be employed in the warehouses packing wool for distribution when she'd done a tour of JoJo's years ago, and Vierra's was much bigger. Yet he knew Isla.

He drummed his fingers along the desktop. "Is there anything else?"

Paislee got up before she told him what she thought of his incredible lack of compassion. "Thank you for seeing me."

He lifted his hand and studied her with a guarded expression. Had he figured out that she wanted to know more about his relationship with Isla? "Bye."

She slung her bag over her shoulder and left the building feeling as though she was missing something. The man was odd—he'd been sad to hear that Isla was dead, though he'd already known. Then he'd seemed more than a little angry.

Glancing at her watch, Paislee realized that she needed to hustle to pick Brody up on time.

She hurried to her car, thinking that maybe just a few miles over the speed limit couldn't hurt. Headmaster McCall's disapproving brown eyes urged her to step on it. As she dodged the occasional sheep, she thought about Tabitha running into the back office in tears. She imagined the florist must feel guilty over stealing Isla's boyfriend. But the image that her mind wouldn't let go of was Isla's scarf around Tabitha's neck.

Her phone dinged an alarm and she let out a breath of air. She'd completely forgotten about Brody's appointment with Doc Whyte.

So much for giving her grandfather the afternoon off. How *had* she managed before him?

Chapter 13

Paislee pulled into Fordythe right behind the last car in the pickup queue, and praised the angels when Mary Beth Mulholland, driving a brand-new silver minivan, entered right after her so that Paislee was not the final car in line—her twin girls were two years younger than Brody.

Paislee waved at Mary Beth in the rearview, and the woman waved back without her usual exuberant smile. Paislee wondered what could be wrong. She pulled up and Brody jumped in wearing an annoyed expression as he slammed the door.

"And good afternoon tae you, too," Paislee said. "What's wrong?"

"Headmaster McCall is being too nice tae me, in front of the other kids."

Good! Maybe something Paislee'd said had reached the man's arrogant, know-it-all brain. It was no easy chore juggling so many things at once. If she occasionally had to race the clock to be on time, well, she did her best, didn't she?

"That's no reason tae be mad." Paislee pulled out of the school property and took a left toward Doc Whyte's office.

Everything around Nairn could be reached in fifteen minutes, though the Earl of Cawdor's plan to enlarge the place might change things—for the worse, in her opinion. For the best, in Lydia's.

As Paislee got older, she appreciated the quaint *shireness* of Nairn and already saw the town bursting at the seams as it sprawled outward.

"And then Mrs. Martin asked if I wanted tae talk tae the counselor. Like there was something wrong. What did ye say tae them, Mum?"

Paislee tightened her grip on the wheel and snuck a glance at Brody. "Uh, I just told the headmaster that we Shaws don't lie, and that we've had a few bumps—I *may* have brought up Isla's death."

Brody scowled as only a ten-year-old could do. "I hate school."

"Well, I'm not going tae homeschool ye." She would certainly not have the patience for that. "And we cannae afford tae send you tae Drumduan." Lydia knew Tilda Swinton and had suggested the independent school, until she'd found out the price, at over eight thousand a year. "So, you'll have tae do your part. It will be summer before ye know it."

He perked up at hearing that—then realized they weren't headed toward Cashmere Crush or home. "Where are we going?"

She braced herself—Brody was like every kid who didn't want to go to the doctor or the dentist. "We have your physical today with Doc Whyte."

"*What?*"

It was like she'd just told him she'd set Wallace's tail on fire. "Brody, it's not a big deal, just your annual checkup."

"Do I have tae get a jab?" He rubbed his arm.

Paislee gritted her teeth. "Don't know."

"I don't want tae go." His chin jutted out stubbornly.

"We've rescheduled three times—if we do it again, we might as well wait until next year."

"Aye. Let's do that."

"No, Brody. We are going." They parked in the crowded lot of a 1950s brick building that housed ten different medical offices.

She and Brody went inside the first-floor office and the waiting room to see Doc Whyte. A scent of antiseptic layered the air. Potted palms and a fish tank didn't change the medicinal atmosphere. There were over ten people on chairs in the square space —she recognized Colleen from the market, and Flora.

Paislee signed in and she and Brody found two padded chairs by the far wall where Flora was sitting, a cloth handkerchief in her hand and a daisy tucked behind her ear. Flora's long skirt reached the floor, vibrant with deep blues and jewel-tone greens.

Brody dug his tablet out of his backpack and plugged in his headphones to play video games while Paislee scanned the room, setting her brown leather hobo bag by her feet. Flora, eyes red, dabbed the end of her nose with her hankie.

"Flora, are you awright?"

Brody rolled his eyes at her dafty question.

The poor woman's energy was visibly drained, her shoulders slumped. "Allergies. As much as I love me springtime flowers and the colors they bring tae my yarn, the bog myrtle does me in."

"Sairy tae hear that." Even the daisy in Flora's long hair was limp.

"The doctor gives me medicine, and I'm good through spring, until the heather gets me in September."

"I hope you're getting enough rest." Paislee commiserated

with a pat on Flora's wrist. "You have so much on your plate."
She didn't say since Donnan's stroke, but she didn't have to.

Flora cupped the handkerchief in her palm. "I'm not complaining. Donnan's healthy as a horse, while I'm sneezing and
wheezing half the night. Probably keeping *him* up."

Tabitha exited the back office into the waiting room, and
Nurse Sandy suggested she take a seat. "I forgot tae get the
prescription from the doctor, one minute, Tabitha, and then ye
can go, poor dear."

Paislee half-stood to corner the girl about her lies but realized that now was not a good time. She slowly took her seat.

Tabitha's face was pale and pinched, her brow furrowed as
if she was in a lot of pain. Yes, that was the sage scarf visible in
Tabitha's bag. Did the girl have no shame?

It wasn't right what she and Billy had done to Isla. If there
weren't a crowd of people she would—Flora elbowed her in
the side.

"What's wrong?" Flora gestured discreetly toward Tabitha
by tilting her head.

Paislee'd never been good at hiding her feelings, and her
dislike must have shown on her face. "Do you know why
Tabitha is here?"

"I dinnae ken the girl, but she mentioned a migraine to
the nurse."

"She *was* Isla's best friend."

"Ah." Flora fixed her droopy daisy. "You always had a soft
spot for that lass—none of us understood."

Paislee shifted toward Flora. "How so?"

"Isla took advantage of ye, Paislee, askin' for special hours
and then not comin' in." Flora leaned in. "She told ye she
wanted tae learn to knit, but behind yer back, that's not what
she said at all."

Paislee straightened. "What are you talking about?" Her

mind scrambled to the year or so that Isla had worked for her. "She had her reasons." Doctor's appointments, or therapist appointments. Sometimes Isla was just too tired to come in.

And not everybody had to love knitting—so what if Isla had preferred to crochet?

Lydia didn't do either.

"I've upset ye, and that wasnae my intent," Flora said, empathy in her bloodshot eyes.

Paislee blinked back a tear. "I know she wasnae everyone's cup of tea, but I did care about her . . . and now she's gone, and . . ." Nobody to claim her body. She couldn't say anything else about it without breaking Amelia's confidence, so she shrugged and kept quiet.

The nurse returned with Tabitha's prescription.

The cheating best friend florist didn't look at Paislee at all before escaping the reception area. It was just as well.

Granny used to say all the time that if ye did good, ye got good, and Tabitha had not done good—it would come around.

"I hope you feel better by tomorrow, for the Knit and Sip. I've got tae get more of my flowers crocheted for the festival."

"I'll be right as rain after I see the doctor. I've got a new color I'm workin' on that I hope tae show you girls. A shade of green ye wouldnae believe."

"Flora Robertson!" the nurse called.

"Here!" Flora stood and waved at Paislee before reaching the nurse.

Nurse Sandy greeted Flora with a concerned expression and Paislee overheard her asking about Donnan, who was due in for some bloodwork.

"I'll make an appointment for next week. He doesnae like tae leave the house—says it's a bother."

The nurse gave Flora a half hug. "Let's get *you* taken care of." The two disappeared behind the door and down a hall.

Mary Beth's husband, Arran Mulholland, entered the office, a man of medium stature who wore his success like a tailored suit. Today he was more subdued in khakis and a polo, his jaw tightly set. Arran averted his eyes as he sat on the opposite side of the room, pinching the bridge of his nose, his complexion pasty.

Something going around? Maybe her husband's illness had been why Mary Beth hadn't been so exuberant in the queue, picking up her daughters.

What had caused Tabitha's migraine? Lying, cheating, or both?

Paislee recalled Isla's will to thrive—one day Isla'd had a scare with her heart skipping irregularly, but rather than whinge or cry, she'd laughed loudly, as if daring death to try to take her; Paislee had seen fear as well as determination in her eyes. "Not my time yet," she'd said.

No way would Isla have committed suicide. And she was way too careful to accidentally overdose.

Paislee remembered the way the dog had run out of the flat. Her neighbor, Gerald, peeking through the window at them. Something did not add up.

What if Isla had been murdered?

Paislee gasped and Brody looked at her with alarm. "Mum?"

She waved him back to his video game, her mind spinning. "It's nothing." What if someone—namely, Tabitha—had killed Isla in cold blood to get Billy for herself?

She thought back to the packet of shortbread beneath Tabitha's worktable, and the shortbread on Isla's dining room table—Isla didn't eat sugar. Had Tabitha taken Isla's scarf then? But why?

Her stomach churned as she considered such a crime.

The detective must have discovered something to make him ask the coroner for more tests. She thought back to what she'd seen in Isla's flat.

She clenched her hands into fists and propped them on her

knees, focusing on the bright yellow fish darting this way and that in the aquarium. Tea—Lipton. Shortbread—the most popular brand in Scotland, which was no help. A prescription bottle. Isla's blond hair splayed beneath her, her eyes fixed, lips blue. Her wee hand palm up, fingers curled. The silver of a crochet hook. The merino yarn.

Gerald's dog running out with the wool, the wool that Detective Inspector Zeffer had asked her about.

Gerald had been down to the station. What had he and the detective discussed?

Some of the wool samples on Roderick Vierra's desk were a similar shade and texture to what Baxter had in his mouth when he'd run from Isla's flat. That suggested to Paislee that Gerald had been inside Isla's home with his dog, and she and Grandpa Angus had both gotten the impression the young solicitor in training had been lying about something—either his relationship with Isla or where he'd been the night she'd died.

Possibly *murdered*.

Brody elbowed her. "Mum!"

"Ouch!" She held her side. "What?"

"The nurse's been callin'."

She looked to Nurse Sandy, who grinned and lifted a clipboard.

"You were far and away!" the nurse called.

She and Brody stood, and Paislee slung her hobo bag over her shoulder.

"Embarrassing," Brody mumbled. "Yer losing your mind, Mum."

"Hey, now. It was a momentary lapse." One she had to bury in order to get through the rest of her day. But how could she? *Poor Isla.*

Paislee and Brody quickly brushed by the friendly nurse to the back area and the scale. Nurse Sandy made note of his weight and then took his height measurement. "Two centimeters taller."

Thank heaven for shorts over the summer, or she'd need to buy him all new clothes. "Now I can stop feeding you."

He shook his head as if she was being ridiculous. "Not funny."

They were led into the exam room and told it would be a few minutes.

Brody climbed up on the exam table while Paislee took the chair, leaving the wheeled stool for the doctor. Nurse Sandy left with a smile.

"This isnae so bad, right?" Paislee set her purse by her feet.

"It's not playing football with me mates," Brody informed her.

Ah, the real reason he was upset about having a doctor's appointment.

"Tomorrow, then."

"We cannae have the field on Thursdays. The band kids have drill."

"That's right—well, there's always Friday." God bless her, but where had the week gone? The festival was three days away, and she wasn't at all prepared.

"I have a project due tomorrow." His heel kicked back against the exam table as his legs dangled over the edge.

"What kind of project?"

He glanced at her from behind auburn bangs. "I have tae make a kite that really flies."

"By *tomorrow*?" What did she know about making kites? It sounded complicated. "When did you get this assignment?"

"I dunno."

"Brody."

He didn't look at her. "Last week."

She counted to five. "You know I dinnae like it when ye

give me these things last minute, Brody. We could have worked on it over the weekend and then—"

"Then we wouldnae have hiked with Wallace in the park," he interrupted. "We would've stayed home."

It had been such a fair day with blue skies that they'd bundled up and taken a picnic to the hills. It had been a magical, although brisk, Sunday afternoon.

Which wasn't the point—Brody couldn't fib about things just to get his way. "Not telling me something like that is a form of dishonesty, and here I just told your headmaster that we didnae lie."

"It wasnae a lie," Brody insisted. He pulled his headphones for his tablet from his pocket.

She arched her brow. "If you dinnae tell me something that I should know, that is called a lie by omission."

"What's that?" He put in one earbud, as if to tune her out, so she shook her head and held out her hand for them.

"Sentences when ye get home, then, so ye don't forget. The definition of *omission*, ten times."

"Mum!" He reluctantly gave the headphones to her.

Doc Whyte entered the room. The only change, after all these years she'd known him, was the color of his hair, which had gone from red to white. He was trim and affable, and she adored him, as did all of Nairn fortunate enough to have him as a doctor. "A few sentences never hurt anybody, Brody Shaw. You've sprouted up, lad, haven't ye?"

He smoothly changed the subject—supporting her decision while not taking sides. He had a brood of children, eight in all, spread out in age, and now some with bairns of their own.

"Two centimeters," said Brody.

Doc Whyte read the report. "Gaining weight, too. Let's have a look at your eyes and ears." He sat on the rolling stool and pulled out his stethoscope, doing his checkup while cracking jokes. The doctor pointed a silver circle toward her. "He must eat you out of hearth and home?"

"Cheese sandwiches and crisps." Paislee was just grateful that Brody was healthy, and gave a prayer of thanks. "Oatmeal is a stretch."

"I never liked porridge, either," the doc said, whirling round on his stool.

Brody forgot he was mad at her by the time Doc Whyte offered him a choice of candy or a pencil eraser. Brody took the sucker, unwrapped it, and had it in his mouth before Paislee could tell him a thing about waiting on sweets before dinner.

They left with a promise to be back in August.

He was growing up so fast that she felt time slipping between her fingers like water—no matter how tight she tried to hold on, it slid through.

Sniffing back tears, Paislee cleared her throat and started the Juke. "Before we go home, what supplies do ye need for the kite? We can stop at the hardware store."

Brody scrunched his nose, unzipping his backpack and pulling out a sheet of paper. Mrs. Martin had given very precise directions with photos for examples, something that would have been very helpful last week.

"I want tae make a dragon," Brody said.

"A dragon?" Paislee eyed the complicated instructions, a sense of unease rising in her belly. "What's wrong with the one that's shaped like a diamond?"

"Boring."

"If ye wanted a dragon, ye should've told me last week."

He shut up about the dragon. "A diamond's fine." He read aloud. "We need wooden dowels, twine, glue, and a plastic garbage bag, then paper for the tail."

She scraped back her bangs. They could do this.

Her mobile rang—her own number? "Hello?"

"It's five o'clock, lass—where are ye?"

Grandpa! Still in the doctor's parking lot, she pounded the steering wheel. He had no keys to lock up the shop, and she hadn't gotten used to him being around. "I'm on my way right now, sairy."

"Mum—we need supplies for the kite." Brody rattled the paper.

"I thought ye were only going tae be gone a while, and I'm famished," Grandpa said. "All the candy's gone."

Paislee's blood pressure rose as each Shaw complained.

"I'll be right there, Grandpa. As a treat"—she ignored the groan of her credit card—"we'll get Chinese takeout."

Brody stopped glaring at her and nodded.

"That'll do," Grandpa said. "I've straightened the shop—we only had two sales of yarn and one blanket pattern. I don't know how ye keep a roof over yer head with such dismal sales."

Really? She shook the phone. "I'll be there in ten minutes."

She hung up and pressed carefully down on the gas, having Brody call the Chinese restaurant and order chicken lo mein and sweet and sour pork with extra fortune cookies.

Those were two sales she wouldn't normally have had. She hated to admit that having an extra set of hands was more help than bother.

Chapter 14

Paislee dropped Grandpa and Brody off at home to set out dinner, while she raced to Rex's Hardware for kite-making supplies. From there, she headed toward Cashmere Crush with the proper-sized dowels, according to Mrs. Martin's list. Paislee had pattern paper that would make a sturdy tail. When she passed the police station, Amelia was leaving for the day, her lightweight navy-blue jacket zipped up to her chin.

Paislee made a split-second decision and pulled in next to Amelia's car in the lot. She rolled down her window, letting in the chilly sea air.

"Amelia! I had a quick question. Were they able tae find Isla's mum?"

Amelia walked to the Juke's open window, her hands in her pockets. "Not yet."

"I just missed talking tae Billy today tae see if he had her number, but I'll try again tomorrow."

"You shouldnae get involved," Amelia said with a guilty look back at the station. "Detective Inspector Zeffer gave us all a lecture today on protecting a citizen's right tae privacy." She leaned in. "Between us, I think Norma got tae talking tae the postman and the detective overheard her."

Paislee bit her lip, not sure what to say. She wanted to know about Isla!

"He's no Inspector Shinner, that's for sure. Shinner used tae tell us all the nitty-gritty details of his cases." Amelia glanced at Paislee and then away. "He said that I'd make a good constable."

She pulled back. "Inspector Shinner did? I didnae know police work interested you." Since Amelia was a receptionist at the station, maybe it shouldn't be such a surprise.

Amelia shrugged shyly and met Paislee's gaze. "I'm not smart enough tae be a police officer."

"Says who?" Paislee was all about breaking expectations, even one's own. Especially one's own.

"The whole lot back at home. I was the only one tae graduate high school. My brothers went into fishin' and me parents barely scrape by."

Paislee could easily imagine being held fast to earth, but her gran had helped her fly. "If ye want," she said, "I'll help you study."

Amelia sucked in a breath. "You would?"

She would make the time, if it meant that Amelia could follow her dream. "Aye—that's what friends are for."

Amelia stared down at the pavement, a grin on her face. "I'll think about it some more—it would be eleven weeks of training. I dunno." She clapped her hand against the car. "I have tae go. Dungeons and Dragons tonight at the pub."

It cracked her up that a bunch of gamers gathered in a dark pub with their laptops to play online D&D and drink beer. The drinking beer part she got, but what happened to pool or darts?

She got to Cashmere Crush, collected the paper for the kite tail, and counted out the till. Before she knew it, the time was a quarter past seven and her cell phone rang—Brody.

"Mum—where are ye? Yer food is cold, and Grandpa doesnae know how tae play the fortune cookie game."

"I'll be there in a few minutes with your supplies. If you have free time, get the rest of your homework done, or you can write out ten times the definition of a lie by omission."

"Lame." He hung up.

She flicked her gaze to the ceiling of her shop and said a quick prayer to Gran for patience.

When she reached the house and went inside, Brody was seated at the kitchen table and Grandpa had his arms crossed, glaring at her son. Wallace darted toward her, his black tail wagging.

The other two didn't say a word, at risk of breaking their standoff.

"What is going on?" She looked at her grandfather.

"Yer son willnae do his homework."

She shifted to Brody, who said, "He's no' in charge of me."

Paislee exhaled and entered the kitchen all the way, dropping the bag of kite supplies next to Brody's chair.

"That is true, but your grandfather is an adult and deserves respect." She faced her grandfather. "Brody is very self-sufficient, and I trust him tae get his work finished."

The last thing she needed was to be a referee. She gave Wallace's ears a scratch and saw a dish of food had been saved for her on the counter. "Is that for me?"

"It's cold," they said in unison.

Great. She took the clear wrap off of the dish and dug in. Even cold, chicken lo mein was delicious, and when was the last time she'd eaten?

After she finished half the plate, she set it aside. Her grandfather had retreated with his mug of tea to the stool by the counter and Brody wrote something on a math sheet.

"Done," Brody said, sending visual daggers toward Grandpa.

Grandpa slurped.

"Wonderful—let's get started on the kite then. Want tae get the box of scissors and glue?"

The tall, narrow cupboard under the stairwell held both crafty stuff and miscellaneous collected odds and ends she was going to get around to sorting one day but never did. Lydia joked that most people had a junk drawer, while Paislee had a whole closet.

Brody ran back with the box, Wallace chasing him in hopes he might drop something fun and tasty.

"In my day, we didnae let children run in the house," her grandfather intoned.

She didn't pick up the argument but kept her focus on Brody as they laid out the dowels, glue, paper, plastic bag, and twine.

It was the longest hour of Paislee's life as Grandpa Angus offered barbed critique on the angle of the diamond shape to the length of the paper tail. Since Paislee had never made a kite before and Grandpa had, she took what bits of advice sounded plausible and ignored the rest.

"We need tae fly it," Brody said once it was assembled.

In the dim kitchen light, it didn't look half-bad, until you peered closely at the lumps of glue and uneven twine.

"It has tae dry," Grandpa instructed.

"It's nine o'clock—we cannae fly it right now anyway." Paislee, in between cutting and supervising and refereeing, had also done a load of wash. The twenty-year-old combo washer dryer machine didn't always get her clothes dry, so she had a rack set up next to the back window to catch the sun. Oh, for modern appliances one day. A separate dryer would be heaven. For now, she dumped the semi-damp socks into a laundry tub to hang before she went to bed. If she was lucky, they'd be wearable by morning.

"If it doesnae fly, I'll fail. Mrs. Martin said it *had* to fly."

"We'll try after breakfast, Brody. If you'd have told me last week when ye received the assignment, then this wouldnae have happened."

"Ye've got tae stay on top of these things," her grandfather advised.

She and Brody both whirled toward him.

He smugly drank his tea.

Hands on her hips she said, "Brody, time for bed. Brush your teeth, and I'll be up in a minute." She turned to her grandfather. "You and I need tae have a wee chat."

Brody gathered his things, muttering about how unfair it all was. He stuffed his homework in his backpack, then froze when he saw something inside.

"What?" She imagined a bad grade on a math quiz.

He brought out a manila envelope with her name addressed on it. "Oops."

Paislee reached out her hand. "What's this?"

"I dunno. I was supposed tae give it tae you today and I forgot because of the doctor's appointment."

Grandpa Angus left his stool and washed out his teacup, setting it upside down in the dish strainer on the counter.

She accepted the envelope with trepidation. They couldn't kick Brody out of Fordythe because Paislee had mouthed off to the headmaster, could they?

"Thanks." She cleared her throat. "Scoot. I'll set the alarm early so that we can try tae fly the kite in the back garden. You better pray for wind, me lad."

Brody scuffed past her to the stairs, where he ran up them as soon as he was by her. "Brody!" she warned out of habit, following him to make sure he didn't bounce off the narrow walls. "Careful now."

"Night!" His bedroom door slammed closed. She gritted

her teeth. Envelope in hand, she returned to the kitchen to
have it out with her grandfather, but the old man had taken
the opportunity to duck into Granny's room.

She couldn't get used to calling it his room.

That made this difficult arrangement too permanent.

Sinking into her chair at the kitchen table, she opened the
envelope.

Rather than a rebuke on her behavior, Headmaster McCall
had sent her a leaflet on government services for the elderly
with a handwritten note, in superior cursive that put her
chicken scratch to shame, apologizing for the misunderstand-
ing. He expressed his condolences for the loss of her associate.

He'd signed it "Hamish McCall." *Well now.*

She flipped through the pages and highlighted some of the
helpful numbers in yellow marker from the craft box still on
the table. Grandpa could make the calls for himself in the morning, instead of coming with her to the shop.

As she cleaned up the mess and then pinned the socks to
the wooden air dryer, all Paislee could think of was how kind
an action that had been, to send a sincere apology.

Had she thought him arrogant?

She hoped that she'd been wrong about him, just as he had
been about her.

Chapter 15

The next morning, Paislee was at Fordythe with Brody five minutes early—which would have been ten, except for Wallace stealing the tail of the kite, which had to be retrieved and reattached.

"Bye, Brody—good luck!" The kite had flown, barely, if Brody ran really, really fast.

"Thanks, Mum!"

There was no sign of Headmaster McCall, *Hamish,* waiting outside in the car queue. The man had apologized, and rightly so, with his well-meaning gesture of assistance.

Paislee had left Grandpa at home with a breakfast of toast and eggs and instructions to call some of the numbers in the leaflet to see if he was entitled to more financial support.

He'd taken offense, but she'd been firm. He was welcome to stay until they found Craigh, which she promised to help him with more on Sunday, but until then it wouldn't hurt to see if there were some perks for making it past seventy.

She trudged into Cashmere Crush completely knackered, but she had to wake up. Tonight was her Knit and Sip, and she'd gotten a custom order in online overnight—paid in full for a hundred pounds—to be delivered for the husband's birthday in two weeks, which meant she had no time to do *anything* but knit a crew-necked fisherman's sweater. The customer lived in London and had admired the sweater of a friend, who had gotten it from Paislee and Cashmere Crush while on vacation in Nairn.

The color requested was Oxford Blue, and she chose one of Jerry McFadden's dyes to work with—the soft yarn always kept the color. Setting up at the counter, she turned the radio on low for background music and let her mind wander.

Grandpa had offered to stay home with Brody tonight. Her son complained about being in the back area on Thursday nights, but he had his headphones in to watch movies or play videos on his tablet, same as at home, so she didn't pay his grousing too much attention.

This might give the two Shaw men a chance to mend fences, so she'd agreed.

She started the rib-knit pattern and hummed along with the music—then stopped with a pang of guilt. The feeling that Isla had been *murdered* hadn't left her all night. But how? And who? How had Gerald not known his neighbor was dead when his dog was inside Isla's apartment? And probably him, too? She and Grandpa had seen the pup run out. Did Detective Inspector Zeffer even believe her? And what had Gerald told him?

She slipped a stitch as she recalled Isla's dead stare into nothing and bit back a cry. She'd tried to make Isla's life easier—but had Flora been right? Had Isla taken the tiniest bit of advantage?

It didn't matter now. Paislee would see that Isla was not forgotten. If her mother couldn't be found, Paislee would cover the costs of a burial. Somehow she'd find a way. Maybe Father Dixon could help and ask the parishioners to chip in for a simple service? Local folks cared about one another.

Her mobile phone rang, and she thanked all the heavens

for the interruption, as her knitting wasn't flowing with its usual ease. She tore out the stitches and put the mess aside.

"Lydia! Good morning. Do you have wonderful news for me?" An affordable location, or perhaps an answer for her grandfather—either would be welcome.

"I dinnae ken how wonderful, but if you're willing to stretch yer wings . . ."

That didn't sound so good. "You mean, my budget?"

"Don't be a stickler—a place by the harbor just popped up on my site as available, starting May first. It's an up-and-coming area, and you would be smart tae get in there before any of the others on your row find out aboot it."

Paislee exhaled loudly, took a look around the empty shop, and let a curse word fly.

Lydia laughed.

"Did you say by the harbor?" That was where Isla had lived.

"Yes."

She pulled up the address and gave it to Lydia. "Can you see what flats at Harborside are going for?"

Lydia did some typing and whistled. "These are dear. Are ye thinking of leaving Granny's house altogether? I can find ye something much better suited for you and Brody."

"No, no. Isla lived there."

"Dead Isla, in need of a job?"

Paislee glowered at the phone. "Aye. And just wait until I catch you up with everything that's gone on."

"Since day before yesterday?"

"A lot, Lydia, I am not kidding."

"I'll be there in ten."

"I cannae close the shop."

"Just for an hour? Yes, ye can. You've done it before."

True, but it seemed irresponsible when there was so much to do. She glanced at the blue yarn and her knitting needles, all tangled. There would be no sorting this mess until she had a few answers. "Fine. But I cannae be long—and I want tae drive by Isla's."

"What for?"

"I'll tell you on the way. You can help me find a good reason tae talk tae her next-door neighbor."

Paislee ended the call and taped a sign on the door reading that she would be back by eleven. She was waiting on the sidewalk when Lydia drove up in her shiny red Mercedes.

"Spill," Lydia said by way of greeting when Paislee climbed in. "Is the neighbor hot? He's certainly got money."

"Yes, actually. You are the perfect weapon."

Lydia flashed her dynamite smile. "Intriguing."

The interior of the car smelled like expensive leather, even better than James's leather shop next door. Though the business owners didn't talk every day, there was still a sense of belonging and to move away would be hard.

"Isla's is only five minutes from the building I want tae show you." Lydia slid on her black designer sunglasses. "I can hold it with a ten percent down payment."

"Don't rush me, Lyd. I've got more pressing matters."

"You have an eviction notice giving you thirty days—what could be more pressing than that?" Lydia turned onto the main highway toward the harbor.

"I think Isla was murdered."

Lydia gulped, checked for traffic, and then veered to a stop on the side of the road. She whipped off her shades to stare at Paislee as if she'd lost her head. "Excuse me?"

Paislee held up a hand. "It's true."

"Why in the world would ye think that?"

Where to start? "Lots of reasons."

"Since when?"

She recalled the yellow fish in Doc Whyte's aquarium. "Since yesterday, at the doctor's office."

"And why didn't ye call?" Lydia demanded.

Paislee went through what she knew about Isla's return to Nairn, and her death. She ended with, "I'm not supposed tae know about the coroner's report, which states that Isla committed suicide." She speared Lydia with determined eyes. "We both know that's not what happened."

"*I* don't know that." Lydia held up a palm.

"Well, I do. Don't be mad. There hasnae been an instant for me tae do anything other than stomp out the fire in front of me."

Lydia sat back, her long black fingernail tapping her black skirt as she considered everything Paislee had just said. "Fine," she relented. "What do ye think's going on?"

Paislee gave her the rundown on Billy, who might have Isla's mother's number but wouldn't call her back. Jealous Tabitha, who she knew had to have called Billy to warn him that she was on her way, and for good measure she tossed in her grandfather and Headmaster McCall. To top it off, she shared that Wallace had tried to eat Brody's kite.

Lydia slowly shook her head, her perfectly styled hair bobbed to showcase her pert nose and sculpted jawline. "I cannae believe it. Next time maybe text me *after* the Grandpa/Brody showdown, and before hanging the socks?"

Paislee chuckled. "I'll do my best."

Lydia slid her glasses back on and continued toward their destination. "So . . . do you think the neighbor—what's his name?"

"Gerald Sanford."

"You think he was inside Isla's flat, and that he left his dog behind after possibly killing Isla?"

Paislee blew her bangs back and dug in her denim pocket for a hair tie, sweeping it up in a tail. "It sounds silly when you say it, but why on earth would Isla dog-sit? Her health issues made her leery of animals, even Wallace, who is a sweetie pie."

"What are you trying tae prove by going there? What if he did do it?" Her best friend sliced her finger across her throat.

"Lydia!"

"Sairy."

They followed the road toward the pier and the harbor apartments.

"I just want some answers, that's all. It doesnae make sense that she would move back tae Nairn alone—why wouldn't she have called me sooner? I thought we were friends."

Lydia glanced at Paislee as she drove. "She was a user, Paislee. She liked you as long as ye were valuable tae her. Trust me—I know plenty of people like that in real estate. It's why me sales are so high. I only take out the clients that I trust have the money tae follow through, and then I show them their dream house. Cha-ching—everybody's happy, but it isnae a friendship, ye ken?"

Paislee didn't want to hear it. "That's no way tae speak of the dead."

"You had a blind spot for her." Lydia made a right down the road and reached Harborside Flats. The large tree that shaded the building waved its branches in the slight wind from the harbor across the street, and the fishing pier. "This is the place? Brilliant!"

Paislee let her annoyance on Isla's behalf go as Lydia chose a spot in the lot next to Gerald. Despite the morning hour, he was washing his silver BMW, bare chested, music blaring.

"Oooh la la," Lydia said with appreciation. "Look at those hips. Please tell me this is the hot neighbor."

"That's the hot neighbor."

"This *will* be fun." She peered at Gerald over the top of her shades. "What do we want again?"

"The truth about how well he knew Isla—and why he'd been in her apartment, and left his dog there. And, if he killed her." The words sounded surreal.

Lydia lifted the car's visor to get a better view and switched off the engine. "Law school isn't cheap," she said. "Neither is that car. And those muscles are hard earned. I wonder what he does for his money?"

"He'd mentioned working as an actor, doing reenactments, but I don't know. I have the same question about Isla—how could she afford this place? What I paid her certainly wasnae going tae cover it."

"Roommate?"

She recalled the mug in the sink, and the empty feel to the flat. "I don't think so."

Gerald realized they were there and switched the music off with a bashful grin. Charming—but Paislee gave a wide berth to charming. She'd learned that lesson the hard way.

"Hey!" His eyes locked on Lydia, who was the whole package at five ten, black fitted sleeveless blouse, black pencil skirt, and boots with stiletto heels. With her black bob and black nails, Paislee was reminded of a sexy Russian spy, though Lydia had been born and raised in Nairn.

"Hiya," Lydia answered with a sly smile.

Gerald dropped his sponge into a bucket of soapy water. His skin was tan even below the waistband of his jeans, which were rolled up at the ankles, and his feet bare.

"Hi, Gerald." Paislee pulled his attention away from Lydia.

"Hello." He kept his friendly smile as he tried to place her. "Have we met?"

"The other day—I'm the one who found Isla." The memory brought a sorrowful emotional punch.

He paled and reached inside the bucket for his sponge, wringing it out in his large palm. "That's right."

"I saw you at the police station?"

He shuffled from one foot to the next, water dripping by his toes. Now that he wasn't dancing, his skin broke out in goose bumps from the chilly morning air, and he rubbed his muscular arms. "Yeah. I got called in tae answer a few questions, but I havenae heard anything since. You?"

"No." *Nothing new today, anyway,* she amended silently.

She saw that he didn't want to talk to her, so she tilted her head toward Lydia and told her bestie, "Gerald here is studying tae be a solicitor."

Gerald nodded shyly.

Lydia stepped closer and cooed, "I love your car—what do ye do for the daily grind?"

Under her stare Gerald stammered, "I'm an a-actor in the reenactment battles in Inverness." He gave his car a halfhearted swipe of the sponge.

"I can see you now in nothing but a kilt," Lydia said approvingly.

Gerald's cheeks went crimson and he shifted to Paislee, who was the safer of the two. "The detective just had some questions aboot Isla that he thought I could answer as her neighbor, but I told him we werenae close. She'd only moved in two weeks ago."

Right after being fired by Roderick Vierra. "She used tae work for me," Paislee said, and laughingly motioned to the gorgeous wooden building with ornate doorknobs and window frames. "I didnae pay well enough for this—do you know if she had a job somewhere else?"

His brow furrowed before he cleared his expression. "She mentioned a severance package—but she wasnae happy with it and wanted more."

"That sounds like the Isla I knew," Lydia said, her hand finding Gerald's forearm.

Sensing an ally, Gerald said, "Right? She was no angel even though she looked like one. I heard her and her ex going at it—fightin' hard enough tae make me walls shake."

"Billy?" Paislee asked.

"Some guy with a beat-up old truck that didn't match the

neighborhood—neither did she. Isla got fired for shagging her boss, and her ex, that Billy guy, was pissed. Dinnae blame him. I wouldnae put up with that, either."

Paislee's mouth opened in shock as she thought of Roderick sitting nervously behind his desk, staring at the silver-framed photo of his wife and kids. He'd been cheating on her with Isla?

"I knew it." Lydia smacked Paislee on the arm. "Didnae I tell you? Isla was not a nice person."

Gerald rubbed his fingers together. "She wanted more than what her boss gave her for a 'severance' package, if ye know what I mean."

Had she been so busy protecting Isla that she'd been blind to the truth?

It didn't matter; the girl was dead and had no champion.

"Were you and Isla secretly an item? Is that why your dog was in her flat?" Paislee didn't look away from him. She needed answers.

"I dinnae ken what you're talking aboot," he said, his easygoing manner fading behind a solicitor's fake smile. She'd thought he'd been too open to lie—but he'd just proved her wrong.

"Let's go," Lydia said. "Bye."

Lydia waved at Gerald while Paislee got into the passenger side of the red Mercedes.

"He knows more than what he's saying," Paislee said. How had her Isla been sleeping with a married man? How could that married man have taken advantage of Isla?

"I agree with you, but you'll get more flies with honey, honey."

"Gran used tae say that—you know what Brody said?" She tucked a loose strand of hair behind her ear. "'Who wants flies?'"

Lydia chuckled. "He *is* a prodigy. I'm just waiting for the rest of you tae realize it."

"I love my son more than life itself, but he can barely do his times tables."

Lydia pulled out of the complex's parking lot. "There's more tae life than math."

Chapter 16

Lydia drove to a row of brick storefronts with modern everything, set back at least a mile from the water. Bare steel posts, a corrugated roof that looked as flimsy as a piece of tinfoil, and a smooth cement parking lot. Not a single plant or tree livened it up.

She had flower boxes in the front of her shop, as did her neighbors down the row. The narrow sidewalk separating the shops had moss growing in the aged cracks. The sea was close enough that she could smell it when she stepped outside of Cashmere Crush.

Paislee's heart sank. "Here?"

"Give it a chance." Lydia practically bounced from the driver's seat.

Paislee pulled herself from the Mercedes and studied the brick façade—was that not even real brick? The place had zero character. "You said it was by the harbor."

Lydia palmed her keys. "It is."

She looked at Lydia like she looked at Brody when her son attempted to stretch the truth.

They went inside the vacant space tucked between a solicitor's office, the lawyer specializing in divorce, and a psychiatrist's office. Each had a single car parked before their door, and she was willing to bet it belonged to the owner.

"This is plain. Too dull." She twirled around, taking in the blinding white-on-white interior. She couldn't bring Wallace with her to work like she did some days, or Brody—heaven forbid he scuff the white wood floors.

"You can paint," Lydia said. "You have a creative touch."

"This would take an entire palette, and I dinnae have the energy."

"You could still put your shelves up as dividers and that would create color. It's only a wee bit smaller than what ye have now."

Paislee didn't like the feel of it—it was too white and new, when she had an affinity for the homespun and unique. "Thank you, Lydia, but I dinnae think this is for me. Let's keep looking." She exited fast, and her friend slowly followed.

Lydia begrudgingly got back behind the wheel. "If ye don't snap it up it will be gone within the week," she said.

"What's the price?"

She named something three times what Paislee was paying now for Cashmere Crush.

"I cannae do that! And there isnae foot traffic like I have now. I know it doesnae bring in a lot of customers, but I just got a sweater order from a tourist from London. I need to be visible."

"I hear you. I just want the best for ye, that's all."

"Your idea of the best would be this," Paislee agreed as she gestured with her thumb behind them as Lydia drove away. "My idea is a little more old-fashioned. And . . . I cannae believe I just said that."

She'd been fighting against old-fashioned her whole life only to realize now that the traditions and ideals suited her after all.

"Me either." Lydia glanced at her and sighed. "But I know you're right. Sairy for wasting yer time."

"You didnae—you met Gerald, and you agree that he's hiding something? He's shady. Too fit, too charming, too—"

Lydia smacked her palm against the dashboard.

"What?" Paislee jumped in her seat.

"I got it." Lydia snickered. "I remember now."

"You've lost me."

"Gerald Sanford—I thought I'd recognized him from somewhere."

"He's an actor. Probably one of the parades."

"His arse, Paislee, I recognized the swing of that tanned bum."

Her brow arched as she turned to face her friend. "What?"

"My boss's sister's wedding shower. For a little extra he would *do* a little extra, if ye know what I mean."

Paislee blew out a breath. "What are you talking about?"

"Gerald was an exotic dancer known as Highland Hung."

"You're kidding."

Lydia's smile broadened. "Naw, I remember all right."

"Don't solicitors have some code of conduct?"

"With an ass that nice, who's gonna tell?"

"I guess ye have a point." There were some things that Paislee was glad to hand off to Lydia, and socializing was one of them. She would have died of mortification to have a man wiggling his bum before her at a bridal party.

"I'll refine yer search when I get back tae the office with things that you actually like," Lydia said teasingly. "Our system picks up listings as soon as they're available. You want tae know what's odd?"

Paislee nodded expectantly.

"Your building still hasn't shown up."

"What on earth? That's strange. This Sunday Theadora's holding a meeting for all the business owners tae see what can be done. I said I wasnae sure about going, but maybe I need tae be there. Especially if there's a chance the sale fell through?"

"I didnae say that; it could be financing woes. But you have tae go," Lydia said. "I'll watch the laddie. We can get an ice cream at Finn's."

"You're the best." She tapped her lower lip. "Is there any way you can find out Billy Connal's mobile number for me?"

"If it was a landline I could, but unless he has his cell listed I willnae be able tae find it. I'll try, but don't hold your breath."

"The police cannae reach Isla's mother." Her eyes stung again, but she didn't cry. "What a nightmare—as a mum, I can't imagine anything worse."

Lydia stopped at a red light. "You care—it sounds like her mother didnae."

"Not enough. Just like mine."

"Another thing you felt you had in common?"

Paislee shrugged. "If Gran hadnae taken me in, and shown me how to knit, where would I be now?" The poorhouse or living off the government. Neither appealed to her.

Lydia sniffed. "You would have been fine, Paislee, because yer strong. You would have found a way—but we can agree that your grandmother was a blessing in yer life. And, vicariously, mine. I get compliments every time I wear a Paislee Shaw original."

"You were my guinea pig, at the beginning, remember?" One sleeve a bit longer than the other, or the hem a mite crooked, Lydia was patient with Paislee's first attempts at fingerless mittens and knit hats with a hole in the center for a woman's ponytail.

"Aye. I've kept a few of the throwaways for blackmail, when you get so famous for your knit goods that you forget all about poor Lydia."

"It'll never happen." They'd been best friends since they were Brody's age.

Lydia had moved away for five years to marry and divorce before coming back to her family in Nairn, and Paislee.

"I'll call ye later if I find Billy's phone number, but I dinnae want you feeling guilty about Isla. You were a good friend tae her—you don't owe her anything."

Paislee disagreed. Lydia slowed before the front of Cashmere Crush, right at eleven. The clock tower, a few blocks away, could still be heard as it chimed eleven times. "I've made a promise tae see that she is at peace."

"Now, why does that sound ominous?" Lydia tilted her head after she put the Mercedes in park. "I'll see you tonight, love. I'm thinking of a melted Gruyère over baked green apples."

"Yum." She didn't care that Lydia didn't knit—so long as she brought snacks. "Can I pick up a bottle of wine?"

"Naw—I have the perfect white in mind."

Paislee climbed out of the car. "Thanks again."

"Stay out of trouble?"

"I live a boring life."

"Liar!" Lydia honked her horn and drove off.

When Paislee entered her shop, her gaze was drawn to the blue yarn on the counter and the sweater she had left to knit. She was responsible, and responsible people did not just close shop to go chasing after lying, sneaky ex-boyfriends.

Isla's wan image came to the front of her head, demanding justice.

Paislee called her house number from her cell phone. There was no answer. Was Grandpa all right? He'd seemed in fine spirits, but what did she know? According to the leaflets, old age often led to dementia and physical ailments. What if he'd had a heart attack or something?

In a panic, she amended the sign on the door to read Gone Until Twelve and left out the back to drive home.

She burst through the front door and blinked in surprise. Her grandfather had swept, mopped, and dusted. Wallace greeted her with a tail wag, then went back to Grandpa Angus, who was finishing a toasted cheese sandwich at the kitchen table.

"Wallace, no beggin'," she said. "Grandpa, this place looks great."

"I can earn me keep."

What would make him think that he had to? A wave of apprehension tickled her nape and she rubbed the back of her head. "Oh?" Her gaze went to the envelope of papers from the headmaster, put away near the phone. "How did the calls go?"

His wrinkled face turned pink. "They treat ye like it's a crime to reach the ripe age of seventy-five. I should be in diapers, eating mush. Well, I have all me teeth, thank ye verra much." His voice rose with indignation as he widened his mouth to show her, then snapped his teeth together.

She sat down across from him, resting her elbows on the table. He appeared in decent health, especially for a man of his years, and heaven knew his pride was intact. "What did you discover?"

"We need tae find Craigh, and then I'll be outta yer hair, but don't expect any extra from the government fer keepin' me."

"I wasnae expecting anything!" Paislee said in shock. "I thought ye might be eligible for assistance for yer own place, that's all."

"I called the *Mona* again, and the number just rings." His brown-eyed gaze held a hint of fear behind his glasses. "Those bawheids at the station dinnae know anything. Craigh will have a good explanation when he comes back, and we'll joke about it over a pint."

"No answer? Should I try?"

"The number is there." He tapped a business card.

She called, and he was right—no answer.

"I may not have a lot of money, but I can fish, and keep the house. Give the mangy dog a bath."

Wallace whined and tucked his body low behind Paislee's feet at her chair. "He is not mangy. I take him tae the groomer."

It was a sad fact that the dog had a standing appointment every three months while Paislee had to do her own nails and brows.

"I can manage the clippers well enough."

"I dinnae want you tae do too much, Grandpa."

"Ye sound like that woman on the phone now, insultin' me with her questions—like I cannae take care of meself." He frowned as if just realizing that something was off. "Why are ye here before noon?"

She had a feeling if she said to check on him that wouldn't go over so well and she'd never get her floors swept again.

Gerald had mentioned that Billy's old truck had been outside—had the exes been hooking up, behind Tabitha's back, perhaps trying to get back together? What would Tabitha have thought about that? Could be why she hadn't been keen on giving out his number.

She'd make a surprise visit to Billy and ask him the truth about his relationship with Isla. Why had they been arguing so loudly at Isla's flat?

"Any chance ye can help out at the shop for an hour?"

He scowled, but she caught a pleased look before he wiped his face with the napkin.

"What fer?"

Feeling protective of Isla, she didn't tell Grandpa about Isla sleeping with Roderick and possibly Billy, too. "I want tae try Billy at Lowe Farm again, tae get Isla's mother's number."

Grandpa Angus rose and washed his plate, then placed it in

the dish strainer on the counter. "Awright, but I have a call in tae the police station in Dairlee about Craigh. I gave them this number."

"Fine. You should be back by two at the latest. No doctor appointments today."

Wallace went out back with a treat; then she and her grandfather walked out the front door to the Juke. She snuck a peek at the older man, in khaki trousers, boots, and a thin sweater. He'd left his trench coat in the house due to the mild weather.

"Do you have everything ye need? I can take ye shoppin', if you'd like."

"I'm fine."

"All right." Pulling her thoughts from shopping, her brain went to the next thing he might want. "We should get you a key made."

He glanced at her quickly. "I dinnae mind using the one under the flowerpot."

She shook her head. "And a set for the shop, so you have yer own."

"You're going tae be moving, I thought."

She scowled and drove them to Cashmere Crush, parking in the back. She hated that he was right. What was the point of getting an extra key? She needed her Knit and Sip tonight to be buoyed by the communal energy of her ladies as they crafted and harmlessly gossiped.

They went in and she got Grandpa set up with a deck of cards so he could play solitaire. She'd refilled the candy dish, but she would have to make a stop at the grocery store for fruit and crackers. What other snacks could she leave around that might be healthier for him?

"I didnae mean tae upset ye," he said. "About the shop."

"You didnae." She shrugged and admitted, "I just hate not knowing what's going tae happen next."

This would be the opening where Granny would offer sage advice to lift Paislee's spirits. Grandpa considered this and scratched his beard. *"It's a sair ficht for half a loaf."*

Basically, life was not a fair fight and she wouldna be getting her fair share.

How she missed her grandmother.

Chapter 17

Paislee left Cashmere Crush in her grandfather's hands—it was better than not having anybody there at all.

She had a bad feeling about Isla, Billy, and Tabitha. And Roderick. What a mess affairs of the heart were. She'd thought she'd been in love once, but what did anybody know at seventeen?

As she drove, she didn't bother with the radio like last time she'd made the picturesque journey through cliffs and green fields—instead, she used the twenty minutes to imagine scenarios that ended with Isla sprawled on the floor like a lass's broken doll.

She slowed twice on the open rangeland for sheep ambling across the road.

Billy had to know something about why Isla had returned to Nairn. If the detective was too busy making a name for himself to dig deeper, then it was up to Paislee to bring the truth to the detective.

Flies and honey, she reminded herself as she made the right-hand turn into Lowe Farm. *Don't jump to conclusions.*

She followed the dirt road past the stream, until she reached the barn. Like yesterday, the shorn sheep herded together as if chilled without their coats, spindly legs and tummies bare, while the others waiting to be clipped meandered in the pens. *Poor things—in one door heavy with ivory matted wool and out skinny and needing sweaters of their own.*

How many sheep did Farmer Lowe have? There must have been at least a thousand, if not more, of the blackface variety.

She recalled from a school trip that each sheep, depending on size and breed, could produce two to thirty pounds of wool a year. Unlike the Scottish cashmere goats, famous for the softest cashmere that only molted in the spring, when the down from the underbelly could be combed or shorn. Sheep made more financial sense on a farm, though Paislee adored the sheer luxuriousness of cashmere.

Paislee parked in the dirt driveway by the barn, next to a couple of pickups. Gerald had said that Billy had driven a beat-up old truck.

She eyed them, hoping he was here and that she could catch him off guard. She noticed a very beat-up silver pickup with a rusting back end that hadn't been there yesterday. She would have remembered seeing it because of the Belle and Sebastian sticker on the back window. They were one of her favorite bands.

Tabitha must've warned Billy of her arrival yesterday, and it smacked of guilt to her. Otherwise, why hadn't he called her back? Left just before she'd arrived?

Farmer Lowe saw her and lifted his hand, then shouted into the barn, where he was overseeing the shearing process. She heard the sheep baaing over the whir of electric clippers.

A few minutes later, a young man she assumed was Billy hoofed out, his expression somewhat menacing, and Paislee stepped back. His hair was shaggy blond and dirty, his physique lean and wiry. He was thin, yes, but strong. Sheering sheep was very physical labor.

Could he have hurt Isla—maybe fired up at her about Tabitha

*and decided to . . . do what? Choke her? Hit her? Naw, Amelia said
that Isla died of an overdose.*

A breeze reached Paislee from the stream, carrying with it
the scent of shorn wool and farm muck—pungent, aye, but
not as odorous as Billy. He charged to a stop an arm's length
from her and pulled a towel from his back denim pocket, wiping sheep oil from his hands. He didn't offer to shake hers.
"Who are you?"

"Paislee Shaw." She was more than a little glad to be meeting him where there were witnesses. She hadn't expected to be
afraid of him. "I was Isla's boss."

"She talked about ye," he said, somewhat begrudgingly.

This was for Isla. "I'm sairy for your loss."

At that, he gave a surprised laugh, quickly glancing back to
Farmer Lowe, who watched from the open door of the barn,
his straw hat tipped forward.

"Loss?" His tone suggested that she was way off the mark.

"You loved her, at one point," Paislee said. "Or at least, she
loved you. She told me so."

Billy grimaced and stuffed the towel in his pocket. "Don't
matter. Why are ye here?"

"I hope you have her mother's phone number. The police
are trying tae contact her about Isla." But that wasn't the
whole truth—she wanted to know why he'd broken Isla's
heart.

"I dinnae—talked tae the police already." He peered back
and then to her. "I gotta go. Can't lose this job."

Paislee brought her hand to her thumping heart—this was
so unfair. He had cheated and now acted like nothing was
wrong. What if Isla had been so overwrought by his callousness
that she'd actually taken those pills on her own? Paislee couldn't
accept that.

"Don't you care at all? Isla followed you here tae get a job
and be with you."

Billy scrubbed his palm through his greasy hair. "You have it all wrong. Isla didnae love me; she didnae love anybody but herself."

Paislee wasn't buying it. "Weren't you messing around with Tabitha in Nairn?"

His upper lip curled. "I was with Tabitha before Isla came along. Isla blinded me with her great legs, but Tabs is the real deal."

Nobody cared about Isla. Maybe it was Tabitha who had shown up with shortbread cookies, tempting Isla with—what? How could Tabitha have forced Isla to swallow a dangerous amount of pills? Billy would know that Isla took heart medication, and Tabitha, her supposed best friend, would, too.

Filled with righteous anger on Isla's behalf, Paislee locked eyes with the young man. "Where were you the night she died?"

He scoffed. "Getting drinks with a pub full of witnesses. Me and Tabs were together, and I can prove it a dozen times over."

She couldn't let him just leave! Paislee needed answers. She pressed harder. "You *cheated*. Why? Did you do worse tae her?"

"Our relationship was complicated, but I wouldnae hurt Isla, no matter how mad she made me. Now go, will ye?" Billy half-turned toward the barn.

Paislee caught his arm. "One more thing, please. Did you know that she was blackmailing her ex-boss?"

Billy scuffed the grass with his boot heel. "Not just her boss," he admitted with a sly smile. "Isla wanted my help tae find the dirt on the locals in Nairn. Promised me a percentage of the blackmail money. Me doing the dirty work, but her keeping her nose clean. I'm not that daft," Billy sneered.

"Billy!" Farmer Lowe shouted. "I'll dock yer pay!"

"Isla was not who you thought she was!" Billy yelled over

his shoulder as he ran back toward the barn to shear sheep.
"Why don't ye ask her boss?"

Stunned, Paislee slowly climbed into her Juke, and stared at
the dashboard.

What did all this mean? How could she have been so de-
ceived? She had to discover who was lying, and who was
telling the truth.

Detective Inspector Zeffer had talked to Gerald, and now
Billy. Neither man was in jail for the crime. Was he flaunting
his authority or proving his ineptness? Paislee didn't know for
sure.

What about Tabitha? Why did Tabitha have Isla's scarf, the
one that Paislee had made?

She thought about getting out of the car to ask—who else
would help if she didn't? But when she looked out, she saw
Farmer Lowe in front of the barn, his arms crossed, scowling at
her. There was no way that she could ask Billy any more questions today.

As if her friend could read her mind, a text from Lydia
*ding*ed through saying that Billy Connal didn't have a landline
or a listed number and the last known address was in Edinburgh, when she knew for a fact that he'd been in Inverness.
Farmer Lowe had said he was moving—but why was that?

"Stuck," she muttered aloud. *Now what?*

If Billy wasn't lying about his and Tabitha's whereabouts
the night Isla had died—who else could want Isla dead?

Her mind twisted like knotted thread when she was in a
rush. It required patience to tug each strand, one at a time,
until the knot was free. She breathed in, then exhaled.

Who?

Maybe someone who didn't want to pay Isla blackmail
money anymore. Her pulse hummed.

Someone with a guilty conscience and a bonny family

waiting for him at home while he stepped out with a pretty girl.

Paislee clapped her hands together. "Roderick Vierra."

Vierra's Merino Wool Distributor was only five minutes away. Maybe she could ask Roderick point-blank about his being blackmailed by Isla regarding their affair. She'd probably be able to read the truth on his face. If she had to, she could insinuate going to his wife with the information.

The idea made her feel dirty.

But who else would get to the bottom of this? Regardless of who Isla truly was, no one had a right to kill her.

Chapter 18

Paislee reluctantly left Lowe Farm, feeling as if she had unfinished business.

It was half past one—she had two hours until Brody was out of school. She would not be late again if she had to sprout wings and fly. But why had Billy said for Paislee to ask Isla's boss about the truth of who Isla had been?

Just a quick drive then, to glean what she could from Roderick. Honey, rather than vinegar, as Lydia suggested.

Six minutes later, she arrived at the fancy distribution center, painted white with black trim, large trees and warehouses in back. She'd been pleased for Isla to get a job at Vierra's. Due to the reputation and size of the business, there would be room for Isla to move up if she worked hard. The samples of wool on Roderick's desk had been a small selection of the quality they provided.

If Isla had been desperate enough to blackmail Roderick, what else might she have done? Paislee couldn't think of it without feeling sick.

She recalled Isla's hint in her email about getting quality wool at a discount. The skein that Detective Inspector Zeffer had brought in for Paislee to identify was fine enough to have come from Vierra's.

She parked and walked into the black and chrome lobby, as out of place as her grandpa the first day he'd been in Cashmere Crush. She still didn't care for the sculptures.

The receptionist, company headphones around her head as she waited to answer a call, greeted her with a smile. "Hello again."

"Hi. Is Roderick Vierra in?"

"He just ducked out back toward the warehouse—if ye hurry, you can catch him." She pointed down a long hall with metal double doors.

"Thank you!" Paislee rushed down the black marble tile floor, her boots squeaking and her pulse speeding. What would she say when she confronted him?

She pushed on the door and it opened onto a courtyard with shade trees and picnic benches for the employees to eat their lunch or take a break. Roderick was seated at one of the tables, in a cocoa suit jacket and slacks, scanning his phone, a mug of something at his elbow. *Coffee?* He glanced up when the door shut behind her.

His smile wavered as he placed her. "Paislee Shaw?"

"Hello," she said, gesturing to the table. "May I join you?"

His manners required that he say yes, so he did, adding, "My brother will be here in just a minute. What can I do for you?"

She got right to the point. "I know that you were having an affair with Isla."

His dark brown brows rose and he glanced around guiltily. "Naw, I wasnae," he said.

She didn't argue. "I also know you were paying her blackmail so that she wouldnae tell your wife."

"What?" He sounded incredulous, but he didn't move. An

innocent man would act differently. He smoothed his dark brown goatee.

"I want tae know why you fired her. Was she really so depressed about Billy and Tabitha getting together again?" *Depressed enough to kill herself . . .*

His jaw clenched. "I dinnae ken what yer talking aboot." His eyes flicked over her shoulder. His brogue deepened. He must not want his brother to know about what he'd done.

Paislee peered behind her toward the row of wool warehouses—she didn't see a soul. "I need tae know if she was truly broken up by Billy, or was it *you* that broke her heart?"

Roderick glanced around like a cornered animal, his knee bobbing nervously. "Now isnae a guid time tae talk. Roger—"

"Hurry, then," Paislee urged. "I dinnae care if anyone else knows, but I'm not leaving until you give me answers." She wasn't sure where her bravado was coming from, but she welcomed it.

Roderick's shoulders bowed in and he picked up his mug of black coffee.

"Me brother discovered us together in the warehouse, in flagrante, so tae speak," he said, his face flushed beneath his olive skin tone.

Unfortunately, she could easily imagine that. "And?"

"He's the one who said I had tae fire her." Shrugging with a half smile, he admitted, "This was not the first time it's happened. I have a weakness for bonny women. . . ." He stared into his mug.

He was a charming slug of a man. Paislee straightened, her bravado metamorphosing into real courage. He'd preyed upon Isla. Paislee had sent her protégé into the lion's den. "How did Isla take her dismissal?"

"Not well. Screaming, crying. Cursing." Roderick shuddered as if appalled by her unseemly behavior.

Paislee asked coldly, "*How* did the two of you happen?"

"She'd discovered her ex, Billy, texting his girl in Nairn and was overcome with tears. I sought tae comfort her, that's all, and one thing led tae another." He waved his hand in the air.

What a pig.

"Does your wife know?"

"God, no. She would divorce me"—he paused—"and take Vierra's down." His voice was disengaged, as if he weren't actually part of the problem.

She'd wanted answers from Roderick, and as hard as it was to hear them, she'd gotten them. Almost. She had to make sure that it wasn't possible Isla had been so distraught that she'd taken her own life as the coroner had concluded.

"Did Isla seem in low spirits?" Billy had claimed Isla hadn't loved him, though she'd seen for herself that Isla had been swept up by the idea of romance. Which left the possibility of her loving Roderick. "After you fired her?"

"She was furious," he said, his brown eyes melding to almost black as he relived a memory she was grateful not to see. "Isla had such fire, such *passion*."

Paislee got to her feet, grabbed his coffee cup, and dumped the contents in Roderick's lap. "How dare you take advantage of someone like that!"

He jumped up and brushed at the front of his expensive slacks, the damp spreading over his lap like a urine stain. She shook with adrenaline. He'd used Isla and tossed her aside. For a moment, Paislee was glad that Isla had taken money from him.

"What's going on here?" a male voice shouted from behind her.

She whirled to see a man very similar in appearance to Roderick with dark hair and eyes but without the slick charm or goatee.

Paislee let Roger have it. "Isla Campbell is dead, in case

you haven't heard. Next time your brother 'misbehaves' maybe you should fire *him*, instead of the victim."

Roger reared back. "Isla was no victim. We're missing forty cases of our finest merino wool. Roderick, should I phone the police?"

Roderick glared at her with malice in his eyes. "Naw. Ms. Shaw was just leaving." His jaw tightened. "Dinnae come back."

"Gladly." Paislee held her head high as she left the Vierra brothers in the courtyard. Her spine tingled. Their joint fury followed her to the door. She left in fear that they might harm her.

Had they hurt Isla? Roderick certainly had reason to want to keep Isla quiet. And now her.

She rushed past the reception desk, the woman oblivious as she spoke on the phone, and jumped into her Juke, locking the door once inside. Her fingers trembled as she started the engine. Good heavens, but now that the confrontation was over, she couldn't stop shaking.

Isla had not been depressed—she'd been a fighter, turning the tables on the man who had used her so poorly and demanding her due. Was it the "right" thing to do? Probably not, but Paislee couldn't blame her.

Looking back at the now ominous white walls of Vierra's, she had a sinking feeling. Had Roderick, or Roger, or both, killed Isla?

One thing was certain—Isla would not have overdosed on purpose. Paislee knew that now with every fiber of her being, and she would prove it to the detective and the coroner or whoever would listen. She couldn't change the outcome for Isla, but she could provide the truth.

Paislee checked the time. *Oh no.* How had it gotten to be quarter till three already?

With one wary eye on the front door of the distribution center, she called Grandpa at the shop.

"Hello," he said.

"Grandpa—if you answer the phone you have tae say, 'Cashmere Crush.'"

He hung up.

Paislee shook the phone and dialed again.

"Cashmere Crush," he answered.

"Grandpa!"

He waited a beat. "How may I help ye?"

"I'm running behind—I know I said I wouldnae be gone long, but I need tae pick up Brody before I take you home. I cannae be late tae school."

"Aye, I know it. And I need a raise."

"What?"

"Flora Robertson delivered a box of yellow yarn about an hour ago, but I dinnae know how tae pay her, or put the things away, so you'll have tae do it yerself."

"Fine—I'll see her tonight." She swallowed and her nerves calmed. Nobody exited Vierra's. "Is it pretty?"

"It's yellow."

She sighed.

"She also brought more of the light green ye like so much. I'm not pricing things for ye unless you give me a raise. I've had three phone calls from ladies about tonight's event, and two customers walkin' in, as well as a yarn delivery. This was not the light work ye implied."

Paislee braced her shoulders. "Can't do it?" She made a deliberate poke at his pride. "Or is it too much for ye?"

He roared back, "I can handle it just fine. Take yer time!"

"Thank ye, I will."

"I want a ten pence an hour raise."

She scoffed. "Deal. I would have given ye fifty."

"Wait a minute now, lass—"

"See you in an hour." *Ha!* She ended the call, very pleased with getting the last word. Time to leave the parking lot and never return to Vierra's.

Whingeing aside, Paislee admitted that Grandpa'd been more help than hindrance. She said a prayer to her gran for guidance on what to do about the business. Her small but steady income would be stretched with another mouth to feed.

Paislee knew only knitting and yarn. She took a right to the main road toward Fordythe.

If needed, she'd sell yarn by the skein at the Saturday festival to help fill the coffers. She'd concentrate on finishing the specialty fisherman's sweater, put together four hundred signature flower keychains, and help her grandfather find Craigh.

Her heart raced at the list before her—but she would get it done.

As she drove, she wondered why Lydia couldn't find a record of the sale of her building. And whether there was a penalty for Mr. Marcus breaking the lease.

Today's showing with Lydia had clarified for both of them what Paislee really wanted. She'd take cracks with character over trendy and new without a second thought.

She rounded the curve and slowed for a sheep crossing the road, then continued on her way. She passed Lowe Farm on her left and made her way down the hill toward Nairn.

With a glance in her rearview, she saw the glint of afternoon sunshine glow silver from a car behind her.

An all-too-familiar niggle of apprehension tickled her nape, warning her to take care and mind the sharp cliff on the left. She lightly pressed on the accelerator even as she remained aware of possible sheep in the road.

Paislee looked again and the car was right on her tail, and getting closer.

She took the next curve a wee bit faster than she liked. Did the car not see her? Were they on the phone, or messing with the radio?

Silver dazzled off the fancy sunshade of the car behind her.

Heading out of the turn and down a steep hill, she suddenly jolted forward—out of control—as the car nudged her bumper.

She tried to straighten the Juke, but the car behind her crashed into her bumper, harder this time.

Paislee spun.

The world whipped around her, her senses reeling as things moved fast yet in slow motion.

Until the Juke smashed with a great crack into a guardrail.

Moments later, she came to. Her head throbbed. Her muscles burned where she was secured to her seat by the seat belt's straps; the deployed airbag pressed her firmly against the backrest.

A feeling of immense gratitude washed over her that Brody had not been in the car. And peering out, at where her car had stopped, the guardrail bent and mangled, that she hadn't gone over the cliff.

Had it been Roderick Vierra or his brother behind her?

Paislee roused next when medics were attending to her and loading her into the ambulance.

"My phone," she told a female medic with a broad face and freckles. "I have tae call my son's school."

The woman retrieved Paislee's bag and purse. "Here ye are, but settle down, now. They'll understand."

She knew they wouldn't, but didn't have the energy to explain. Her head and neck twinged, but she dialed anyway, biting her lip as the school secretary answered.

"Headmaster McCall, please."

"One moment."

Time ticked by like a leaded weight. Her body pulsed with waves of heat.

The medic pulled down straps, securing her for the ride to the hospital. "You lost consciousness. We're taking you to Town and County Hospital."

Paislee groaned.

"Are ye in pain?" asked the medic.

"Headmaster McCall," the headmaster said on the phone.

"This is Paislee Shaw. I just wanted tae let you know that Lydia Barron will come for Brody today."

"Ah. She's on the form?"

What was with this guy and his forms? "I'm not aware of any form."

Paislee winced as a stab of cold, a new pain from the heat, pierced her temple.

"Is everything fine?"

"There's been a small accident," she said.

He sucked in a breath. "Are you all right?"

"A car accident—I'm okay. Please don't alarm Brody, but I wanted tae make sure that you understood if he was a bit late being picked up."

She could feel his emotions spill toward her over the phone. Embarrassment despite him believing himself in the right, and concern.

"Do you need any assistance?"

"That's all. I have tae go." She ended the call with her eyes closed. Cold had churned back to heat once more and her stomach twisted with nausea.

"No more now," the medic said. "I gave ye somethin' for the pain."

"I have tae call Lydia, tae pick him up. I'll be quick. I can't be late."

"My two bairns are with me mum until they start primary," the medic said. "I didnae realize schools were so strict."

"Fordythe. They like ye tae be on time."

Rather than call, she texted Lydia, asking her to pick up Brody. She gave a brief rundown of what had happened, and where she was going to be for the next few hours.

Lydia immediately texted back that she would pick up Brody, was Paislee really all right, and what else could she do to help?

Paislee gave her phone to the medic and politely passed out for the ten-minute drive to Town and County Hospital.

Chapter 19

Paislee stirred as they transferred her from the stretcher to a hospital bed. She hadn't been in a hospital since Brody's birth, and she didn't care for the cold, antiseptic feel.

A doctor read her chart at the foot of her bed. " 'Car accident.' " He ran his finger down the page as he went. "Let's just see what's going on." He set the chart down on the nightstand. "I'm Dr. Raj. Can you sit up for me?"

She tried, gritting her teeth at the pull of sore muscle.

"What hurts?"

"My neck and head."

"Not your back?"

She took stock. "No. My shoulders a little."

"The airbag deployed, which explains the bruise on your cheek, and your seat belt the soreness in your shoulder." Dr. Raj pressed on her collarbone, and she squealed.

He flashed a penlight in her eyes, then put the instrument back in the pocket of his white coat.

"Can you turn your head?" Dr. Raj's Indian accent was thick, making him hard to understand—or, she acknowledged, it could be the fact that her mind was foggy.

She did—gingerly.

He pressed gently along her neck and had her move her fingers and arms. "Good," he said. "I do not think anything is broken, but let's get you an MRI—just to be sure."

"I'm fine," she said, not liking the sound of that. Anything needed by the doctor would be covered by National Health Insurance, so it wasn't about the money but her own fear.

"It's better to be sure." He tapped his lower lip and studied her. "Do you want to stay overnight?"

"No! I have a son that needs me at home." And a dog, and a grandfather . . .

"Then let's make a deal. You get the MRI, and if it is clear I will sign off on your release."

A doctor who liked to bargain. She really didn't want to spend the night, so she accepted his deal with a painful nod.

Dr. Raj flagged down a nurse from the hall. "MRI for Ms. Shaw please—let me know when they're done?"

The nurse was a tall man in his early twenties wearing dark green scrubs, his carrottop hair tied back in a tail.

"I'm Scott. This willnae take but a minute. Ready?"

"Aye." There was no time for her to be anxious, and despite Scott's optimism, it was more like an hour before she was in and out. She'd changed into a hospital gown in the adjoining dressing room, but the 3-D imaging machine hadn't hurt after all.

Paislee shuffled back into her room, boots loosely tied, to find Detective Inspector Zeffer waiting. He rose from the single armchair. She tried to finger-comb her bird's nest hair. What was he doing there? All she could think of was that she was glad she'd changed back into her jeans and sweater. "Detective Inspector!"

"Ms. Shaw."

" 'Paislee,' please."

"Paislee. Are you all right? They said you needed an MRI."
He searched her face, and she touched the bruise on her
cheek. She knew she must look something awful.

"I'm fine, fine. My head aches, but that's normal, right,
Scott?"

"Right-ee-oh." The nurse told the detective, "The doctor
just wants tae make sure nothing is broken."

DI Zeffer nodded, then asked Paislee, "What happened?"

Scott took that as his cue and bustled out the door with a,
"Be right back. Images should be ready shortly."

She sat on the edge of the hospital bed, and the detective
reclaimed his chair. The clock hanging on the wall above him
read five thirty. Brody would be out of school by now—where
was her phone?

She had to make sure that Lydia had Brody. Apprehension
simmered in her belly as she scanned the room for her purse.
Paislee slid stiffly off the thin mattress and searched the counter.
Nothing. On the verge of a panic attack, she rummaged through
papers on top of the bedside table. Where were her things from
the ambulance?

There—a plastic bag tagged with her name and room
number had fallen to the floor. She lifted it and dumped the
contents on the bed. "I have tae check on my son."

"You have someone tae help?"

Her phone peeked from the side pocket of her hobo bag.
"Aye." She skimmed her messages with a sigh of relief. Lydia
had sent a picture of her and Brody with sad faces wishing her
well. "My best friend picked him up and took him home.
There's a key under the flowerpot."

"How many people know that? I suggest moving the key."

"You, Brody, Lydia, and Grandpa. Other than you, they
need tae know where it is. Dinnae go burgling my house, now."

What she meant as humorous came out sharp.

His pale green eyes narrowed below russet brows. Dressed

in a blue suit, something he seemed to favor, he folded his arms before him, balancing his elbows on the armrests of the chair. "I can guarantee yer house is safe from me."

She rolled her eyes, but even that hurt, and she carefully perched back on the hospital bed. Her jeans and sweater were no match for the chill, so she tugged the top blanket around her shoulders like a shawl. Lydia would die of hypothermia before committing such a fashion faux pas.

The detective offered to help, but she waved him off. "I'm fine."

"Why do I think you'd say that even in a body cast?"

That made her laugh. "How'd ye know I was in hospital?"

He leaned back comfortably. "I heard yer name on the police scanner. What were you doing away from yer shop?"

"Visiting Bi—someone." He'd warned Amelia against talking about Isla's death, and she doubted he would appreciate Paislee searching for answers on her own.

His stare had a demanding quality. Charismatic.

She caved beneath the cool green gaze. "I went tae Lowe Farm tae see Billy." No matter what, she couldn't get Amelia into trouble by sharing she knew about the coroner's report of suicide. She was glad that he hadn't accepted the verdict and had ordered more tests. She wished she could ask why. What had he seen that made him think there was more to the story?

"Oh?"

She thought back—*Lowe Farm. Billy.* "To offer my condolences. Isla had told me that she and Billy might be married one day, so I was surprised tae find out they'd broken up."

Zeffer felt at his coat where he kept his notepad but didn't pull it out. "Why didn't ye just call him?"

"Tabitha wouldnae give me his phone number when I asked her for it." She watched his face to see if he already knew why not. "It seems Tabitha and Billy were messing around behind Isla's back."

His expression remained as fixed as a champion poker player's.

"I cared for Isla. As a mum, I cannae imagine not knowing about my child's death." *And if that child had been murdered?* Her heart skipped. "Have you found Isla's mother?"

"Aye. Charla Campbell. She'll be here in the morning."

Paislee relaxed, pushing her bangs back from her eyes. "Thank heaven."

"You can rest now," the detective proclaimed somewhat sarcastically.

She crossed her legs at the ankles and ignored his comment. "Billy confirmed what Gerald Sanford told me, about Isla blackmailing her ex-boss, Roderick Vierra."

"Blackmail?" His voice hitched as she finally got a rise out of him.

Paislee quickly explained, ending with, "I wanted tae confront Roderick about it, so I went there this afternoon, after I talked tae Billy."

"Confront him about what?"

"He and Isla were having an affair."

At this, the detective pulled out his black leather notebook. "Affair?"

Feeling rather pleased with herself, Paislee said, "Roderick was cheating on his wife with Isla, who blackmailed Roderick tae keep quiet. Billy said he didnae get back together with Tabitha until after he discovered Isla with Roderick, but Roderick claims it was the other way round."

He wrote without looking up. "When did Gerald tell ye this?"

"This morning." It felt like days had passed since she and Lydia had gone to question Gerald. "According tae him, Billy often showed up at Isla's flat and the two would argue loud enough tae shake his walls."

He briefly closed his eyes. "We are getting off track. Can you please relay tae me what happened on your way back from Vierra's?"

"The sun was shining bright behind me."

He clenched his jaw.

"It matters," Paislee said. "The sun made it hard tae see the driver behind me because of the silver sunshade in their car. Billy drives a beat-up pickup truck, so it wasnae him; this car seemed fancier. It might have been Roderick, or his brother, Roger—the accident happened right after I left there, and they were both upset with me."

"Did ye see the make or model of vehicle?"

"It was silver, and not a truck, but that's all I can tell you."

He scribbled something down. "Whoever it was, they didnae stop."

She recalled waking up in her Juke, afraid, and tightened the blanket around her shoulders. "I think they ran me off the road on purpose."

He glanced up from his notebook. "Why so?"

"They nudged me once, and then bumped me again until I lost control."

He leaned forward with an incredulous expression. "Why would anybody do that?"

"Like I ken?" Paislee splayed her hands. "Isnae that your job tac find out?"

He rubbed his lower lip and hummed. "Could be somebody doesnae like you asking questions about Isla."

She chilled. "I never saw what Roderick drove, but Gerald has a silver BMW."

The detective made a note. "I remember."

Dr. Raj entered with Scott, who held the film images of her neck and shoulder. "We are here to go over the MRI," Dr. Raj said. He gave a pointed look at the detective. "Are you her husband?"

"No!" He shot up, tucking his notebook away into the pocket of his stylishly tailored suit.

Paislee would have laughed if her head didn't hurt so badly. She didn't invite the detective to stay and review the MRI. *A girl deserved a little privacy.*

Detective Inspector Zeffer made his way to the door. "See me tomorrow tae finish your statement, all right?"

"Aye."

"Ye have a way tae get home?" He waited.

"Aye. Lydia will pick me up."

He nodded and left, shutting the door behind him.

Paislee faced the doctor and nurse as Scott hung the MRI images on the wall. Dr. Raj rubbed his hands together.

"Whiplash, but no breaks. You will be sore for a few days. You should take it easy. I can write you a note excusing you from work."

No work meant no pay. "I own my own company. I'll take it easy, but I have tae be there."

"Rest all that you can." Dr. Raj sat on his stool, the hem of his white coat almost brushing the floor. "I want you to take ibuprofen and limit your movements as much as possible. I'm going to prescribe a muscle relaxer, and suggest a neck brace as well."

She scrunched her nose at the idea. "For how long?"

"At least forty-eight hours," said the doctor. "If you're still tender next week, come back and see me—unless you have a family doctor?"

"Dr. Whyte."

Dr. Raj's face lit up. "I know him—make a well-check to see him soon, that's all I ask."

She slipped off the end of the hospital bed. "Am I free tae go?"

"Let me fill out the paperwork. I'll try not to take your eagerness to leave personally."

Oh—was he serious?

He winked, and Paislee relaxed. "Whatever you say, Doctor."

She texted Lydia while she was waiting to be released to let her know that she could go home.

Grandpa! Ach. He must still be at the shop. Grandpa?

Lydia texted that she and Brody had stopped at Cashmere Crush. Brody had shown them where she kept the emergency key. Lydia had just dropped them off at home and she was on her way. One bestie to the rescue.

Chapter 20

Paislee checked out of the hospital with a prescription for muscle relaxers and a soft brace around her neck. Her cheek hurt and shoulder ached. She wanted to go home and have a strong cup of tea and a whine.

Lydia squealed when she saw her in the lobby. "Are ye sure you shouldnae stay overnight?"

"Positive."

"If this is about money, I can give you some." Lydia cautiously swept Paislee's bangs from her brow.

Her nose lifted with Scottish pride. "No, thank ye."

"Dinnae be dafty. Yer poor face!"

"I havenae looked yet. Am I scary?" She felt at her hair, which had come out of its ponytail at some point during the afternoon and was now tangled around her shoulders. "I don't want Brody tae worry."

"It was all I could do tae convince him tae stay at home with your grandpa. He wanted tae see you for himself. I have makeup in my bag tae tone down the red and blue, and it willnae be such a fright."

"Thanks." Paislee led the way out of the hospital.

"I'd offer tae stay the night, but I have another showing at seven o'clock for a house next tae Cawdor."

Big bucks, then, and explained her black pantsuit with a charcoal silk blouse. "You've done so much already."

"Hardly. I did order you a rental car for three days—the Juke is at Edward's Mechanic. But he cannae even look at it until tomorrow."

"Totaled?" She couldn't afford a new car, or a new car payment. "I wasnae hit that hard."

"Hard enough tae crumple the front end and deploy the airbag," her friend argued. "He didnae say totaled. He said he couldnae look at it yet. Don't borrow trouble."

"Good advice."

The best friends walked to Lydia's red Mercedes. "Did they give ye pain meds? Do we need tae stop at the pharmacy?"

"He did, but I have enough for tonight and tomorrow morning. Regular ibuprofen will be fine after the shot he gave me wears off."

Lydia scrunched her pert nose and got in the car. "I put a note on the shop door cancelling Knit and Sip."

Paislee groaned and checked the time. Quarter past six. She'd forgotten all about it. "I cannae cancel. I have tae finish those key fobs, and a sweater, and Mary Beth has her blanket. The ladies need their night out."

"Reschedule for tomorrow night. I'm disgustingly free, even on a Friday. Do ye ken I havenae had a date in two months?"

"I've told you, men are afraid tae ask you out."

"That's not the man I want in me life then." Lydia sighed and started the car. "But going tae dinner at a nice restaurant would be fun."

"I'd take you, but I'm a little under the weather." She

touched the neck brace and tried to deliver a pain-free smile. "I guess we can reschedule for tomorrow night."

"Do you need tae stop by Cashmere Crush for anything?"

"Naw. All the ladies' numbers are in my mobile." She searched the space by her feet to make sure she had her purse. Her mind was a wee bit fuzzy, and she had a sudden urge to giggle.

"So, what happened?"

She sobered, thinking of the drop past the guardrail. "I was hit from behind, going from Lowe Farm tae the valley. There's that corner, and then the cliff?"

Lydia gasped. "That could have been bad."

"Aye." *To tell, or not to tell?*

"So, hit-and-run then?" Lydia questioned. "Why do I feel like yer holding somethin' back?"

"I think it was on purpose." She peeked at her friend.

"Why on earth would someone do that?"

She drew in a breath, not wanting her painkiller buzz to completely disappear—she had a feeling intense pain would follow. "Detective Inspector Zeffer thinks maybe because I was talking tae people about Isla."

Lydia slowed around the traffic circle, then made a right, toward Paislee's house. "The detective visited you at the hospital? Paislee, what is going on?"

"Billy told me that Roderick was not the only person Isla was going to blackmail, and that he didn't break Isla's heart. So, I went tae Vierra's Merino Wool Distributor, tae visit Roderick Vierra. I dinnae believe that Isla was depressed, like he said, you know? I wanted tae confront him and get the truth."

"I dinnae have a guid feeling aboot this."

"Roderick admitted tae seducing Isla—and then firing her because his brother caught them in the warehouse doing, you know. . . ."

Lydia smirked. "I get the picture."

"And it wasnae the first time Roderick had an affair. He's a real dog. I dumped coffee in his lap." A dormant giggle escaped but turned into a sob. "I should've protected Isla, and instead, I helped her get a job working with the devil."

"Stop that—you cared for her. How could you have known? I would've loved tae see you douse him with hot coffee!"

"It wasnae that hot."

"Still."

"If not for Gran, I could've been just like Isla—"

"That's not true. You have an inner strength that she didnae have, and it didnae have anything tae do with her heart condition."

"She was dealt a rotten hand."

"I agree with you there—but she could have made different choices."

"I really miss Gran right now. She'd heat the kettle and warm the scones and talk it out. She had a way of listening."

"I know. I remember." Lydia reached over and gave her wrist a squeeze.

"I didnae have a chance tae tell the detective before the doctor returned with the results of the MRI aboot Isla blackmailing more people. He wants me tae see him at the station tomorrow."

"I think you should stay home and rest."

"You know I cannae do that." The cars on the street seemed to blur by. "I hope he questions Gerald," Paislee said. "I'm fairly certain that the car that hit me was a fancy silver one."

"That guy's BMW." Lydia tapped a finely manicured nail against the steering wheel. "You think he was that upset about us questioning him? I'll go talk tae him right now, on my way tae the showing."

"No! Lydia, until we find out what's going on, we need tae lay low." Paislee shivered, unable to keep from touching the soft fabric around her throat. "I dinnae want anyone getting hurt on account of me. Zeffer told me that Isla's mum, Charla, will be here in the morning. I feel that once they are together, Isla will be at peace, then."

"Guid. That means ye can leave all this alone."

"I'm not in any condition—"

Lydia arched a black brow over a smoky gray eye. "It sounds tae me like you've been given a warning. Heed it, Paislee, please. No more questions. You can let Isla's mum take care of Isla."

She knew Lydia was right, but her heart wasn't as certain things were settled.

Lydia parked in the drive at Paislee's house next to a white Sentra. "I had it delivered—your grandfather should have the keys. Should you even be driving?"

"I'm fine! Just sore."

"Dinnae overdo it. Let your grandpa help. Funny how he's fit into your life just when you needed it."

"*Funny* is one word for it," she agreed. There were others she could think of. "Good luck with your showing. I'll text you before I go tae bed about the Knit and Sip for tomorrow."

Lydia waved, then rolled up the window and backed out of the drive onto the street. They lived in a quiet, older neighborhood, and at dusk most folks were inside preparing dinner.

Dinner. What was in the pantry? Something easy, maybe cereal with berries, though that wouldn't win her the Mum of the Year award. Her heels dragged with exhaustion.

Paislee entered and had made it two steps down the hall when Brody lunged at her from the living room.

"Mum!" His arms clasped around her middle and things suddenly felt a wee bit better.

"Hey now, it's all right." She hugged him tight and ruffled his auburn hair.

He pulled back to look at her. "Is yer neck broken?" His voice pitched up.

"No, no. It's called whiplash—a sort of sprain."

"Does it hurt?"

"Not much." *Yet.* "I have medicine."

"Grandpa made dinner and put it in the cooker. He set the timer so it willnae burn. I was verra worried, but Lydia and Grandpa said not to call, and I don't have me own mobile to text ye, and it isn't fair."

Wallace pawed at her leg, curiosity in his licorice drop eyes.

She winced as she leaned down to scratch behind his ears. "It's awright now."

Brody dragged her down the hall to the kitchen table. "Grandpa, Mum's home. What happened to yer face?"

Ach, she forgot to put the makeup on her cheek. She raised her hand over the throbbing flesh.

"Just a bruise, that's all."

Grandpa turned off the telly and joined them at the table, taking her in from head to toe. "I'm glad yer home, lass."

The timer sounded and her grandfather opened the cooker, allowing the scent of garlic to waft out.

"That smells wonderful—what did you make?" Ten times better than cold cereal no matter what.

"I helped make potatoes, too, Mum. I got tae use the knife."

Paislee's eyes immediately dropped to her son's fingers—which were all still attached. "Oh?"

Her grandfather took out the pan. "I found some ham and made cheesy potatoes. Used the last of the milk, though, so we'll need tae make a trip tae the grocery store. If ye give me a list, I can go after dinner." Grandpa pointed to the keys on the counter. "For the rental."

"That would be"—her eyes welled—"lovely." It had been a very long time since anybody had taken care of *her*.

"Can I go, too?" Brody looked from her to Grandpa.

"If yer mom agrees, and after the dishes are done, aye."

Paislee wasn't allowed to even set the table as Brody and her grandfather did it all. Then, after dinner, she was shooed to the living room and onto the couch with a cup of tea, while they did the dishes and made a list for supplies at the grocery store.

She gave her grandpa the only cash she had—an emergency twenty pounds in the flour canister.

"I can help when me check comes in," he told her.

"There's money in the grocery budget," Paislee assured him, "but I dinnae think ye can use my card. This will be enough for milk and some fruit. If ye see something that you'd like and have enough, be sure tae get it."

"Well, Craigh never complained about my pot roast."

Paislee nodded. Someone else to cook? She wasn't going to say no.

The two left and she was overwhelmed by the silence. She put her feet on the couch and Wallace jumped up beside her for a snuggle.

She texted Amelia, Flora, Mary Beth, Elspeth, and Lydia about Knit and Sip for Friday night so they could all catch up on their projects—she was fine but would see them tomorrow, if they could make it.

All five immediately responded in the affirmative.

Her eyes slowly closed as she fell asleep.

Chapter 21

Paislee woke up from where she'd fallen asleep on the couch, just before dawn—Brody and Wallace both snuggled on a blanket on the floor at her side.

Bless them, she thought. Her guardians.

She tried to move and groaned—it seemed her muscles had stiffened overnight. Wallace blinked at her but stayed curled up with Brody. She carefully avoided Brody's sprawled body and climbed the stairs, avoiding the creaky ones.

Twenty minutes later, she'd used all of the hot water, but she could move without crying. She swallowed her ibuprofen.

What to wear? Paislee chose a pink plaid button-up shirt that she didn't have to pull over her head with room for the soft brace, jeans, and brown leather flats. No bending or tying. Her hair would be down today. Not having the strength to style it, she'd let it do what it wanted.

Sitting at the vanity, Paislee used a stick of concealer to blot over the bruise on her cheek. It was no longer red but had faded to a pale purple.

When she went downstairs, her grandfather had cereal bowls out on the table along with the milk and the box of

Weetabix. Brody was making his cheese sandwich at the counter.

She didn't care if they'd only called a truce while she was under the weather, and she wasn't going to complain about the amount of butter spread on the bread or that two packets of crisps had made it into Brody's lunch box—nary an apple in sight.

Grandpa handed her a steaming mug of Brodies Scottish Breakfast and she took it gratefully. "Thanks. Sairy that I fell asleep last night on the couch. Were you watching over me, Brody, lad?"

"Just in case you needed me, Mum."

"I hope the floor didnae hurt your back!"

He stretched and touched his fingers to his toes, springing back up. "Naw."

Grandpa Angus chuckled. "It's been a while since I could touch me toes."

"I made you a sandwich, too, Mum. And Grandpa." He tossed the knife in the sink and raced to the table to pour cereal into his bowl. "Grandpa said ye might need him at work today? Lydia texted aye, aboot knitting tonight."

"My messages?" She filled a bowl with cereal, then added milk.

"I didnae mean tae read them," Brody said earnestly, "but when I put yer phone on the charger, Lydia texted."

"I dinnae even remember you coming in last night."

"You were knackered," Brody assured her. "I blew in yer face and everything."

She laughed—that was the true test of whether or not she was faking on a Sunday morning, trying to get a few more minutes of rest.

Paislee touched the brace. "We'll see how long I can wear this thing, but it's already bothering me. It doesnae hurt, but it itches. It's supposed tae restrict my movement."

"What did the doctor say?" Brody scooped a spoonful of cereal into his mouth.

"At least two days, but we'll see."

"You have tae do what the doctor says. That's what you tell me."

And now he remembered every last thing she said? "I'm tae see Dr. Whyte next week tae make sure everything is healing as it should. But I dinnae have a life of leisure—I told the doctor that."

"I can help," her grandfather said. "Ye can show me this morning where tae put the yarn from Flora."

"That would be excellent, thanks." Some of the shelves required a ladder to reach. "My next order from Jerry"—she met Grandpa's eyes—"McFadden? Ye met him the other day?" Grandpa nodded. "Will be in on Tuesday, so it's just a matter of powering through today and Saturday." The festival. "Sunday we'll all collapse."

"Will ye be able tae work at the booth, Mum?"

"I'll be fine." She had to be. In years past, she and Lydia would take turns being inside the shop to ring up orders, or outside at the table to hand out the freebies. Brody amused himself with his tablet and video games.

Brody swallowed a bite of cereal. "I'll hand out the keychains and sit at the table with ye. But I get an elephant ear, right?"

He loved the fried dough treat, and having a bribe guaranteed good behavior. "Right."

"My friend Edwyn said his dad has a comic book booth . . . they're giving away posters!"

She saw where this was going and held up her hand. "Getting the booth set up first is the most important thing."

"But what if they're gone?" His tone implied that it might be the end of his existence if he didn't get a poster.

"I'll take ye," Grandpa volunteered. "I used tae read comics."

"Did they have comics when you were a kid?" Her son chewed a blueberry. "That was a loooong time ago."

Her grandfather scratched his beard. "Or maybe not."

"What?" Brody asked, too innocently.

And so ended the truce. "Lydia showed me a possible new place tae lease, but not only was it out of my price range; it was boring and white."

"Can't ye paint?" Grandpa asked.

"Booooring," her son repeated, slurping the last of his milk.

"Paint wasnae the only problem, so we'll keep looking for a space I can be at for the next few years."

"Are ye buyin'?" Grandpa poured a few pieces of cereal into his bowl and picked at them, eating them dry.

"I wish." Paislee sipped her tea. "Someday I would love tae own me own shop, but that isnae where we are right now."

"No money," Brody said with a scowl. "When I get older I'll buy you a shop, Mum."

"That's sweet, but it is *my* job tae take care of *you*, my lad. Now finish up so we can go."

He bolted upward. "I'm so proud of ye, Mum—four days in a row without a tardy!"

She sat back. "Do ye want me tae sell ye tae the gypsies?"

Brody darted past with an unrepentant grin. "Try and catch me!"

Wallace barked and raced after him up the stairs.

She didn't bother yelling at them to keep it down. It would only hurt her head.

"He's a guid boy," Grandpa said. "Wouldnae think of leavin' ye tae sleep alone last night."

Her heart warmed with love. "Thanks for stepping in. Did you hear back from the police department yesterday, in Dairlee?"

"They think I'm a dodgy old codger without a workin' brain in me head. Makin' up Craigh's job."

She patted his wrinkled—but very capable—hand. "Let me get through this week and I'll do more."

"I know ye will, lass. You have problems of yer own."

"Gran used tae say that God—"

"Wouldnae give ye more than ye could handle. Aye, I remember well, usually after a fourteen-hour day on the fishing boat while she was fixing me a bowl of Cullen skink."

"Her chowder was the best." Smoked haddock, onion, and cream. They shared a smile.

The house phone rang and she jumped, startled, checking the caller ID before she handed the phone to her grandfather. "It's the Dairlee police."

His face lost all color as he took the receiver.

"Hello. This is Angus Shaw."

She only heard Grandpa's side of the conversation—should she leave or stay? He gestured for her to sit at the table.

Paislee held her palm out for the phone and pressed the speaker button.

". . . returning your call from yesterday. As we have told you before, sir, there is nothing more we can do about helping you locate your son."

"Did ye search for a rig named the *Mona*?" Grandpa asked.

"Aye. We have found nothing."

Her grandfather clenched his hands into fists and rested them angrily, impotently, on the table.

"And the missing person's report I filed?"

"There have been no leads in the month since you filed it."

He slammed his fist to the table. "And how much manpower have ye given tae it?"

The police officer spluttered, "I c-c-an promise you that we have explored every avenue available tae us."

"Meaning ye put the information I gave ye into the computer and forgot about it."

"Is there anything else I can do for you today, Mr. Shaw?" The question was asked with forced politeness.

She shook her head at him before he said anything too foul to regret.

He blew out a breath. "You havenae done *anything* for me yet."

"Is this the best number to reach you at if any new information arises?"

"Aye."

"Then have a nice day." *Click.*

They sat in silence for a moment. She had a bad feeling about Craigh. "It sounds like you've followed the right steps. Has Craigh ever been out of touch before?"

Trembling, Grandpa shook his head. "Not like this. A weekend with a lass. I dinnae ken what tae do next." His voice quavered. "He's the only son I have left and I need tae find him."

Paislee understood his anguish. She couldn't imagine her son disappearing.

Speaking of sons, where was hers? Listening upstairs, she heard water running in the sink. "Brody—hurry up!" Her head pounded, but she gathered the empty bowls and piled them in the sink to wash quickly, her eye on the round clock.

They left the house at quarter till nine. Grandpa drove the white rental to Fordythe as Paislee was still a mite sore around the shoulder.

Headmaster McCall was watching for them and hurried over when he saw Brody exit the car. Paislee rolled down her window, and he leaned in.

His gaze dropped to the padded brace around her throat. "How are you, Paislee?"

"Just fine, thank you. Headmaster McCall, this is Angus Shaw, Brody's great-grandfather."

She watched the headmaster assess Grandpa's fitness level and realize that the older man was in better shape than Paislee to drive.

"How'd ye do?" Grandpa asked.

"Fine, thank you. Nice to meet you. I hope ye'll get a chance to rest up over the weekend, Paislee?"

"We'll be at the street festival," Brody informed him. "Giving away keychains. With flowers. You probably don't want one."

Paislee scowled at her son, who stood behind the headmaster. "Bye, Brody. Grandpa or I will be here to pick you up."

The headmaster winced. "It has to be you, unless you put your grandfather on the pickup list."

Ach, his dratted rules. She clenched her teeth. Just when she was thinking he may not be so bad, he reminded her he really was a pain in the arse.

"Fine. I'll be here." She faced her grandfather and rolled up the window on Headmaster McCall. "Can we go?"

The old man chuckled. "Gets under yer skin, does he?"

She refused to look at the headmaster. "Just drive."

"I think he likes ye," Grandpa practically chortled.

"I dinnae want tae hear your opinion. Keep it up and you really will be sleeping on the back porch."

Chapter 22

Paislee had Grandpa Angus park in the alley behind Cashmere Crush and she slowly climbed the four stone steps to the rear entrance of her shop.

She flipped on the switch. "It feels like I've been gone forever." The first thing to catch her eye was the open box of bright yellow yarn that Flora had brought in the day before. Paislee picked up a skein and held it to the light. "This is one of her best colors yet. It's like a bonny daffodil."

"Looks like yarn tae me." Grandpa placed the keys to the rental on the shelf beneath the counter next to Paislee's purse.

"She uses all-natural extracts from flowers and even weeds."

Grandpa examined the yarn again, his glasses sliding a bit down his nose. "Why does it matter what makes the color?"

"It matters tae customers. Do you remember Mary Beth, the lady who wanted the pink yarn for the christening blanket?"

"She's the size of our rental out back."

"Grandpa!"

He shrugged. "She's not petite, lass, and that's no lie."

"Anyway, she only buys synthetic dyes. Says they're better for the environment. We've had some pretty intense discussions about it." Paislee smiled at the memories here. How could she leave?

"What's yer preference?"

"I think there's room for both natural and synthetic dyes, if done properly. Quality matters most. That's why I use McFadden's."

"I've known me share of ladies and they're sure tae take a side. But *yarn*?" He sat on the stool by the register, nudging the box aside. "I dinnae see what the fuss is aboot."

His share of ladies, eh? "Everybody has a right tae believe what they want. My friend Amelia was swayed tae the synthetic side of the argument, because of the danger in natural ingredients for setting the color in the yarn."

He snorted. "Danger?"

"Aye," she said, crossing her arms. "A mordant is needed tae fix the color. Flora uses chrome tae keep her colors from fading, which is very toxic. Before I agreed tae carry her product, I had tae see her setup and make sure she was being safe in how she disposed of the hazardous waste." Flora was very cautious and respectful of the environment, but not all dyers took such care.

He scratched his beard, his tone doubtful. "Sounds like a dull subject. I imagined ye'd all get together and talk about women stuff."

Women stuff? "And what would that be exactly?"

"How would I know? I dinnae go to hen parties." He winked at her. "But that Lydia sure is a looker. Think she'd be interested in an older man?"

She smacked him on the arm with a yellow skein of yarn. "Don't be daft."

Paislee pulled the label gun from a bottom drawer beneath the register. "Let me set this up for you, and then you can price each skein, and stack them." She pointed to the shelves of a lighter yellow yarn, up on the third shelf. "Next tae those would be brilliant. I'll get the ladder from the back."

"No, lass, I'll get the ladder. You do the label thing."

Grandpa was back in two minutes and opening the metal ladder.

She showed him how to price the yarn, noticing the tangled beginnings of the fisherman's sweater lying on the shelf. "Two weeks tae knit the sweater." She glanced at the box of crocheted flowers. "Those are the priority because I need them by tomorrow." Paislee had learned to juggle things effectively by stomping out whatever fire needed attention first, but now that she was injured there seemed to be fires all around.

"Did ye say something?"

"No, talkin' tae myself—usually there's nobody here tae answer back."

He chuckled. "I'm happy to ignore ye."

She picked up the sage yarn, then put it back, remembering that the detective wanted to speak to her. "Do you mind manning the store while I go speak tae Detective Inspector Zeffer? He wanted tae finish taking my statement about the accident yesterday."

"So long as yer walkin' slow, go right ahead." Grandpa lifted the label gun and priced a yellow skein.

"Ta."

She grabbed her phone and left out the front door. Her flower boxes were pretty with red geraniums and mustard-colored marigolds. The storefront had to look nice for tomorrow's festival. She'd thought that she would be running back and forth between her booth and the register, but now with both Lydia *and* Grandpa she didn't have to be in two places at once. *Somehow things will work out*, she told herself.

As she took in a deep breath of fresh spring air, her gaze found the florist shop across the road. Ritchie dragged out buckets of fresh flowers, tempting folks in to buy. Must not be a wedding today, she thought.

Ambling past the leather shop, she waved to James through the window as he oiled a strip of leather that appeared to be a belt. Next was the dry cleaner's, and Ned, who chatted with someone on the phone and didn't see her. The lab didn't have an open window, like the office supply shop did—she lifted a hand to Lourdes—and as she passed the tea shop she promised herself a tea and a scone on the way back for her and Grandpa.

Paislee crossed the street and turned right, walking the half block to the police station. She climbed the steps slowly, her neck brace reminding her of yesterday's accident, and that someone wanted to hurt her.

No, warn her.

From what?

Proving that Isla had been murdered?

She entered the building, the glass door squeaking.

Amelia sat at the front desk. Her big blue eyes in her pale face with her short brunette hair made her look like an elf. She came around to give Paislee a very gentle hug, her gaze pausing at her cheek. "Poor thing! Ach. I hope the DI finds oot who ran ye off the road."

"I'm sure he has other things tae do." Like discover what had happened to Isla.

As if he'd heard his name, Detective Inspector Zeffer barreled from his back office. In another blue suit, this one navy, the detective looked quite handsome with his freshly shaved face. His greeting stopped when he saw the brace at her neck.

"Paislee! What's the verdict?" He joined them in the foyer and eyed her closely.

"Just whiplash, according tae the doctor. I'm fine, remember?"

He chuckled ruefully at the reminder of their conversation

at the hospital. She'd say she was fine even if she needed a full
body cast.

Amelia looked with interest between them.

"Thank you for showing up this morning," he said. "Why
didnae ye take the day off?"

"I cannae afford tae do that."

He shuffled uncomfortably. "Right." The detective swept
his hand toward his office. "This way, and we can finish your
statement."

She finger-waved to Amelia, who returned to her desk to
answer the phone by the second ring. "Nairn Police Station."

Paislee followed him into a spacious office.

The window looked out on the green lawn of the park
around the bandstand, between the road and the Moray Firth;
a sturdy oak provided shade over a picnic table.

Detective Inspector Zeffer's shiny black shoes matched the
shiny black of his new desk. A desktop computer was positioned to the right, and a black leather office chair waited
invitingly. A brass nameplate read: Detective Inspector Mack
Zeffer.

Old field maps remained on the turquoise-colored wall
from when this had been Inspector Shinner's office. A single
wall had been primed in white.

"Excuse the mess," Zeffer said, gesturing for her to sit on a
less inviting gray metal chair. "They keep asking me about
paint, but I dinnae care. I'm fine with beige."

She perched on the hard chair. "You don't like bright colors? I find them energizing."

He sank into his seat, the leather creaking, and surveyed
the room with a shrug. "I dinnae want tae waste my time
looking at paint samples. Inspector Shinner left some pretty
big shoes tae fill here."

"And Isla's death right off," she said, hoping he would tell
her more about it.

He didn't. "Let's talk again aboot who might have run ye off the road?"

"I told you what happened," she said, touching her brace.

He leaned forward and focused on her intently. "Tell me again."

She gave him the rundown of confronting Roderick Vierra regarding his and Isla's affair, and the blackmail.

He listened to every word. "Why did you feel the need tae do that? Isla is dead, and it doesnae matter now."

"Isla was my protégé." Paislee crossed her legs at the ankles and held his gaze—he had to understand that this "case" mattered to her on a personal level. "Not a stranger that I can dismiss. I discovered her."

He straightened and rubbed his jaw. "What did you see in the flat?"

Could she finally tell him about Tabitha? And Gerald? "She had a mug of tea on the table. Her medicine bottle lay on its side."

"What else?"

"Shortbread cookies—she had health issues as you know and it struck me as odd that she would have those in her flat. Made me think she had a guest, as did the rinsed mug in the sink."

He rubbed his upper lip. "It isnae against the law tae have a guest."

"It is for that guest to kill her," Paislee snapped. "And I saw that same brand of shortbread when I went tae visit Tabitha at the florist. She was wearing the sage scarf that I had made for Isla, brazen as you please."

She took a deep breath to calm down.

His mouth thinned and his sea-glass-green eyes flashed. "What makes you think she was killed?"

Oh no. She couldn't rat out Amelia. "What else am I tae

think when ye willnae tell us how she died? If it was heart failure, you would have said so."

"It might be suicide," he said. "She'd split with her boyfriend, and gotten fired after an affair."

"No." Paislee straightened. "It could never be that. She was too much of a fighter tae kill herself. Besides, after talking tae Billy and Roderick, I know Isla wouldnae have let them close enough tae break her heart." She didn't share that Billy claimed Isla didn't have one.

"Is that what ye've been doing? Talking tae everyone?"

"Talking isnae a crime. Was Isla killed?"

He wiped his expression clear, literally scraping his palm across his face. "You were lucky that someone called in your accident so quickly on that quiet stretch of road."

She wished he would just answer her question! "I thought so, too." Paislee brushed her bangs back. "Did you ask Gerald about where he was yesterday afternoon? Or Roderick?"

He waved that aside. "How did you meet Isla Campbell?"

Paislee recalled the day. "She burst into the shop, asking about sage-green yarn tae knit a cap. Well, crochet. She didnae like knitting. Her eyes were red, and when I asked her how she was her lip trembled, but she didnae cry. She was tough. She'd been dumped by her boyfriend, who went back tae Edinburgh without her."

He sat back and shook his head. "You were easy. A mark."

"Think what you like. She might have been brash tae some, but she did fair work—I saw the frightened young girl beneath her exterior." Isla had been aware that death hung over her like a cloud that could rain at any time, if her heart gave out. She'd decided to live to her fullest.

Detective Inspector Zeffer's russet brow arched. "Isla seemed tae have more enemies than friends. So far, you are her only one."

"What about her mother?"

"When Isla left Edinburgh, she took her mother's jewelry with her."

Paislee deflated. "Her mother didn't treat her well."

"Perhaps."

"I'd be interested in speaking with her," Paislee said. "There are quite a few things I'd like tae know."

"You ask a lot of questions."

"Nairn is a small town, and that's how ye show you care." He should remember that if he wanted to fit in here.

He smoothed the lapel of his stylish suit. "Ms. Campbell was supposed tae be here today, but she's postponed her arrival until Sunday. She cannae miss work, she says. She's asked about burying Isla here."

Poor Isla—Paislee would definitely speak to Father Dixon on the girl's behalf. "I meant tae tell you that Billy told me Isla wanted him tae help her blackmail people for a percentage of the profit."

"Hmm." He took his notebook from his interior pocket and read a page as if to double-check his facts. "After you mentioned blackmail at the hospital, I put a call in to Roderick Vierra. He claims tae have been at the Vierra warehouse with Roger all afternoon."

"I know they would lie for one another."

The detective continued, "Billy didnae share that Isla had wanted tae recruit him tae help her with a blackmail ring in his interview."

Why would he have? Billy was sly. "I didnae find Billy very likable, but he didnae run me off the road—it was a silver car, and he drives an old pickup."

Silence stretched between them.

She resisted the urge to fill in the silence as she'd done before in their meetings. He had a way of dragging forth secrets, and while she only had the one, it was a biggie, and she could never give it up.

Rather than look at the detective, she stared over his shoulder out the window to the tree behind him. Spring leaves added color to winter drab. How else could she help with Isla?

He set the notebook onto the blotter of the shiny black desk. "So, tell me, Paislee Shaw, where were you on Monday morning, around eight?"

Stunned, Paislee spluttered in shock, "F-f-feeding Brody a hot breakfast. Why on earth do ye want tae know?"

"I've read through Isla's emails, and saw the one she sent tae you, alluding tae a side deal on yarn. Did ye take her up on it?"

"I beg your pardon?" Paislee was so angry she literally saw stars before her eyes.

His cool green gaze turned glacial. "Did you take her up on her offer tae buy discounted yarn?"

"No." Paislee got to her feet, her voice raised. "You are searching in the wrong place for Isla's killer, Detective Inspector Zeffer, if ye think I did it. I didnae do it! You should look closer at Gerald Sanford. He was in Isla's flat before we were— Isla had an aversion to dogs, so ask him the real reason why his pup Baxter was in Isla's flat?"

Her breaths came in hard flexes of her lungs, but she did her best to keep outwardly cool. Because Isla's body had been so stiff, she'd assumed Isla had died at night, but no, in the morning—right before Isla was supposed to show up for her interview.

Would she have been able to save Isla if she'd gone at nine thirty, when the girl didn't show? She pressed her palm to her chest.

"Let me get this straight." He drummed his fingers along his desktop. "You think Gerald could be guilty because *Baxter* was in Isla's apartment."

She lifted her chin, which hurt her neck. "He wasnae being honest."

"And ye want me to check on Tabitha because she stole Isla's scarf and likes shortbread cookies?"

Paislee didn't care for his tone. "She was so upset the day I spoke to her that I saw her at Doc Whyte's later with a migraine. Guilty conscience, I think."

"And Billy?" He massaged his temple as he watched her, banked amusement at her expense on his face.

She bristled. "Maybe he got tired of Isla demanding things from him—maybe he did it for Tabitha. I don't know."

"We can agree that you don't know."

Ugly silence grew between them.

"Can I leave now?" She spoke stiffly. He would have a very hard time in Nairn if he didn't change his ways. Inspector Shinner had always been friendly and respectful—this *detective* acted entitled and was rude.

"Aye. I'll be in touch."

"You know where I work. Where I live. You even know where I keep my spare key. I have nothing tae hide regarding Isla, Detective Inspector."

She banged out of his office. She hated that she'd lost her composure when it was something she prided herself on.

Norma and Amelia rushed to her. "Are you all right?" The older woman offered her a bottle of water.

Amelia rubbed Paislee's arm. "He can be a tough man."

"Can you believe he asked me where I was when Isla died?" Out of everything he'd said, that stung the worst.

"We heard you shout that ye didn't do it," Norma said. The phone rang and she lumbered around the desk to answer it.

Amelia glanced guiltily to Zeffer's office. "I'll see you tonight, okay? The pressure is on for him tae solve this case, so dinnae take it personally."

Paislee nodded and made her way out the front door in a fog, too upset to stop for tea and a raspberry scone as she hurried back to Cashmere Crush. Her sanctuary.

When she arrived, there were fresh flowers on her counter. Grandpa folded the metal ladder. "Delivery just came for you."

She was still upset as her gaze skimmed over the bright bouquet. "Who are they from?"

She'd never received flowers before, and she couldn't think who might have sent them now. She'd just left the man who owed her an apology—he didn't have time enough to order them. *Ach.*

"I didnae read the card, lass," Grandpa chided before putting the ladder away.

She reached for the sealed envelope. Had Tabitha made the bouquet and maybe stuck something sharp in it? Noting the address, she saw that it wasn't from the flower shop across the street.

" 'Get well soon, Fordythe Primary.' " Her brow arched. "Since when does a school send a parent flowers?"

"I bet that headmaster's behind it." Grandpa stuffed his hands in his khaki pockets.

"Grandpa—I dinnae want tae talk about it. Did you get the yarn put away?" She could see for herself that he had but was too flustered by the events in her world to think clearly.

"What's got you in a dither?"

Leaning back against the high-top table, she recapped what had happened with the detective, her face hot.

Grandpa glowered. "Ye didnae mention that the accident was deliberate."

She smacked her forehead in exasperation, hurting her neck. "*He* doesn't seem tae care!"

"The police have their own way of doin' things; I've seen it aboot Craigh, too." He puffed out his thin chest. "Are ye in danger?"

"Naw." She tried to banish the memory of the silver car

behind her. "I dinnae ken anything about how Isla died. I told the detective she wouldnae have committed suicide. I told him tae question Gerald Sanford."

"The pretty boy that lives next door tae Isla?"

"Yeah. Lydia called him Mr. Highland Hung."

Grandpa chuckled.

"You know what? I bet you Isla was blackmailing Gerald. That's why he killed her."

He straightened and took off his glasses to stare her in the eye. "That is not funny, lass."

Chapter 23

Paislee had no time to discuss with Grandpa why Gerald had killed Isla, because James from next door walked in, a worried frown on his very weathered face.

"Paislee, love, what is this I hear about ye being run off the road?"

"I'm fine."

He gently touched her shoulder. "Tourists come tae Scotland thinkin' all roads are the North Coast Five Hundred, thanks tae Jeremy Clarkson. I have half a mind tae set up a drag race right in front of *his* house."

"You know Jeremy Clarkson?" Grandpa asked.

"Aye. We've tossed back a few pints." James's empathetic gaze paused at her bruised cheek and neck brace. "Nothing broken, then? "

"Naw." She rested her elbow on the high-top table, not willing to admit that the walk to the station and back had tired her.

"I'm glad yer all right." James offered his hand to Grandpa. "And who is this?"

"Angus Shaw," her grandfather said, giving James's hand a

solid shake. She had visions of the pair, wily and wrinkled, roaming Nairn in search of a good time.

"James Young. Name was funny tae me when I was young, but now it's a real crack-up." His grin invited Paislee and Grandpa to laugh with him. "How long are ye here for?"

"At least tourist season," Paislee interjected to get Grandpa off the hot seat. "He's been an immense help."

Jerry McFadden arrived through the back entrance carrying a box of sandy beige yarn that she could hardly keep in stock but she hadn't expected it until Tuesday.

"Hi, Jerry."

"Morning, Paislee. Ach—the rumor is true." He scanned her face with concern. "Are ye feeling better than ye look?"

Grandpa and James glared at the man.

Jerry deposited the box on the counter and gave Paislee a soft hug. "It was just a joke, ken?"

"I know, I know." She shook her head at the older gentlemen and their matching scowls. Jerry would be forty this year and had been a good friend to her always—but just that.

"I wanted tae make sure that yer well, so I squeezed your delivery in, but I cannae stay. I'll visit yer booth tomorrow."

"You're sweet for stopping by—see you then," she said as Jerry disappeared as quickly as he'd shown up.

Next, Ned from the dry cleaner arrived on the pretext of seeing if she needed any help with her booth in the morning—but she could tell he was just checking on her, too. He didn't stay long, either, after seeing with his own eyes that she was all right.

Margot from the lab showed up with an all-natural remedy to reduce bruising. "Arnica pellets under yer tongue, and vitamin K cream for a topical. I can't stay, love, but I'll see you Sunday at the meetin'? Oh." She pulled an ivory card from her pocket. "This is from Lourdes and Jimmy. Jimmy is out sick, so she sent the card with me."

Paislee was overwhelmed by the support of her business family. "Thank you—yes, I'll be there."

"You're welcome, Paislee. Hard to believe I've known ye since you were twenty and ye first moved in. Take care, now." Margot departed in a whirlwind of sandalwood perfume.

Two minutes later, Theadora had sent a girl down with a box of mini raspberry scones and a note to get well. Did they have a grapevine?

James snagged a scone as he gave her a one-armed hug, and left to work on a pair of leather sandals.

"I'm knackered." She wilted onto a chair.

Her grandfather bit into a scone. "I see why these are your favorite."

They didn't even sound good to her right now. She should work on the Oxford Blue fisherman's sweater, but she couldn't picture the pattern in her mind, so she promised to do it later, early Monday.

"Grandpa, can ye get me five skeins of that sage yarn from the third shelf?" She could at least manage to work on the key fobs.

He did, offering unsolicited commentary. "Shame tae have left this job tae the last."

"Have ye not seen my life? This drama isn't that unusual—there's always something. Flat tires, chicken pox, laundry—how much dirt can one boy attract?"

"Yer gran ran the household," he admitted with a shrug. "I didnae start cooking until I moved in with Craigh."

Paislee switched from her chair to a stool and the high-top table to keep her neck and shoulders straight so she wouldn't strain her muscles. She crocheted the raised center of the flower petal using a small hook for the fine work.

"Want tae learn tae crochet?" she asked. "It's never too late."

"No thank ye. Cookin' is as close to me feminine side as I'll get. It's a guid thing for Brody that I've come along or he'll be spoilt by all the women around."

Paislee rose to the argument in a flash. "Brody is not the least spoiled, and if it wasnae for women, men wouldn't know how to—"

The door opened again and she turned with a quick smile of welcome—which fled as Detective Inspector Zeffer entered.

Grandpa settled behind the register to watch the fireworks.

"Hello again," the detective said.

"Morning," she replied begrudgingly. She didn't get up from her stool.

The detective glanced at the ceiling as if she was being unreasonable. "You're upset?"

"It isnae every day I'm suspected of being a murderer."

"I never actually suspected you, but I had tae ask. It's my job."

She supposed she could give him that. She looped sage green around the hook, twisted, and pulled. "And did ye ask Gerald where he was in the morning—and not just then, but yesterday around quarter tae three?"

"Gerald is not at home."

Which meant he'd called or driven by, at least. She set her project down. "What can I help ye with, then?"

"You mentioned that ye know Dr. Whyte?"

"He birthed me and Brody," she said defensively, the older man's smiling visage dear to her heart. If the detective thought the doctor had done anything wrong, the town would run the detective back to wherever he'd come from.

"Something more recent?"

His smug drawl made her want to shake him. "Brody had a checkup on Wednesday, and we saw Tabitha there, with a migraine."

"Brought on by guilt?"

So he remembered what she'd said. "Right—from cheating with her best friend's boyfriend, if not worse. Flora was there for allergies"—she thought back to the full waiting room—"and Mary Beth's husband Arran was in. I'll be going back next week," she said snarkily. "Why do you want tae know? He's a suspect now? He wasnae Isla's doctor—she went tae the heart specialist in Inverness."

"I know that." The detective's jaw clenched. "I'm trying tae put together her life here in Nairn."

Paislee sat up. "She wasn't blackmailing Dr. Whyte. The man is a saint."

"I never said that—don't leap tae conclusions."

"What would ye have me think, then?"

"I would have ye simply answer my questions. I told you, I had access tae her emails."

"If your link tae the doctor is as flimsy as the link you tried tae create with me, then I would give it up. Look more closely at Gerald, for heaven's sake. Maybe police work isnae for you."

Grandpa Angus waggled his silver brows at Paislee.

"What?" She was in no mood for games or being subtle. Lydia's reminder about more flies with honey whispered she should be nice.

"Why don't you tell the detective what you thought about Gerald?"

Detective Inspector Zeffer turned toward her grandfather with dismay. "The two of ye were discussing the case?"

"Just conversation tae pass the time," Grandpa said, bristling at the detective's tone.

Paislee cleared her throat to get the detective's attention

back on her before he recalled that her grandfather had been sleeping on a bench the morning of the murder, with no alibi.

"Gerald was in Isla's flat, and I bet you he was looking for something—not yarn, Detective, but what if she was blackmailing *him*?"

"On what grounds?"

"He moonlights as an exotic dancer."

The detective's pale green eyes narrowed to slits of glass. "He already told me that he was a dancer."

"Highland *Hung*? Couldn't something like that ruin his chances as a solicitor?"

Zeffer crossed his arms.

Paislee tilted her head and arched her brow. "It's not unheard of, dancers offering *extras*."

He flushed.

"What if Isla had proof, like video or something, and Gerald wanted it back—or maybe they argued because she raised the price of her silence, like she did with Roderick Vierra?"

He blew out a breath. "This is all speculation."

"It wasnae speculation that his dog ran out of Isla's flat. She couldnae tolerate animals. When she worked for me I never brought my terrier tae the shop."

For effect, she grabbed a knitting needle and jabbed it down against the counter. "And Gerald drives a silver BMW."

Her grandfather left the cash register to stand by her in support.

The detective looked from her face to his.

"Sounds logical tae me," Grandpa said.

"I want facts, not conjecture." Detective Inspector Zeffer smoothed the lapels of his blue suit, which he had a tendency to tug. "It's my job tae weed through what you're telling me and find the truth."

"Oh?" She quirked her brow. If so, Gerald would be behind bars.

"Do you know how many silver cars are registered in Nairn? For just under fourteen thousand residents?"

She shifted on the stool.

"Over three thousand."

Paislee gasped.

"That's more than a few," Grandpa conceded.

"Aye, but rest assured we're checking on them." Detective Inspector Zeffer swept his gaze from Grandpa to her. "Dinnae think for one minute that I've forgotten you were run off the road."

She opened her mouth to tell him again what she thought, but he cut her off. "It just may not be the same person who killed Isla. Dinnae make the mistake of assuming they are one and the same." He left without saying another word.

Chapter 24

Paislee and Grandpa closed the shop at three fifteen to go pick up Brody from school. "I will add you tae the list next week, so you can get him whenever I can't."

A fairy cranky grandpa instead of a fairy godmother had been dropped into her life, but Paislee was not complaining. At least she had someone.

Grandpa drove, and they entered the queue at Fordythe. Paislee searched the front of the building for Hamish McCall to thank him for the flowers but didn't see him. She waved at one of the school chaperones as Brody climbed in the back of the car.

"I forgot about this white car," her son complained. "It sucks."

"Excuse me?"

"I like our Juke 'cause I can see it over the other cars in line."

"I havenae heard back from the mechanic yet—let me give him a call." Having a chauffeur was pretty sweet, too.

She dialed Edward's Mechanic, the phone to her ear. "Hello," she said when a male voice answered. "This is Paislee

Shaw—I'm calling about a Juke that was brought in yesterday?"

"Hello, Paislee, it's Joseph. I just put on yer tires last month?"

Sucking in a breath she said, "I know."

"Good news is that the tires are fine."

"Bad news?"

"Weel. We have tae replace the airbag in the driver's seat, as
well as the driver's seat belt, which jammed."

Her sore shoulder muscles throbbed their confirmation.

"I know ye're on a budget."

"Aye. But I have collision insurance if the damage is over
five hundred?"

"We are looking at four just for the airbag, with the new
sensor. That doesnae take into account the front bumper—but
since you have insurance, I'll do the work and bill them, and
you can make payments to me on the five hundred. Deal?"

Tears burned her eyes. "Thank you so much, Joseph. And it
will be safe?"

"Like brand-new," he promised. "How are ye getting
around?"

"A rental, so we're okay for transportation. How long will
the repairs take?"

"Give me a week. I have tae order the airbag in from Edinburgh."

"I am very grateful tae you."

"I hope they catch the eejit that ran ye off—coulda been
much worse. I did the tow into the shop."

"I know how fortunate I am—I think I have a guardian
angel." *Granny*.

"Awright, then. I'll be in touch soon. Dinnae worry, Paislee."

She was glad she'd kept the phone conversation private,
because she didn't want Brody to know that the action had
been deliberate or how close a call it had been. "Thanks!"

Hanging up, she shifted to see Brody in the back seat. He wore a look of concern that didn't belong on a boy's face.

Grandpa snorted. "Well? Is it an arm and a leg?"

She smiled wide, exuding gratitude and assurance. "It will all be covered by our insurance." She didn't share about the co-pay. "We should have our car back next week."

Her son exhaled as if the weight of the world had lifted.

"You know I will always take care of you, don't you, Brody? We will find a way, like we always do."

"I know, Mum, but ye can't take one more thing."

She made a vow to stop saying that immediately. "Life is full of ups and downs, and as long as we have each other, that's all that matters."

"Should I drop ye off at Cashmere Crush, like we talked about?" Grandpa asked.

"Aye." She said to Brody, "You and Grandpa get tae order pizza and watch movies."

"Yes!" He fist-pumped the air. "Way better than Knit and Sip. It gets so loud I can't hear the telly."

Grandpa slowed to a stop in front of the shop and Paislee got out, waving good-bye with a promise to see them later. "Lydia will bring me home. Have fun!"

They drove off, the white back end of the Sentra flashing in a ray of sun breaking through the gray sky.

She hurried inside and put away the yarn from Jerry, then crocheted flowers until half past five, when it was time to set out the drinks and crisps for the night. Elspeth was the first to arrive at ten to six, followed by Flora, then Amelia, Lydia, and, last, Mary Beth.

The ladies all fussed over her bruised cheek, cosseting her and showing their care in different ways. Lydia brought an extra cheese dip for Paislee to bring home with her; Elspeth gifted a geranium in a pot; Flora handed over a bag of dried comfrey leaves to ease inflammation and sore muscles. "Bathe in them, or steep them; both are good." Amelia gave her a book on staying positive no matter what happened, and Mary Beth handed her a gift certificate for a pedicure.

"I feel like it's my birthday." Which was actually in November instead of March.

"We're just so glad yer all right, love." Mary Beth squeezed her gently in a hug.

Lydia cleared one of the high-top tables for food and drinks while the other women found seats and brought out their projects.

Mary Beth lifted the gorgeous pink christening blanket from her bag and Paislee admired the uniform bubbles she'd managed to make. "This is lovely," she said.

Mary Beth blushed.

Elspeth worked on a soft blue cardigan sweater for her sister. "Although we had the worst fight earlier today. I'm sorely tempted to unravel the thing and make dishrags."

"What did ye fight about?" Amelia asked, lifting a black knit cap from her backpack.

"Susan says I baby h-h-her." Elspeth's voice wavered. "She wasnae blind growing up, so living with her now because she cannae see is hard on both of us."

"I understand," Flora said. "My Donnan used tae be able tae do things for himself that he can't after his stroke. Don't be too hard on yourself as ye find yer way."

Paislee wondered how often Flora had to give herself that same talk.

"What caused her blindness?" Mary Beth asked Elspeth.

"Macular degeneration, which can happen as you age. She was diagnosed at fifty, which is early, I s'pose. She's sixty now and so angry about it. I try tae make it so that she can be independent, but she complains that I smother her with good intentions. How is that even possible?" Elspeth looked down at the light blue yarn rather than at them.

The ladies swarmed around Elspeth in hugs and solace, assuring her that she could manage what she had to do.

Flora handed Elspeth a tissue from her purse. "Don't we all find the strength somewhere?"

"I do, and this, here, helps me." Mary Beth gestured to their lopsided circle. "Arran's not been well this week and it makes him a bear. I banished him tae his office before I left tonight, and told him that if he so much as raised his voice tae our girls while I was gone, then he'd be eating burned soup over the next week."

Paislee, Flora, and Lydia laughed, as did Elspeth. Amelia wore a questioning expression.

"Arran cannae cook for himself," Mary Beth explained. "I cook *verra* well, and he loves his meals as much as I do."

"You could have stayed home," Paislee said, smiling still at Mary Beth taking a stand. From what she'd gathered over the years, Arran could be domineering.

"Don't I deserve me own time, too?"

They all agreed she did.

Flora brought out the yellow yarn she'd delivered to Paislee, then put it aside for a cherry red she told them she got from the red geranium. "I'm making Donnan a new cap—he's so cold all the time now."

Paislee smacked her palm to her forehead. "Your check for the yarn you dropped off—let me get it." She got up and quickly filled it out.

Flora didn't hide her relief when she accepted it. "Thanks, love."

Paislee saw green and yellow dye under Flora's nails. "Flora, are you not wearing gloves when you mix your dyes? How are your allergies?"

The woman sniffed to prove her sinuses were clear. "Bless Dr. Whyte and his antihistamines. Staying away from nature is impossible, given me line of work. Online yarn sales are booming, and since I'm the only one workin' I have no time tae be sick."

"I wanted tae ask you about that," Paislee said. "In case . . . I have tae move, or cannae find a new shop as big as this."

Lydia stood behind the counter, a black frilled apron over a silky blouse and jeans. "Never worry about that, Paislee, love; we will find something. All right—who wants what tae drink?" She loved to act as bartender, since she didn't knit.

"Whisky on the rocks for me," Amelia said, putting her black yarn aside to collect her beverage.

"I brought me own tea," Flora said. "Do you have lemon?"

"Sliced and ready," Lydia promised.

Elspeth sniffed one last time, then stood. "I'll have a glass of whatever wine you brought, Lydia. You have a guid taste for pairings. I was Father Dixon's right hand when finding quality wine on a budget. Not just for the church, but for entertaining."

Paislee realized that Elspeth had been needed and appreciated at her job, while her sister needed her, too, but resented her help. That would be a difficult adjustment.

Elspeth turned to Paislee. "I havenae forgotten tae reach out tae the historical society aboot this building. I left a message, but the woman I need tae speak tae is on holiday."

"Thanks. We're meeting on Sunday, me and the other businesses, tae discuss what we might do."

"It will be next week at least. Sairy," Elspeth said. She shook her head and her iron-gray hair, straight and thick, fell perfectly into place.

"Don't be." Paislee touched the soft brace at her neck. "Us being forced tae move certainly isnae your fault."

Lydia tossed a cherry stem at Paislee. "Pinot grigio, my injured bird?"

Paislee laughed when it landed beside her. "Aye, I also trust your taste in wine. In buildings not so much." She told the ladies about the new and very white office space.

Lydia actually seemed embarrassed. "I realized my mistake. It will be amended. Though no matter what, you will have more than thirty days tae vacate. I havenae seen a sale posted yet and I've been looking constantly."

"I appreciate that, Lydia. I'll be sure tae let the others know."

Elspeth passed Paislee a glass of white wine, then poured one for herself. The older woman sipped and nodded. "Brilliant flavors."

Amelia perched on the edge of her seat with her tumbler between her hands. "So, Paislee, what do ye think of our new detective?"

Paislee knotted off another crocheted flower. "You don't want tae know."

"I do. I saw sparks."

"Sparks of anger." She glared at her friend. "The man thought I was a suspect in Isla's death. I suppose I ran myself off the road, too?"

Flora and Mary Beth gasped.

"He didnae!" Mary Beth said.

"Not really," Paislee amended at the righteous anger on the faces of her friends. "But he did question me about my whereabouts Monday morning. I told him I was in the kitchen, thank ye verra much."

They all laughed, but she was still a little hot under the collar—her neck brace itched a bit. Dr. Raj had been right to insist she wear it for two days; otherwise she would have done too much.

"He was muttering under his breath after he'd been tae see you and didnae leave his office for an hour." Amelia snickered. "He's from Glasgow, ye know, and thought Nairn would be a boring job, beneath his skills. And he's handed a hard tae figure case right out of the gate. I'm torn between feeling sairy for him and rooting for him. Norma thinks he's cute."

"Norma is twenty years older than him." Paislee knotted the center of another flower.

"Isla was really *murdered*?" Mary Beth asked. She sipped from a bottle of fizzy water.

"Aye," Paislee said. The detective had confirmed he was searching for Isla's killer, perhaps inadvertently, but she'd heard him.

"Nothing tae drink, Mary Beth?" Lydia spread her hands over the array of adult beverages on the high top.

"I feel like water tonight. Do you realize that drinking and driving is up ten percent in Nairn?"

"That sounds like a solicitor's statistic. Does your husband have a new high-profile case?" Elspeth asked.

Arran's success allowed Mary Beth to have the latest fashions, jewelry, a nice home, and a new van—but Paislee suspected that Mary Beth *earned* her luxuries.

"I cannae say," Mary Beth deflected.

"It's all the new people that have moved here the last few years, I bet." Lydia offered Flora a plate with melted Gruyère and crackers.

Flora sniffed the appetizer to detect ingredients. "Green apples?"

"Aye."

Flora piled a bit on a cracker and tasted, her eyes closing in delight. "You are a marvel."

Amelia took a drink of her whisky. "The DI doesnae have a single real suspect. I read in a police procedural that the more time that passes the harder it is tae catch a killer."

"A police procedural?" Paislee asked with a grin.

She blushed to the roots of her short hair. "Inspector Shinner left behind some books that I've been readin' through. You know, just tae see."

"See what?" Flora asked, feeling the marigold positioned beside her ear.

Amelia's bright blue eyes twinkled as she informed them, "If I might like being a constable."

Lydia clapped her hands. "Brilliant. And why not?"

Amelia searched her glass as she admitted, "I never went tae college. I'm a gamer at heart, and a receptionist for pay."

"She's worried she isnae good enough, and I highly disagree," Paislee announced.

"I think you can do anything ye set your mind tae," Flora declared, her eyes filling with tears. "Tae be sure. I have a college degree in literature, but I dinnae use it."

"I didn't go tae college, either," Paislee said. "I had Brody, and had tae earn money right away."

"College is not a sign of intelligence." Lydia brought the wine around to top off her and Elspeth's glasses. "Following your passion to make a living matters—like Paislee and Flora both do. Me too, actually. I enjoy matching people with their hooses."

"It's not a bad paycheck," teased Paislee.

Amelia blinked at Lydia with stars in her eyes. "You think I can do it?"

"I have no doubt."

Amelia finished her whisky, a quiet satisfaction about her.

"What's the latest on Widower Mann?" Mary Beth asked Elspeth. The widower was notorious for the stream of elderly ladies he had visit in the nursing home across from Elspeth's house.

"The Lawson sisters went in tae see him last night—both at the same time!" Elspeth brought her fingers to her mouth.

"I'm tempted tae make my own visit just tae see what the fuss is about."

"You were married, right?" Paislee asked.

"Ach. Thirty years—I know what the fuss is *supposed* tae be about, but we never got on in that way. He was my best friend and I did my duty, but there wasnae passion. Not once did I have cause tae smile like some of the women leaving Widower Mann's room."

They all laughed at that.

Paislee tried hard to banish Roderick's comment on Isla being full of passion, but it was difficult.

Flora sipped her tea and Paislee saw flowers as well as lemon floating atop the mug. "I dinnae miss me nights with Donnan," she shared. "What I miss most since his stroke is being held." A tear slid down her cheek. "But I will do what I must for him tae get better."

It was no secret that Donnan used to get drunk and violent, though none of the ladies ever talked about it. This was her safe place, just as it was for all of them. Paislee didn't blame her for not missing that.

"I'm tempted tae visit Widower Mann myself!" Lydia offered crackers and cheese around. "I havenae had a date in months."

Amelia's shoulders slumped.

Guess they were all having a dry spell—not that Paislee wanted to change her situation. There would be no dating for her until Brody was out of school. She had one job in this world and raising Brody was it.

"Well, be sure tae report the findings. Although you're so pretty ye might be too much for him!" Mary Beth laughed as she knit another row of bubbled yarn.

"What a way for him tae go." Paislee giggled.

"I would never have sex again if I killed someone while

doing it," Lydia declared. "Never mind. I will have tae keep up with my dating sites."

"You should have men lined up at yer door," Flora said. "What is the matter with them all?"

"Paislee says I scare them off."

The ladies all turned to her. "What? She's beautiful, smart, wicked funny, and doesnae put up with idiots. If I was a man I'd be terrified, too."

"How many of those do you have tae finish by morning?" Amelia asked.

Paislee looked at the box filling up with flowers by her side. "Until this is full or I dinnae feel like doing them anymore."

"How do you feel, lass?" Flora asked. "Make sure tae have the comfrey when ye get home."

"I'm awright. Just mad. I wish that the detective would hurry up and arrest Gerald, and then I wouldnae be looking over my shoulder anymore."

"Gerald Sanford?" Amelia asked.

"Oh, Paislee," Lydia said. "I dinnae think it's him. I was so angry when you thought he might have run ye off the road that I called his boss. Gerald was at a sleepover, if ye know what I mean, and didnae leave till noon Monday. Ye said Isla died in the morning?"

Disappointment crushed her and she jabbed her finger with the crochet hook. She took a pound note from her pocket and placed it on the table to let the cursing fly.

Chapter 25

Paislee woke up early Saturday for a hot, muscle-loosening shower. Last night before bed she'd soaked in the dried comfrey leaves from Flora and had a cup of comfrey tea. It had taken a lot of honey to make that palatable, but she'd drunk it down.

She had just enough of the dried herbs left for a mug this morning. Paislee went downstairs to start breakfast, mindful of being at the shop by eight, but Grandpa had beaten her to it.

"Scrambled eggs," he said, lifting the spatula. "Lorne sausage frying in the pan. Toast, with orange marmalade. Brody picked that out at the grocery store the other night."

"It's his favorite."

He peered closely at her face. "Yer cheek looks better," he said. "How's your neck?"

"It's all right." She touched the sore muscles where the seat belt had wrenched. "I willnae need the brace today."

"Mibbe take it with you? Just in case. Ye can keep it in the shop."

"That's a good idea." She patted his shoulder and told him about Gerald having an alibi—he'd gone to bed as soon as she'd come home last night, so this was her first chance to share the news. "I was wrong."

"It happens." Grandpa's brown eyes flashed with humor. "Even tae the best of us."

She smiled. "Let me go wake Brody and Wallace."

But dog and boy were already descending the stairs, lured by the scent of cooking sausage.

She let Wallace out to the back garden to do his business. "It's gorgeous today!"

Blue sky, a slight chill, but a sweater should suffice.

She turned to Grandpa Angus, who was stirring eggs in a pan. "One year it rained so hard that we moved everything into the shop and watched the parade from under the awning. You used tae live around here?"

"I used tae live in this house," he said.

"Oh!"

They each backed away from the subject like it was a sore tooth not to be prodded.

She'd forgotten that.

Luckily, Brody hadn't heard the conversation, as he'd run out back after Wallace. He returned to the kitchen, his cheeks flushed, the smell of spring on his heels. Wallace's nearly black eyes shone brightly as he lapped up some fresh water from his bowl.

Brody sat at the table. "Yum! Grandpa let me get orange marmalade; did ye see that, Mum?"

"I did. It's your lucky day. That *and* sausage."

He licked his lips and rubbed his tummy, his auburn hair up like feathers in a tuft. "Dinnae forget we're going tae the comic booth, right, Grandpa?"

"Right." He brought the pan of eggs and sausage to the table and dished out food. "Sit, Paislee, and eat. We'll be there in plenty of time."

"We just need tae assemble the canopy. They have workers who set up the tables and each business is assigned a number. The paperwork's at Cashmere Crush."

"Can we bring Wallace, Mum?"

It was on the tip of her tongue to say no, but then she shrugged. "So long as you agree tae walk him and take care of him, then, aye."

"Yes!" He pumped his fist into the air.

Brody managed eggs, sausage, and three pieces of toast before Paislee shooed him from the table. "I can make you more, but why don't ye get cleaned up so we can go."

"I'm full." He licked his lips. "It just tastes so good."

"That's like me and Theadora's raspberry scones." She gathered his plate as Wallace watched her with interest from his spot on the floor. Brody ran up the stairs.

"Nothing for you, pup," she said.

She caught Grandpa slipping a bit of sausage to the dog but bit her tongue to keep the peace. He never fed the dog from the table, her eye. Plugging her nose, she drained the comfrey tea and hoped it worked its magic.

Traffic was heavier than usual on this Saturday morning as people headed out to the Spring Festival. All the businesses on the parade route had numbers, booths, canopies, and free gifts to entice customers to buy.

Grandpa parked the white Sentra behind the shop. They were there by half past eight and said hello to James, who was just arriving as well.

Brody gave the wizened old man a high five, chatting about the comic book booth he couldn't wait to see.

"I remember when I liked comics," James said, exchanging a glance with her grandfather. "And then I discovered the ladies."

The two men chuckled. Paislee ushered Brody into Cashmere Crush with a roll of her eyes. It would be some time before she had to worry about that, praise heaven.

Right?

Wallace, on a red plaid leash, stayed at Brody's heels. They'd brought his gray flannel bed to tuck beneath the register and out of the way. She bumped the box of silver charms she'd ordered and groaned. They were so adorable, how could she have forgotten them?

"Can you help me affix the charms with the Cashmere Crush logo?" she asked Brody, who had dropped Wallace's leash to let it drag on the ground. "I only ordered a hundred, so just give those out tae your favorite people."

"I can bring one tae Edwyn's mum—if she's at the booth." He sat cross-legged on the floor by Wallace's bed and opened the box.

She gave him the crocheted flowers to attach to the silver key rings. "Brilliant."

Paislee gathered flyers and postcards with her business information on them. Each advertised a 25 percent discount off a special-order sweater on the website.

"Looks guid, lass," Grandpa said. "How can I help?"

"Let's get the canopy raised over the booth out front, and then we can bring out our goodies. The streets are blocked off for setup right now, but security will allow foot traffic starting at nine. The parade is at two, and the day is over at five."

"Ye sound like ye've done this a time or two," he said with a laugh.

"Eight years, since I first opened." She rubbed her hands together. "One person needs tae always be at the booth, ready with a keychain or a flyer. Someone needs tae be inside manning the register. Lydia should be here any minute. Between all of us, we'll have time for breaks and to walk the festival."

"Sweaters make the most money!" Brody said. This was not his first festival, either.

She centered the bouquet of flowers from Fordythe Primary on the high-top table to be seen through her frosted picture window. She brought the red geranium out to decorate the table in front of the shop. Its bright petals tied in nicely with her pretty flower boxes.

She scanned the blocked-off street where each participating business along the parade route had a booth and was now preparing for a busy, and hopefully lucrative, day. Paislee waved to Ritchie, all in black, from the flower shop, who waved back. There was no sign of Tabitha.

To Paislee's right, Flora was setting up her booth, too. Her white Volvo was parked in the dirt lot of the pub behind her table as she unloaded supplies. Donnan sat on a crate as Flora did all the heavy lifting.

Paislee poked her head inside the shop to send assistance. "Brody, Grandpa?"

But her two helpers were inundated already with affixing charms, and when she looked next, Mary Beth and her husband, Arran, were helping Flora with her boxes and canopy.

Thank heavens for friends.

Paislee arranged a fine-knit multicolored cloth over the table—it was her fourth year with this cloth, and it was still just as nice as when she'd made it. Quality wool lasted a lifetime. There were two folding chairs behind the table and two in front, facing Market Street.

Folks began to trickle by the closer it got to nine.

Mary Beth brought her twin girls and husband to Paislee's table after they'd finishing helping Flora and Donnan. Arran was filled out around the middle, due in part to Mary Beth's cooking, and her two daughters were plump-cheeked, blue-eyed cherubs. They each held a half-eaten chocolate chip cookie.

"Morning!" Paislee gave her friend a hug. "You're here early!"

"Arran and I offered tae help Flora set up and take down. We're going tae check in with Margot at the lab. I think Arran's cold has turned into a sinus infection."

Paislee noticed his eyes were still red rimmed, his nose chapped—not looking much better than he had at the doctor.

Arran nodded his greeting and then waved good-bye as Mary Beth tugged him by the hand. Paislee'd never seen him so complacent.

"Margot will fix him up—why suffer? I say." Mary Beth said in a lower voice to Paislee, "Doc Whyte can call something in, and he will be right as rain before the parade starts."

Mary Beth, holding tight to Arran's hand, urged her daughters before her to the lab a few doors down. Paislee hoped so, for Arran's sake. Bagpipes were no comfort for an aching head.

Lydia burst out the front door of Cashmere Crush preceded by her expensive perfume. "Paislee, morning, lass—ach, you look a bit better today. How are ye feeling?"

Without waiting for an answer, Lydia sat down next to Paislee at the long table and admired the array of keychains, flyers, and postcards displayed on the table. She caressed the petal of the red geranium. "I parked next tae ye in the back. It's already crowded and just nine! Appears a beautiful day for a festival."

"I think so, too. I'm torn on what tae display —I willnae do Flora's since she's here selling her own. Look." Paislee pointed to the right and down, to Flora's booth, where she could see her greens and yellows. "You can see her yarn from here."

Donnan had been tucked in the corner in the shade, made cozy on a wide camping chair with a cupholder. Flora had a yellow gerbera in her hair today and a floral tunic with short sleeves over yellow leggings.

Lydia and Flora exchanged waves.

Paislee's bestie was dressed "casually" as in no business attire, but the cost of her designer jeans could keep Brody in cheese sandwiches for a month. Black boots and a lightweight black cashmere mock turtleneck Paislee had made for her, tucked in to show off her waist, with a black leather belt and silver buckle, made her look like a fashion model.

"Thanks for spending your day off with me," Paislee said.

"My pleasure. I heard the two Shaw boys bickering over comics when I passed through the shop."

Paislee grinned. "Brody has a friend who has a dad with a comic booth this year—Grandpa is walking him down right on the dot, tae get a poster before they're all gone."

Lydia fanned the postcards. "Did ye ever think tae have him in your life?"

"No. I imagine Granny spitting nails. I don't know why I didnae think of it, but he used tae live in my house. With Gran."

Lydia's gray eyes widened. She hadn't used so much black liner today, or smoky shadow, and the color of her eyes was like a river pebble.

Paislee had more than a touch of envy—not for the difference in their looks, as that couldn't be helped, but for Lydia's ability with makeup. Lydia had tried time and again to show Paislee how to create contour and make her eyes pop—but when ye didn't sleep more than six hours a night, calling attention to the circles under her light blue eyes wasn't the best choice.

Practical, that was her, she thought with a shrug. *Let Lydia be the glamorous one.*

"I didnae ask details, but he says she was the love of his life. I think Gran couldnae forgive Craigh's birth."

"Proof of infidelity." Lydia shrugged. "I dinnae blame her. I didn't stick around for it, either. I would rather be single and confident in myself than constantly wondering what's happening behind my back."

"I'm glad you came home tae Nairn."

"Me too. Oh—who is that?" Lydia perked up as two muscular men in khakis and polos passed from the direction of Flora's booth and the pub toward the water.

The brown-haired man held a clipboard and Paislee made sure the number on her booth was visible. "He looks official."

"I like the blond. Do we have a problem they could solve?"

Paislee shook her head, laughing. "You are incorrigible."

Lydia stood as the men passed by. The man with the clipboard did a double take. She fluttered her fingers, but he didn't come back.

Paislee tugged on Lydia's elbow. "Will you handle the register while Grandpa and Brody go in search of his free poster?"

"Sure thing. Any specials this year?"

"Twenty percent off merchandise today only." Her breath caught. "Oh, Lyd, what if this is the last time we get tae do this?"

"Stop that. I have three properties I printed out and left in the car—I'll get them. We'll find ye something brilliant."

Lydia disappeared into Cashmere Crush and Brody, with Wallace on the leash, exited with Grandpa.

Brody raced toward her. "Can we go now?"

"Aye. Take your time and mind yer manners. Stay with Grandpa."

"I will." He pulled the flower keychain and charm from his pocket. "I found a good one, Mum."

She shook her head and kissed his cheek, ruffling his hair, which he hated. "Good luck getting one ye like."

The pair strode off with Wallace's short furry legs keeping pace, black tail sweeping down the crooked sidewalk.

Gran had told her time and again not to fear change. But this had been her life as a business owner, these people on this row her friends and family.

James had an array of leather goods on his table. She ambled over to give it a closer inspection. "What's your giveaway this year?"

"Money clip." He showed her a handcrafted strip of leather the size of her finger that closed by using magnets. "Let me use up me scraps."

"Clever!" Inside the shop behind him, his fifty-year-old daughter stacked squares of leather. "Nora's helping today?"

"Aye. Promised her dinner out afterward."

"And not just the pub!" Nora shouted.

Paislee studied the Lion's Mane behind Flora's booth. The single-story pub was made of dark gray stone, had a blue tin roof, and the owners made a decent shepherd's pie.

He scowled. "Nothing wrong with the pub. But it'll be packed because of the festival. I heard on the news that this will be the biggest turnout yet."

She glanced back at her table. "I only made four hundred keychains."

"You better get to making more then," James teased. "They find who ran ye off the road?"

"Not yet." She gave a half shrug. The reminder that Isla's killer was still out on the loose cast a pall over the blue-skied morning. "Detective Inspector Zeffer promised he would."

She wasn't sure if she believed him.

Chapter 26

By eleven that morning, Paislee had given away fifty crocheted-flower keychains. She stood beneath the canopy of her booth with a basket as folks passed by, making sure to smile and greet as many as would meet her eye. She passed out Cashmere Crush postcards as well, which directed people to her website and the festival special. Was it time to go back to a website-based business?

The idea made her feel lonely.

Change is opportunity, and only a fool fears it! Gran's voice shouted in her head.

"Go to Cashmere Crush online for an extra discount," she told a mum of three, handing each of the woman's children a keychain.

"Thank ye," the woman said before being tugged ahead. "I love your shop."

"Check out our Thursday night Knit and Sip event!" she called to the lady's back. *Three bairns? How did she do it and stay sane?*

Paislee's eyes lifted. Was that Detective Inspector Zeffer striding toward her? It was. The throng of festivalgoers instinctually parted to make way. Maybe it had something to do with his tailored blue suit. It was too fashionable for a detective and more like he was playing a part in a drama.

She thought of Amelia's observation that she'd seen sparks and her cheeks warmed before he arrived at the table. Sparks of anger, aye, when she did her best to control her temper. She didn't care for his rude dismissal of her observations. But his wanting "facts" made her realize that she had no way of knowing for sure if Gerald had actually been on a "date."

What if his boss was covering for him and had lied to Lydia?

"Morning," she said once Zeffer reached her table, offering him a keychain with a flower from her basket.

The detective started to take it out of reflex but then held his palms up and shook his head. "No, thanks."

"I'm assuming you're here for a reason. Did you find out who sent me into the rail?"

"I'm down to a hundred silver vehicles unaccounted for."

She stifled a laugh. He'd warned her not to presume that the killer and the person who'd caused her accident were the same. Yet she wondered if he knew otherwise or was just doing due diligence. "That's what you wanted tae tell me?"

"No." His voice lowered. "Gerald's 'dancing' alibi checked out and I thought tae put your mind at ease."

"My mind will be at ease once Isla's killer is caught." She stepped out of the flow of foot traffic and sat down behind her table, inviting him to do the same. She took the opportunity to refill her basket with more keychains from the box by her feet.

Lydia's source had been correct. "Did you discover if Isla was blackmailing him, too? There had tae be a reason he was in her flat."

He leaned forward with his forearms on the table, scooting aside a skein of red yarn on display. "Aye. Seems Isla had video footage of his . . . activities . . . and was tightening the screws for a hundred pounds a month."

"Oh." Disappointment in Isla's behavior weighed on her. "That doesnae seem like much—what was the point?"

"It added up. We're going through her bank records."

She remembered Granny saying, "Many a mickle makes a muckle"; every penny counted. Paislee sighed. "Will that help you find who did this tae her?"

"I'm getting closer." Today his blue suit was cobalt, with darker blue pinstriping, and dark blue leather shoes. His eye for fashion seemed at odds with his no-nonsense demeanor. She'd never met a man who dressed so well.

"Good." Paislee chided herself for noticing and spoke sharper than she intended. "It's coming on a week."

"Monday morning," he said, a muscle by his eye twitching. "I'm well aware of the time."

Paislee didn't envy him the pressure of an unsolved homicide. "I should've realized she'd died in the morning. She was careful with caffeine as well as sweets, and only had one cup a day. She wouldnae have had regular Lipton at night."

He tugged his lapel. "You have a good eye. Is there anything else ye can think of that might make her seek out Dr. Whyte? She'd made an appointment for Tuesday but was dead by then."

Such a cold relaying of facts. Paislee knew he was sharing with her because he was desperate to get this case closed.

"I dinnae ken. His nurse is Sandy; maybe she remembers something?"

He shrugged. Had he already talked to Dr. Whyte and Sandy? Why wouldn't he tell her so? Frustrated, she reluctantly said, "Tabitha eats the same brand shortbread cookie as what was on Isla's table—but that's the most popular brand. I buy it myself."

Zeffer sat back and rubbed his smooth jaw. His sea-glass-green eyes bore into her. "A cookie."

Just then Elspeth and her sister dropped by the booth; Elspeth had her arm linked with Susan's, and Susan had a white cane in her other hand, tapping the asphalt before her.

"Oh—is this a bad time?" Elspeth asked, seeing Paislee with the detective.

"Of course not." Paislee made the introductions. She could kiss her for interrupting the conversation.

"If ye think of anything that's actually helpful, call me." Detective Inspector Zeffer stood, nodded to the ladies, and quickly departed.

"Any news?" Elspeth asked, guiding Susan to a chair on the street side of the table.

"Nothing yet." Paislee clasped her hands together so she didn't toss her precious yarn at the detective's retreating back. "Hello, Susan."

"Paislee—Elspeth told me about yer accident. I'm so sairy. That's one thing I dinnae miss aboot my blindness, driving."

Lydia darted out of the shop to the sidewalk, waving to Elspeth. "Was that Detective Inspector Zeffer, the man with the spark?"

"Stop it!" Paislee kept her back turned to her bestie. As soon as this situation with Isla was resolved she would never speak to Zeffer again.

Elspeth laughed. "He was very attractive. A wee bit tense."

Susan shifted toward Paislee, lifting her barely lined face. She too had gorgeous iron-gray hair, though hers was cut short. "You have a new man in yer life?"

"Naw. I do not want a man in my life. Especially *that* man. Me and Brody are just fine."

Elspeth wisely changed the subject to the lovely day for the festival, joining Lydia at the doorway to Cashmere Crush.

Susan didn't care for knitting or crocheting, calling it a waste of her time, but she could sit for hours, she said, and listen to life bustle around her.

Elspeth and Lydia went inside the shop, leaving her and

Susan to converse in between Paislee handing out keychains and postcards.

Headmaster McCall strode toward the booth, wearing uncharacteristically casual beige khakis and a navy-blue polo shirt. His blackish-brown hair had been styled back from his face. He removed black sunglasses to reveal dark brown eyes and thick black lashes.

His shoulders were quite broad in the polo. Did he work off the pressure of managing Fordythe Primary at the gym?

"Hello, Headmaster."

He smiled. " 'Hamish,' please, when away from the school." He held out his hand to shake, his gaze falling on Susan, and then the flowers visible through Paislee's front shop window. His smile widened.

"Please thank Fordythe for the flowers," she said, her tongue awkward in her mouth. Was her grandfather right— did he fancy her? "Hamish, this is Susan Booth."

The two exchanged greetings. Paislee offered him a keychain, making sure he had a silver charm, which he accepted.

"You made this?" He held the keychain in his palm to admire.

"Four hundred of them."

He studied her yarn on the table, then chose an ivory skein, rubbing his thumb over the silky strands. "When you were in the other day, you mentioned that your shop was a specialty sweater shop. What makes it special?"

"I use locally sourced wool and local dyers. That's merino wool."

He exchanged the ivory for a lavender cashmere skein. "Oh, this is great, and much softer."

"That's real cashmere." She smiled as she explained, "It's made from the underbelly of a goat. This"—she tapped the ivory—"is shorn from a sheep. Are ye interested in some yarn?"

"Not for me, thanks," he quickly said. "My sister knits. She lives in London. What would be a guid gift tae send her?"

"What's her favorite color?"

"Orange, I think."

Elspeth arrived in a flurry. "I can stay here at the table, if you'd like tae show him inside? Hi—I'm Elspeth Booth, loyal Cashmere Crush customer."

"Hamish McCall, headmaster at Fordythe."

Elspeth's groomed brow rose and she practically pushed Paislee in the direction of the shop.

Amused, Paislee brought Hamish in with pride and showed off her many shelving units full of colorful yarn.

Lydia stepped from behind the register. Hamish was polite to Lydia but didn't seem to lose his mind at her beauty.

"Lydia, Hamish from Fordythe." Her bestie's gaze flicked briefly to the flowers. Paislee walked to the row of orange yarn. "What's your sister's skill level?"

"She made us all uneven scarves last year for Christmas."

Paislee laughed and Lydia melted back with a thumbs-up.

"If she's a beginner, perhaps a thicker yarn? I have a simple knit cap pattern, if you'd like something matching for next year?"

He grinned. "I'll take it." Hamish peered around the shop and the many colors. "But my favorite color's blue. Are these all cashmere?"

"I do carry some cashmere, but most of what you see here is merino—sheep's wool. Cashmere is verra expensive because the goats only molt once a year."

Hamish tilted his head at her. "Yer not pulling my leg aboot the goat?"

"Naw. JoJo's Farm raises the Scottish cashmere goats. They're about ten miles from here."

"Is cashmere better?"

"Depends what you're making."

"And what ye can afford?"

"Aye, that too." She chuckled.

She loaded him up with supplies, and they were easily laughing as Lydia rang him up and put his things in a bag. He was very different outside the school.

"Did ye get a keychain?" Lydia asked.

"Aye." He removed it from his pocket to show Lydia, who nodded as she noticed the silver charm and added it to the paper sack.

Brody raced into the shop. "Headmaster McCall! Guess what I have?" He thrust out two rolled posters.

"What is it, Brody?"

"Edwyn's dad gave me two, when I gave him the keychain, Mum. He asked if ye were single and I told him that ye were, but ye couldn't take one more thing."

Lydia burst out laughing.

Paislee turned crimson in mortification as her son tossed her words back at her. "Gypsies, Brody, gypsies. I could get a good hundred pounds for ye."

Hamish's blackish-brown brow arched.

"I'm joking." *Sort of.* She glared at her son.

Brody tugged at her arm and glanced to Hamish. "Did ye give him a special keychain, Mum, with the charm?"

Her face was so hot that it hurt.

Hamish rubbed his top lip and pulled the keychain from the bag. "Is this the good one?"

Brody saw the charm and relaxed. "Aye."

"My godson is a prodigy," Lydia announced.

Paislee was not so sure. She crossed her arms. "Where is your grandfather? And Wallace?"

"He's flirting with Elspeth." Brody swung his posters before him like an imaginary double-bladed sword. "Is that woman blind?"

"That's Susan, Elspeth's sister—aye, she is."

"Wallace licked her."

"I hope Wallace is a dog?" Hamish asked, trying to keep track of the conversation.

"Aye." Paislee's face began to cool, but she didn't dare look at Lydia, or she would never stop laughing.

"They found him in the park." Brody peered up at Hamish.

"Your dog?"

"No, me grandpa."

Paislee bit her tongue to keep a straight face. Hamish probably thought they were all mental—but she'd warned him, hadn't she?

With a peek back at Paislee, Hamish took Brody by the shoulder. "Well, let's go meet him."

The two walked out, the headmaster carrying the gifts for his sister and Brody his new posters.

Lydia poked Paislee in the middle of her back. "I think the universe is letting you know that it's time tae stop hiding behind your mum jeans."

Paislee didn't grace her with a response, and followed them outside to the table beneath her canopy.

Susan had Wallace in her lap and the dog seemed in nirvana as she petted him.

Paislee's grandpa and Elspeth exchanged a meaningful glance.

"Grandpa, did you meet Hamish McCall?" Paislee asked. She wasn't sure she could stomach watching her grandfather date one of her knitting friends. She didn't recall him and Gran together but a few times when she was younger, for holidays.

Grandpa and Hamish shook hands; then Hamish petted Wallace. The dog wagged his tail but remained content on Susan's lap.

Paislee handed out her crocheted-flower keychains, greeting people as they passed, smiling at the conversation behind her. This was a community, and she was a part of it.

Sneaking a glance at Hamish, who chatted at ease with her family and friends, she dragged up a mental image of her clothes. She didn't own "mum" jeans, did she? Her wardrobe might need an update, but she was the same size she'd always been and didn't have money to spend on an elaborate wardrobe, like Lydia.

After an hour or so, Hamish said his good-byes. "I'll let you know how the cap project goes," he said.

She smiled. "My number's on the card." She realized how that sounded and stammered, "If your s-s-sister has any questions."

As she watched him stride away, she rubbed at a painful tinge in her neck. What an odd day it had been, but she couldn't forget that Isla's killer remained on the loose, and was probably in Nairn.

Chapter 27

Paislee shivered as a chill of apprehension snaked down her spine. A killer in their shire was hard to fathom. Detective Inspector Zeffer's caustic remarks aside, she would do what she could to help him, for Isla's sake.

Brody's exuberant laughter brought her back to the present. She gave out another flower keychain, and returned to the table.

"How are ye feeling?" Elspeth asked Paislee, patting her own neck in sympathy.

"Fine." Truth was, she could use more ibuprofen. "Grandpa, are you ready for a break? Why not wander for a while?" She'd handed out cash this morning before they'd left so that Grandpa and Brody had pocket money.

Grandpa stood and sniffed the air. "I smell popcorn, fresh popped."

Brody leapt off his chair to tackle her in a hug. She tried not to wince when his enthusiasm hurt her shoulder. "Is it time tae get an elephant ear?"

"How about we let Grandpa and Lydia go first, and after that, we'll go. Do you want your face painted?"

"That's fer bairns." Brody scowled at her as if she'd lost her mind. "I'm ten."

Grandpa whistled. "That would be a no, then."

"They grow up so fast," Elspeth remarked. She turned to Susan and Wallace. "Are ye ready, Susan? I'd like tae stop at the tea shop for a sweet treat myself."

Susan nodded. "What a wonderful pup you have, Brody." She reached for her cane.

Wallace hopped down from her lap and wandered toward Paislee and Brody to sit at their feet, as polite as you please. She scratched behind his ears to reward him.

Elspeth said good-bye with the promise to meet up next week about the historical society possibly preventing the sale of the building.

"Thanks!"

Grandpa also left, and Paislee sent Brody inside the shop to let Lydia know she'd be on break once Grandpa returned. She filled up her basket of keychains from the big box below the table and stood before her booth. The fine sunny day had folks laughing and smiling, and eating ice-cream cones as they enjoyed the festival.

Her gaze was drawn to Tabitha and Ritchie across the street—Tabitha handed out a single rose per person as they passed the flower booth. Tabitha occasionally glanced Paislee's way.

Paislee was pleased by the people milling around Flora's booth. A lot of folks walked by with a bag of Flora's yellow or green yarn, which meant sales.

By the time Grandpa and Lydia had each gotten something to eat, Paislee was hungry, too. "Ready, Brody?"

He fist-pumped the air. "Finally!"

He'd been patient, considering this was his favorite treat. They made their way down the sidewalk and she stopped to say hello to each of her fellow business owners. James and his daughter, Nora; Ned, who gifted free closet sachets; Margot and her team at the lab, who handed out neon-colored bandages. Lourdes and Jimmy donated pencils, and Theadora offered her freshly baked sugar cookies.

Paislee and Brody strolled to the bandstand and she breathed in deep of the seaside air. The park was crowded with picnickers at tables or on blankets, and booths selling food of all kinds dotted the lawn. Seagulls cawed and swooped through the sky. It was difficult to believe that bad things could happen in such a beautiful place.

"Over there, Mum!"

Brody practically dragged her and Wallace across the grass to a red and white awning and a wheeled cart where a man sold deep-fried dough sprinkled with powdered sugar and cinnamon.

From the cart, she could see the police station and the large oak tree outside the detective's window. Was he too hard at work to enjoy the sunshine, even for a few minutes?

Tomorrow morning she would find time for a mug of Brodies Scottish Breakfast and knit the fisherman's sweater on her back porch in the quiet to let her mind untangle the threads surrounding Isla and her death. Her gran had taught her to gather her thoughts while her hands were busy.

She purchased an elephant ear for Brody, and candied nuts for herself. They took their time returning to Cashmere Crush, eyeing the wares at every booth. Even the comic book booth, where Paislee met Edwyn, and Edwyn's gorgeous single dad.

He was just the kind of guy that Lydia would love—tall and charming with a lean body, big jade-green eyes, and blond waves around his long face. Thirty, if she had to guess, and very friendly.

"Bennett Maclean," he said, introducing himself. "I just opened up the comic shop six months ago and we're goin' strong. I have a few arcade games in the back for the kids tae hang out and play." He tugged his son's blond hair. "I dinnae want him gettin' bored and looking for trouble, aye?"

"Smart thinking." Paislee palmed Bennett's card and decided to send Lydia his way.

By one thirty, Paislee and Brody had made the loop back to Market Street. Tabitha was still giving away roses for the florist's booth, and this close Paislee could see that Tabitha was wearing Isla's scarf. The young woman gave her a sly smile as she handed over a pink blossom. Paislee checked first to make sure there wasn't a thorn.

Tabitha's plain brown hair had been pulled up into a ponytail. Her brown-eyed gaze challenged Paislee to dare ask a question about Isla, or Billy.

She smelled the rose and decided to keep the peace.

Ritchie's silver earrings glinted in the sunshine as he transferred more roses into a bucket. "How's it going over on your side of the street? I can hardly see, there are so many people."

"Tae be sure, it's packed this year. We're doing well—I sold a few sweaters, which is always good."

Brody tugged her along, and she said her good-byes. Tabitha had turned to the next person walking by to give the young woman a rose.

"Let's go say hi tae Flora and Donnan." Paislee'd seen Mary Beth head that direction earlier and assumed it was to give them a break, but she wanted to at least say hello.

When she and Brody reached the Robertson table and canopy, Donnan was resting in his camping chair against the back crates of their yarn, away from the foot traffic. Flora greeted them with a smile and a flushed face, the yellow gerbera in her hair minus half its petals. "Paislee, Brody—ach, what is that?" She pointed to Brody's fried dough that had been devoured down to half its original size. "Looks delicious."

"An elephant ear," Brody said, offering her a bite.

"No, no, you finish it, lad. I have my own treats here." Flora glanced to the platter of cookies next to her stack of yarn, then sat and plucked a square shortbread from the selection. "Help yourselves."

"Would ye like a break?" Paislee offered, choosing a thin orange lace cookie with nuts. "I can sit with Donnan." She perched against the edge of the table. Wallace dragged Brody to sniff crumbs on the other side of Flora's table, near a man selling ceramic vases.

"We're fine," Flora said, looking back fondly at her dozing husband. "Mary Beth and Arran were here, and he helped Donnan tae the bathroom. My husband just isnae the same, but . . ." She dabbed her eyes. "I cannae imagine being without him. Well." Flora blew out a breath. "How are sales on your end of the street?"

"Good." *Surprisingly good.* "I'd hate tae lose this location."

"Maybe ye willnae. I know ye asked me about online business, but things are hard tae manage since Donnan's stroke. I'm doing the work fer us both." She snatched another cookie and took a bite. "What I need is a third person at no extra cost, and then I'd be just fine." Flora laughingly gestured to Grandpa Angus, who ensured each person going by Cashmere Crush had a postcard at least. "Mibbe send him my way for room and board if ye don't get on?"

Grandpa Angus belonged to her and Brody now, and she wouldn't be passing him on, though he might be flattered that there was a line forming for his cranky services. Brody was now on the left side of Flora's booth, feeding ants crumbs of sugar by the curb, before Wallace licked them up.

"Funny how quickly life changes." You couldn't take anything for granted. She looked at Donnan with empathy for Flora. He must've felt the weight of her gaze because he startled; his eyes opened wildly as if waking from a bad dream.

"Donnan?" Flora jumped up. "What is it, love?"

He twitched and his leg jerked, knocking over the crate of yarn in front of him. Skeins of green spilled to the cement.

Paislee sprang to his side and righted the yarn. "Hey, Donnan."

Flora offered her husband a mug of sweet yellow tea—honeysuckle? He drank it, not fully awake as he murmured something about the flower's bloom.

She rubbed Flora's arm. "What does Doc Whyte say, about his prognosis?"

The stroke had been two months prior. "He's getting better—I shouldnae have expected an immediate rebound. I could hire help, but it all costs money." Her smile turned sad as she caressed her husband's short brown hair.

Paislee thought of Lourdes and Jimmy, who might give up the office supply shop if the building sold to run an adult day care. Donnan would be a perfect candidate.

"Rest is supposed tae be the best thing for him, but I dinnae dare leave him alone for long stretches of time. Tomorrow is our wedding anniversary," Flora said. "At Saint Ninian's fourteen years ago. Time goes by so fast."

Paislee was feeling the speed of time firsthand herself, whenever she looked at her son—who was ten, thank you, and not a bairn wanting his face painted.

"Happy anniversary," she said. "What will ye do?"

"I'll make him his favorite—leek and tattie soup, and fresh-caught salmon." Flora brought her fingers to her mouth. "He's lucid for hours at a time, and we talk aboot the old days."

Cheers and bagpipes sounded as the parade began. It would start by the clock tower and end at the park to the far right of the police station. "Brody, get Wallace. It's time for the parade." She hugged Flora and called good-bye to Donnan.

They crossed the throng of people to the other side of the street and the corner of their building. Grandpa stood with his arms at his sides in the doorway, the shop empty of customers. She and Lydia sat at the table as folks gathered on the sidewalks to watch the parade, Brody and Wallace on the chair in front of their booth.

The high school bands marched by with flags, drums, and horns. A dance troupe of girls from three to teens, all in pink ballet costumes, twirled and tossed candy to the folks on the sidelines; then acrobats—both boys and girls—came flipping and doing handstands. A pair of jugglers tossed bowling pins. Then, Scottish dancers in tartan and plaid whirled knives as they pranced in tempo to the band of bagpipers behind them.

She whispered in Lydia's ear, "How do you feel about comic books?"

Lydia waved the comment away and pointed to a man in Highland garb.

"Is that Gerald?" Shirtless and in a kilt suited him; Paislee would give credit where it was due.

When he noticed them watching, he flashed a peek of his backside. "More than nice legs," Lydia said admiringly.

Grandpa chuckled.

The parade lasted an hour, and by the end Paislee'd clapped and whistled until she'd given herself a headache.

"I want tae play the bagpipes," Brody declared.

Imagining the noise that'd bring compounded the pressure behind her eyes. "Why is that?"

"I could wear a dirk," he told her.

"You want tae play the bagpipes so you can wear a knife?" She looked to Lydia to see if her bestie understood this logic.

"You can play the bagpipes without a knife," Lydia assured him.

His nose scrunched. "What for? Mum cannae tell me no tae a dirk if it's part of me uniform."

"You arenae getting a dirk," Paislee said, cutting to the chase.

He threw himself back in his chair. "I'd be careful with it."

Did he really think she'd allow him to have a sharp blade like that, ever?

"A knife isnae a bad thing," her grandfather said from behind them.

Brody's eyes widened and he shot up at the unexpected support from his crotchety great-grandpa. "Yeah!"

Grandpa said to Paislee, "We gave yer da a wee pocketknife at twelve, for cutting fishing wire."

She glared at her grandfather, and then her son. "This is not the time or place for this discussion."

"How aboot tomorrow?" Brody pleaded, his hands folded together as if he were a starving beggar child praying for a crust of bread.

"Aye. But the answer will still be no."

He pouted at the ground. "Why bother talking aboot it then?"

"I'll explain tae you *why* the answer will still be no."

He kicked his heel against the chair leg. "I'd rather play video games."

She smiled, accepting the victory. "Tomorrow is our Sunday Funday. We can go tae the beach in the afternoon, but I have a meeting with the other business owners that shouldnae take more than an hour."

He started to complain, but Lydia shook a long finger at him. "Not a peep, laddie, I am taking you for an ice cream at Finn's. You can have two scoops."

Brody bolted from his chair and gave Lydia a kiss on the cheek. "Double chocolate!"

He brought Wallace inside Cashmere Crush to Grandpa, who had chosen to sit by the register and out of line of Paislee's ire—the pair probably discussing a fishing knife.

Lydia rested her chin on her fist. "Brody's a Romeo. And a prodigy. Heaven help us."

"Be serious for a moment." Paislee pulled the comic store business card from her pocket. "Bennett Maclean."

"Bennett? That's a nice name." Lydia flicked the card with doubt. "But a comic book shop? I have a mental image of a geeky guy with a vintage toy collection."

"You are so wrong. Have Brody take you over."

"Brody might be a little too candid for this mission." Lydia stood and smoothed her hands down the front of her designer jeans—as if anything would ever dare to be out of place.

"You won't be disappointed."

Lydia quickly applied a soft red lipstick to her mouth. "Intriguing."

A young lady with spiky purple hair stopped at the table and held up a skein of blue yarn. Lydia left and Paislee talked to the young woman, who was interested in fingerless gloves.

Paislee was in her element, sharing her love for crafting with local yarn, and invited the young woman to next Thursday's Knit and Sip. What would she do without such a convenient venue?

She sent the girl inside to buy three skeins of the blue she liked from Grandpa as Tabitha and Billy strolled by. They walked hand in hand and said nothing, Tabitha tossing the tasseled end of the scarf over her shoulder.

Paislee knew that Tabitha knew she'd made it for Isla. What was she trying to tell Paislee with that childish move?

Paislee wondered if the detective had questioned Tabitha about the scarf. Was this Tabitha's way of tweaking Paislee's nose?

Billy scowled at Paislee, his shaggy blond hair windblown around his face, his jaw bristly as if he hadn't shaved in a couple days. Had he worked on the sheep farm this morning?

She had to trust that the detective had properly interviewed them both.

They crossed the street, stopping at Flora's table. Donnan

was awake and sitting in his chair, watching people pass by. Was he like Elspeth's sister, Susan, content with her thoughts?

Tabitha sidled up to the table—shoulders back. She'd been shy and quiet when Paislee had met her before, but she'd changed.

Billy nodded to Donnan, who nodded back. Paislee could see Flora's face flush red from across the street.

What was going on?

Tabitha whispered into Flora's ear, and the woman pulled back as if physically struck.

What had she said?

Flora pointed for Tabitha to leave, saying something Paislee couldn't hear.

Tabitha laughed at Flora, knocking skeins of yarn off the table as Billy pulled her away. The two scuffed off toward the pub, away from the festival, which was winding down.

Disturbed by the scene, Paislee checked the time. Only twenty minutes until the festival was over. Handing out the last flower keychain, she started to pack up so she could make sure Flora and Donnan were all right. Tabitha was a rotten girl.

Mary Beth and Arran hurried by—Arran less pinched around the sinuses, so Doc Whyte must have called something into the lab for the poor man—with their daughters trailing exhausted behind them in limp pink sundresses.

Mary Beth reached Flora, who had regained her composure. The little girls each gave Flora a hug. She hadn't realized that Mary Beth and Flora knew each other so well, outside of her shop and their Knit and Sip nights.

Lydia returned, demanding her full attention. "Sign me up. I am officially interested in getting tae know Bennett Maclean. I know nothing about comics, so I'll have tae borrow Brody."

Unsettled by what she'd just witnessed, Paislee halfheartedly laughed.

"What?" Lydia searched her face.

"It's nothing."

"I don't believe you."

Yesterday Paislee had insisted that Gerald was guilty—and she'd been wrong. She hesitated to toss an accusation at Tabitha or Billy without proof.

Normally, she was not one to judge another's actions, considering her own path of single motherhood. Rather than spread tales that might not be true, Paislee poured her energy into cleaning up and taking down the canopy before going inside.

As she counted the money in the till, her shoulders relaxed. It wasn't a million euro, but they'd had a very good day.

"Verra good," she announced, zipping up the money bag to put in the shop safe.

"Good enough for Chinese?" Brody asked from behind her.

"Do we want something else?" There was Indian, or the new German restaurant downtown.

Brody shook his head. "Orange chicken, yum." Grandpa nodded.

"Awright then—Lydia, are you up for it?"

Lydia agreed. "Spicy pork."

Chinese food it was. Paislee could meet the co-pay for her Juke without making payments to the mechanic and that soothed her pride. She was grateful to get assistance when she needed it but hated to need it all the same.

They'd packed up and she'd signed off with the town official—the blond gent now had the clipboard. She made a last visual sweep of her space, checking that she hadn't left anything behind.

Flora and Donnan were already gone and she hadn't had a chance to say good-bye. Now that the festival was over, she had a clear view of the Lion's Mane pub's back entrance. Stone walls covered in tired old graffiti, a dirt parking lot with half a dozen vehicles that would fill up once the roads were open again and folks had access.

She recognized Billy's beat-up old pickup.

Just then, Tabitha exited the back door of the Lion's Mane, her arm wrapped around Billy's waist. Billy bumped into the back end of a car and sprawled to the dirt as if completely smashed.

Tabitha leaned down and helped him up, then awkwardly managed to push him inside to the passenger seat of his truck. He had his hand to his head. According to Paislee's watch, only thirty minutes had passed since they'd gone into the pub. Who could get wasted that fast?

She took a few steps toward the pair, calling out for Tabitha, but the girl jumped behind the wheel of the truck and peeled off.

Chapter 28

Paislee stared at the road for a moment after Billy's pickup was gone. Had Tabitha even heard Paislee call out?

Lydia joined her on the sidewalk. "What do ye see?"

Paislee needed her bestie's advice to stay grounded. "Remember Tabitha and Billy? Well, Billy just fell hard leaving the pub. Then Tabitha sped off, driving Billy's truck."

Lydia's gray eyes focused on the street, which was now busy with cars. The festival was over and the roads open again. "And?"

"She made a scene earlier with Flora—Billy pulled her away. What if she's gone mental?" She tapped her temple. "Or drugs?"

"This is Nairn, not Glasgow," Lydia quipped.

She couldn't shake the bad feeling. "Just listen. Tabitha was Isla's old roommate. She would know that Isla took heart medicine, and that too much could kill her. She has Isla's scarf. How did she get it? Isla wouldnae have given it tae her."

Lydia nudged her elbow into Paislee's side. "Yer starting tae sound like a TV drama."

"I'm not done. Billy told me that Isla wanted him tae help

her track down people's secrets; she would blackmail them and give him a percentage for doing the dirty work."

Lydia tilted her head, the bob of her haircut brushing against her jaw. "And so what, he told this tae Tabitha?" Her gray eyes expressed doubt.

"What if Tabitha decided that Isla was causing problems in her relationship with Billy . . . so Tabitha killed Isla tae keep her out of their lives?" Following a killer's logic, was that so unreasonable?

Lydia's mouth dropped open. "Killed."

The fact remained: Isla was dead and *somebody* had killed her.

Paislee bit her lower lip and looked from her shop toward the sea, then the police station farther down the road. "Detective Inspector Zeffer confirmed this morning that Isla"—this version of Isla nearly broke Paislee's heart—"was blackmailing Gerald, as well as Roderick, her boss, who paid tae keep the affair from his wife."

"You were right aboot that then," Lydia said. "What did she have on Highland Hung?"

Paislee paced before her flower boxes, feeling Lydia's gaze. "A video of his extracurricular activities—"

"A gig vid?" Lydia giggled and started to sing, "He was just a gigolo—"

As beautiful and talented and smart as Paislee's bestie was, she couldn't sing a note, bless her for being human. "Stop!" Paislee laughingly covered her ears.

Lydia zipped her lips.

The somber mood had been broken, allowing Paislee to think again. "Let me place the Chinese food order, and Grandpa can drive Brody home. We'll pick up dinner. Can you see on your superfancy search engine whether or not Tabitha still lives on Dartmouth Street?" Farmer Lowe told her that Billy had been moving. Probably in with Tabitha since he'd broken up with Isla.

"Aye, but what are you going tae do with that information?" Lydia tugged the collar of her cashmere mock turtleneck.

"I dinnae ken—yet. Billy fell in the dirt, stumbling out of the pub. He couldnae walk straight on his own, Lydia." Tabitha's arm around his waist had been the only thing keeping him upright, and even then, he'd taken a dive.

"It's called too much tae drink," Lydia said with a straight face. "Blitzed, sloshed, hammered, pished."

"In half an hour?"

"Wrecked, minced, buckled, tanked up—"

Paislee held up her palm. Scots were known for their love of drinking and had almost as many terms for being drunk as they had sheep.

"It could be just that. It willnae hurt tae check, aye? The worst that can happen is Tabitha slamming the door in my face."

"Why would Tabitha harm Billy?" Lydia brought her phone from her back pocket. "She's always wanted him."

"What if Billy and Isla were doing more than arguing over her wanting him tae dig up dirty secrets—what if they'd started shagging again?"

"A woman scorned I understand, but if Isla is out of the picture, Tabitha has what she wants. Billy."

"You make an excellent point." Blowing out a breath she said, "I'll go give Grandpa the keys." She darted inside her cozy shop. "Do ye mind driving Brody, Grandpa? Lydia and I will bring home the food."

The two Shaws pulled apart from what they'd been whispering about—looking guilty.

"Aye," Grandpa said.

Brody gathered Wallace's bed and emptied the dog's water dish before attaching the lead to Wallace's collar.

She took the coward's way out, and didn't ask what they'd been plotting. She had her own plan to devise. "We'll be home in thirty minutes."

The two left, Brody, next to Grandpa, followed by the dog. That image swept away any feelings of wrongness about the change happening, and replaced it with something right.

Brody no longer only had her—he had his great-grandfather, too.

She pulled her phone from her pocket along with Detective Inspector Zeffer's business card. The detective had said to call him if she had anything that might help. Billy being unable to walk from the bar counted as something of interest, right?

Lydia had closed the front door, giving it a jiggle to make sure it was locked, and then joined her at the register. She lifted her mobile. "What's Tabitha's last name?"

"Drake."

Fingers flying, Lydia typed in the name to her database.

"The good thing about living in a small place—there are only two Tabitha Drakes, and one is out near Dairlee; the other lives in an apartment building, five minutes from here on Dartmouth."

"The same place she used tae live," Paislee said. "Let me call the detective and tell him about Billy."

"That's a better idea than going over tae Tabitha's uninvited."

To her surprise, the detective answered, and she put the call on speakerphone. "Detective Inspector Zeffer."

"Hi! It's Paislee . . . Shaw."

"Yes?"

She could imagine his glare and cleared her throat. "You asked me tae call you if I had any information?"

"Something better than a cookie. Aye?"

"I saw Billy Connal leave the Lion's Mane just now, completely wrecked after only being inside the pub for half an hour."

"Was he driving?"

"Naw—his girlfriend, Tabitha, drove off. He didnae look at all well."

"There is no law against consuming too much alcohol and being a passenger in a car. In fact, we recommend that."

Sarcasm fried the phone line. Lydia's brow winged up.

Paislee knew, though she wasn't supposed to know, that the coroner thought Isla had overdosed on her digoxin. What if Tabitha had somehow taken Isla's medication to poison Billy with? The bottle had been on its side, empty. "What if Tabitha put something in his drink?"

"Why would she roofie her own boyfriend?" The detective's tone grew chillier. "I have tae go and follow actual leads." He hung up abruptly.

Lydia said, "I hate tae say it, but I agree with that rude man."

Paislee held her friend's gaze. "You werenae there when I found Isla, Lydia. Somebody did that tae her. Billy fell on his face in the parking lot when there's no way he could be that drunk. It isnae right."

Sighing, Lydia said, "Fine. We do a drive-by. If his truck is there, we can stop. Dinnae forget tae call in the dinner order."

Five minutes later, they passed a four-story building of flats, and Billy's pickup was parked out front. "This is it."

"Now what?" Lydia asked. She'd parked three spaces over from the truck, the red Mercedes a beacon in the less affluent neighborhood. Isla had been making enough money from her blackmail to afford a much nicer flat. It had all added up, the detective told Paislee.

Paislee stared at the familiar door, and number 204. "I cannae very well just ask her if she killed Isla, now, can I?"

"I wouldnae suggest it," Lydia said. "What if she really is guilty and decides tae push ye over the railing? For the record, the only reason I am okay with this is because I dinnae believe Tabitha is a murderer."

The reason she was here, searching for answers, was for Isla. "I know she was trying tae tell me something earlier when she flicked Isla's scarf at me."

"Aye—tae piss off," Lydia teased.

Her bestie was a freaking riot today. "I'll just ask how Billy is feeling."

"It's a stretch. Maybe you can pretend tae sell magazine subscriptions?"

Paislee blew her bangs back.

"Religion?" Lydia laughed, hitting her stride. "Flat recommendations?"

"You arenae helping."

"I love you like a sister, Paislee, but you have no reason tae knock on that door, except for being nosy." Lydia tapped her perfect nose.

"What if Billy is in danger?"

"And what if he just drank too much?"

Paislee considered this from the safety of Lydia's passenger seat. "I'm going tae knock on the door, and ask how they're doing, just being neighborly."

"You dinnae live in this neighborhood."

"I want tae know how she got Isla's scarf. Stay here. I'll wing it."

"I feel like the driver in a getaway car," Lydia said, revving the gas.

Paislee exited the car and climbed the center stairs to the second-floor landing with no idea what she was going to say. What had Tabitha said to Flora to make the poor woman upset? What had happened to Billy in the short time they were in the pub? She didn't believe he could drink so much to be ill, unless he'd slammed back twenty shots of whisky.

What if Tabitha *was* the killer and Paislee was just bold as brass knocking on the door? Number 204. The nameplate beneath read: Tabitha Drake, and "Isla Campbell" had been blacked out, below that "Billy Connal" written in.

Swallowing past the large lump lodged in her throat, she rapped on the door. The material was so thin, the sound echoed.

Her heart hammered.

She glanced behind her to make sure that Lydia's red car was still in the parking lot.

Lydia waved her fingers.

Nobody came to answer.

She knocked again.

Nothing.

This was eerily reminiscent of when she'd discovered Isla.

She discreetly shook the knob, but it didn't budge, as she checked to see if the door was open, like Isla's had been. What if it was Billy inside on the floor this time, instead of Isla?

The doorknob rattled and was slowly pulled inward. Billy's bleary, bloodshot eyes peeked through the crack. He had a gash on his forehead from when he'd fallen. "Tabs?"

"Naw. It's me, Paislee."

"Whatchya want?"

"I saw ye leaving the pub and ye didn't look good. Can I help?"

"Tabs will be back innaminute," he slurred. "Ate bad cod at the pub."

Paislee immediately felt ashamed of herself.

She'd imagined the worst, except for food poisoning. . . . "I'm sairy." It was on the tip of her tongue to ask about the scarf, but it really wasn't the right time. "I willnae keep you." Maybe if she hurried she could be gone before Tabitha returned.

He slammed the door and she jumped back, her heart hammering hard and loud.

She hurried down the stairs to the lot, and ducked into

Lydia's car. Lydia was biting her lip to hide a smile. "How'd it go?" she asked in a too-innocent tone.

"Billy has food poisoning," Paislee said. "We should probably go before—"

"Och, what's this?" Lydia began to reverse from her spot when a silver car nestled in between Billy's truck and Lydia's Mercedes. Paislee, on the passenger side, was hidden from view.

Silver? She'd known it couldn't have been Billy's pickup that hit her—but what about Tabitha? *Naw.* This car had a wide black bumper. There was no silver foil at her window, and the shape of the car seemed different. She didn't trust her memory, as she'd been under duress.

Tabitha climbed out of the driver's side of the car with a white pharmacy bag, clearly worried by her frantic expression.

"She's trying tae make him better, Paislee," Lydia said in a gentle voice. "Not kill him."

Embarrassed, Paislee would have to warn Amelia that police work was more difficult than it appeared. "I see that."

"Can you let it go now?" Lydia faced her as Tabitha raced up the stairs to her flat and burst inside. "Isla's mother has been located. Isla was not a nice person, Paislee, even if she did have reason. She was blackmailing Roderick and Gerald."

Paislee bowed her head, feeling foolish. "And who knows who else?"

"We dinnae, and that's the point here. You have a caring heart, but let's leave it tae the professionals tae do their jobs."

She glanced back at the building. She'd been wrong, twice now, about who she'd thought had killed Isla.

Forcing a light tone, she said, "Our Chinese food should be ready. Let's go home and celebrate a good day at the festival. You mentioned you had some other places tae show me for Cashmere Crush?"

"Three places we can see on Monday," Lydia said, sounding relieved that Paislee was willing to move ahead.

Paislee was determined to let it go before making a fool of herself—who was she, asking questions like she had any right? And it bothered her, that she'd made a judgment and been wrong.

She knew better, and if Gran had been alive she would have reminded her to mind her business and let other folks tend to theirs.

Chapter 29

Sunday morning, Paislee was up before the birds, and she cautiously made her way down the stairs, avoiding the creaky ones, so as not to wake Brody or Grandpa.

Lydia had stayed until ten last night, playing Stramash with them. Grandpa had been the biggest winner of the strategic board game, crediting his years of experience.

They'd feasted on chicken lo mein and her fortune cookie had suggested she give love a chance; Lydia had vigorously agreed. Paislee'd tossed the fortune in the trash. There was no time in her life for romance.

She plugged in the electric kettle and chose the mug Brody had made for her two Christmases ago, with a picture of him and Wallace on it.

Paislee shrugged a heavy sweater on over her flannel pajamas, collected her tea and sack of knitting, and sat outside on the enclosed porch. She missed her gran terribly.

She hadn't slept well, feeling out of sorts about everything and, worst of all, that she'd wrongly suspected two different people of Isla's murder.

Lydia had been right to suggest she let the detective handle it—and she tried not to worry that he hadn't already caught the killer. That was not her job.

She settled the Oxford Blue yarn in her lap and began on the sweater where she'd left off, recalling Hamish McCall telling her that his favorite color was blue.

Detective Inspector Zeffer seemed too uptight to have a favorite anything—yet he also favored blue suits. Very stylish blue suits. What was his story?

Before she knew it, her tea was gone and she had the first sleeve done for the fisherman's sweater, the sun just peeking between the trees in her back garden. Knitting soothed her better than a dram of whisky, and she liked seeing results from the efforts she put forth.

A scratch sounded on the back door from the kitchen and she got up to let Wallace out.

He wagged his tail in thanks, brownish-black button eyes shiny as he licked her hand before racing out to the green lawn, scaring two birds from the grass to the branches of the sweet chestnut. Her gran had planted flowers in neatly rowed containers, but Paislee hadn't kept up. So, she'd let the flowers grow wild. Semi-organized chaos, yet beautiful all the same. Very much like her life, she thought.

Out of that beauty jutted the practical poles of their clothesline. Two poles six feet apart, with four strands of sturdy rope running across the lawn.

She mowed with a gas mower as needed—though Brody was old enough this year that she might pay him to do it. He would earn an allowance to spend on comic books. That made her smile as she could see Lydia and Bennett together, gorgeous in their togetherness.

Brody burst out the back door with a grin. "Sunday Funday! Morning, Mum." He planted a smooch on her cheek.

"Morning, love. Did you have pleasant dreams?"

"I dreamed of going fishing."

"Fishing?"

Her son's eyes turned crafty. "I asked Grandpa if he could take me and he said yes."

"Is that what you two were talking about yesterday?"

He nodded.

"And why was this a secret?"

"It's not a secret." His long auburn bangs brushed his brows. "It's a plan."

"For?"

"I cannae tell ye till I'm twelve."

"Brody Shaw, you are not getting a knife. Nothing sharper than nail clippers, aye?" She rose, lowering her knitting to the bag. "And I willnae have you and your grandfather conspiring against me on this."

He crossed his arms angrily. "What does that mean?"

"Why don't you go look it up?"

"I dinnae want sentences."

"That's enough of yer cheek, then. Drop those arms."

He did.

"*Conspiring* is another word for planning, but it's planning behind someone's back."

"Oh." He considered this for a moment. "Your da had one, though. Didnae he have all his fingers?"

Brody'd never met his grandparents—with her da deceased and her mum in America. She could tell her grandfather had coached him a bit on what to say. "Aye. He did."

"Will ye think on it?"

Twelve was both a long way away and too short a time. "Aye—if ye don't nag me about it."

"Deal." They shook on it and went inside, Wallace scampering around their feet. Grandpa sat over a steaming mug of Scottish Breakfast tea.

Paislee arched her brow at him.

"Aye, I heard ye," he said, tapping his finger to his ear. "I'm not deaf."

Brody leaned against the table. "Mum said we can go fishing today."

Paislee poured herself a fresh cup, her nape tingling that she'd been outplayed.

"You have rods, lass?" Grandpa asked.

"No."

"We can rent 'em," he said, as if money were no bother. "Or I have me things in storage in Dairlee if ye'd rather drive me?"

She remembered him saying he had a storage unit. "Do ye need tae go there?"

"Naw. I was just thinkin' tae save the cost of rental, but it isnae much."

To be honest, Paislee wasn't in the mood for the twenty-minute drive to Dairlee and back, or the mysterious contents of Grandpa's storage unit.

"Let's do that, then."

He rubbed his hands together. "I'll make homemade fish and chips for dinner tonight. You willnae have tae lift a finger."

"I like my fish already deboned and cleaned." She'd never fished and hadn't planned on starting. "The way the grocer does it."

Her grandfather eyed her as if she hadn't lived. "I'll do it, I said."

"Please, Mum?"

What was the point in saying no when it would be a nice outing for all of them? Besides, he'd asked so sweetly. "Fine. I'll pack a picnic lunch. But I have a meeting at Theadora's first. I'll text her and find out what time."

Paislee found her phone and sent off the text. Lydia had

put the printouts of the three possible properties on the counter by her phone, so she read them at the table while drinking her second cup of tea.

She'd need at least one more for today's plans. *Fishing. Ew.*

She was intrigued by the open warehouse plan of the first listing. Shelving could divide the space, and the price was right. The downside, and it couldn't be overlooked, was that it was five miles on the far side of town.

She passed the sheet of paper to her grandpa and read the next. Two-story, which she could make work, but high priced for the location on the west side of Nairn. Would Mary Beth or Elspeth be able to navigate stairs?

She hated to admit that Lydia had been right that the first property, white on white as it had been, was the best so far.

"Ah, but wait," she murmured as she read the third.

"I hope it's better than these, lass." Grandpa rattled the sheets of paper.

"It might be, it might be." Single-story brick, only fifty pounds more per month, three blocks back from downtown. No parking, but there was a lot across the street.

"May I?" Her grandfather held his hand out to see.

She passed the listing over. "Lydia is going tae take me tae see them tomorrow after we pick up Brody."

"This looks all right."

Paislee agreed but didn't want to get her hopes up. "I wish my shop could stay where it is." Yesterday's festival foot traffic had been the boon for the year. It wasn't all about the day's sales but people knowing Cashmere Crush was there. "I need tae check the website and see if we got any orders in."

"Mum—ye're supposed tae take the day off. No working. Yer already going tae that dumb meeting."

"It's a special circumstance. And you get ice cream with Lydia."

He balanced one foot on the other, his arms out to the sides. "Fishing, fishing, fishing . . ."

Her phone *ding*ed. She read the message from Theadora and chuckled. "Well, me lad, yer in luck. Theadora cancelled for today." She wondered why.

Brody grinned and raced around the table.

Theadora added another message: *Looking forward to hearing what the historical society has to say.*

"Maybe they dinnae have enough information to act?" she mused aloud. She received another text. *Meeting next week.*

Paislee sent Lydia a message that she was off godmother duty, unless she wanted to join them for fishing at the pier.

Lydia answered with a green-faced emoji with its tongue out. *See you tomorrow.*

"Awright. Let me cook up some sausage and biscuits and then we can picnic on the pier—you two fish, and I'll lounge with Wallace like a lady of leisure."

Grandpa had done some of the chores already that she tried to fit in on a Sunday so she didn't feel too guilty about taking the day to relax. She could make some progress on the sweater while he and Brody fished. Other folks liked to read to escape, but Paislee preferred having her hands busy while she either listened to the radio or watched the telly.

It was close to noon by the time they arrived at the fishing pier across from Harborside Flats, where Isla had lived. She'd let Grandpa drive since she was still a wee bit sore.

"Why did you choose this park?" she asked.

Grandpa shrugged. "I knew they had fishing poles for rent. There are less crowded piers, but they dinnae have the amenities. Is it a bother?"

"Naw." Paislee got out the picnic basket she'd loaded with cheese sandwiches and crisps, and the packet of shortbread cookies for a sweet. She kept Wallace on his lead, giving Brody and Grandpa cash to rent rods and buy bait.

She hadn't quite released her hold on the money as she looked them both in the eyes. "I am not going tae clean or fry."

They both nodded. Brody had on a mesh cap with a blue bill, while her grandfather wore his dark green tam. The weather was warm enough that they were all content in sweaters.

Off they went to the office on the pier, leaving her with Wallace. She snuck a peek back at Isla's apartment building. Beside Gerald's silver BMW there was another silver car, too shiny to be Tabitha's old clunker.

An Audi?

That was fancy.

Brody and Grandpa waved from the office with their rods and bait and headed down the pier to find a spot midway to drop their lines. They were close enough that she could see them. Dogs were not allowed on the pier in case of hooks in the paws, so Wallace stayed at her side.

Paislee took a seat at the picnic table and watched Isla's flat. Her body tensed when a man in a dark suit walked out, a cardboard box balanced in his arms. Was that Roderick Vierra? She hadn't recognized the make of the car behind her when she'd been hit, too focused on the silver sunshade on the windshield, but he'd sure been mad at her when she'd left his warehouse.

Couldn't get too much fancier of a vehicle than an Audi. The detective had said that Roger and Roderick had been together that afternoon at the warehouse. She truly believed they would lie for each other. Didn't Roger cover up Roderick's affairs?

He brought out another box. Was he stealing his own yarn back? She doubted that he had permission to remove items from a possible crime scene.

It wasn't right. She had to see the front of his car to check for damage, and get a picture of him going in and out of Isla's flat to send to the detective. She didn't dare call after his last response about Billy. Paislee moved quickly so that Roderick didn't leave before she caught him in the act.

She waved at Brody and Grandpa, but they were engrossed in hooking bait to their fishing line.

Making sure she had her phone on silent in her cardigan pocket, Paislee walked the leashed Wallace across the street from the little park on the harbor to the apartment complex. Just a lady taking her dog for a stroll on a beautiful spring day.

And what if Roderick was the killer? Wallace was no bodyguard. Paislee could scream very loudly, though, and dash toward the main road to safety. It was best to stay out of sight.

Nerves tingled along her shoulders. She stopped at the corner of the building, flat number 14. Then 12. She waited for Roderick to cross from Isla's to the parking space in front of Isla's door, and discreetly snapped a picture. He loaded the boxes in the boot before hurrying back inside.

On the walkway before the apartments, she sidestepped toward the Audi that had been parked facing the flat.

Paislee scanned the front of Roderick's car. Not so much as a scratch to mar the silver paint, and there was a black grill that she didn't recall seeing in her rearview. Not to mention that his windows were tinted.

What was he doing in Isla's apartment?

"What are *you* doing here?" Roderick asked. She whirled, her heart in her throat. He glowered at her from the threshold of Isla's flat, a box balanced on his hip.

Wallace barked and Paislee tightened her grip on the dog's leash, tugging him back from Roderick's pant leg.

Guess he was still upset about the coffee incident. "I was going tae ask you the same thing." She laughed softly, but he didn't join her, his expression shuttered.

"I dinnae owe you an explanation, but I'm getting *my* property before Isla's mother arrives tae collect her daughter's personal items." Roderick's chiseled jaw clenched. "I spoke tae the police and they're having an officer escort her after I'm done."

She glanced inside the boot of his silver Audi and saw ten boxes of yarn. There were more in the back seat. Roger had said forty had been missing from the Vierra warehouse.

He followed her gaze. "I had no idea Isla had stolen this much. Roger thinks me a fool. What was she planning tae do with it?"

She blew her bangs back from her eyes and avoided Roderick's question—if he gave it enough consideration, he could probably figure out that Isla was going to sell it on the sly. Isla had been far more in survival mode than Paislee had ever suspected.

"Do you live around here?" He put the box in the boot and closed it, his movements very controlled.

"I have a friend next door." Gerald would be very surprised to hear it, she thought, but it was the best she could come up with.

A gold key dangled from the front door handle and she suddenly realized why he would have access to Isla's apartment and be allowed inside. "You own this place?"

"Vierra's does." He winked. "You didnae think she could possibly afford this place, did you? You may not think much of me, Miss Paislee Shaw, but the women in my . . . employ . . . never go hungry." He walked briskly into the flat and shut the door behind him.

Clear communication, that. He'd set Isla up in this flat away from his wife to continue seeing her. *Pig* was too good of a word for the man.

Gerald glared at her from behind his front window curtain, then opened the door. "If ye don't leave right now, I'm going tae call the cops. This is harassment."

She didn't argue that she wasn't harassing *him* but his neighbor.

"Sairy tae bother you," she said, taking Wallace across the street to the park.

Even with her back turned she heard the bang of Gerald's door as it closed. Roderick hadn't run her off the road, but could he have killed his lover?

Chapter 30

In a melancholy mood, Paislee considered the "facts" as she returned to the picnic table and their plaid blanket. Grandpa and Brody were immersed in fishing, so she took out her knitting and got cozy on the grass with Wallace at her side.

She petted her pup, enjoying the silky feel of his fur between her fingers. His steady chuffs of breath were a comfort, and she liked that he kept his gaze fixed on Brody—Wallace was her boy's dog for sure.

It made no sense that Roderick would leave Isla dead on what was essentially his floor, to be found who knew when. The trail would lead right back to Roderick Vierra as the owner of the flat.

Roderick lived in Inverness with his fancy silver car, and the detective had only been checking Nairn's registered vehicles. Perhaps there was a way to check into whether he'd gotten repairs as of late?

Didn't matter. Roderick had tinted windows, and she hadn't recalled a black grill behind her.

It had happened so *fast*, though. She didn't remember a front plate on the vehicle, either, now that she thought back.

She pulled the pattern with the measurements for the

torso of the man's sweater from her knitting bag and began to stitch, knit one, purl one, starting from the bottom up. She would attach the sleeves and collar last.

Isla's mother would be in town today—at this very flat. Did the two ladies look alike? Was the woman sorry now that she hadn't been kinder to her daughter?

Paislee looked up as she heard Brody's laugh, smiling automatically. He'd had something on the line, but it slipped off and back into the harbor's waters.

Grandpa clapped Brody on the shoulder, and helped him attach another bit of bait. Wallace didn't relax his vigil.

She returned to her knitting, and musing. Gerald had an alibi that satisfied the detective. Did Detective Inspector Zeffer even consider Roderick a suspect? She was glad she hadn't sent him the pictures of Roderick. Tabitha and Billy claimed to have alibis for that night, but Isla had died in the morning—

"Mum!" Brody shouted from the pier.

She stood right away, her pulse skittering at his yell. Shielding her face, she narrowed her eyes—Brody had caught another fish! Silvery white and the length of her shoe.

Joy filled her and Paislee raced to the edge of the pier with her phone to snap a few pictures. "Well done!"

This was a first, and deserved her attention. Wallace barked from behind her, racing around her feet, his tail wagging.

Grandpa grinned proudly.

Well, Gran? What would you make of this?

Four skinny size-eight fish later, the Shaw men were ready to eat their sandwiches and crisps. They'd returned to the picnic spot for shade, the fish cleaned and deboned, on ice in a plastic cooler.

Her son had a blush of color across his pale cheeks and a sprinkle of freckles along his nose.

"Sunscreen next time," she said, ruffling his hair.

He ducked but grinned.

At four that afternoon, Paislee cleaned up the remains of
their sandwiches and trash from their picnic and suggested a
movie when they got home to rest before the big fish fry.
"Something superhero?" Her son loved humans with super-
powers more than magical beasts.

She looked up as she was folding the plaid blanket and
sucked in a breath. A police car had parked at the complex, and
an officer was opening the door to Isla's flat.

Isla had been an exact replica of her mother and for a
minute Paislee'd thought she'd seen a ghost. Blond hair and
cute nose, a petite frame.

The two disappeared inside the apartment.

Brody and Wallace played fetch with a yellow tennis ball.
Grandpa Angus sat on the picnic table watching, too.

"What's goin' on now?" He shoved his tam back on his
head.

"Isla's mother. They could be twins." She patted her rapidly
beating heart. "Thought it was a ghost."

He glanced at her. "Ye want tae have a word?"

"I would, but I wouldnae." Tears burned the backs of her
eyes. "Does that make sense?"

Her grandfather shrugged. "Sometimes what we feel doesnae make sense."

"Isla didnae have nice things tae say about her—and now
Isla's dead. I wonder if she's sorry for how she treated her only
daughter."

"You'll probably never know that, lass."

"Yer right. I just wish that things had turned out differently. Isla had good in her. I know she did." Her heart ached.

Minutes later, the front door of the flat opened and Isla's
mother marched out, her arms crossed. The police officer
scrambled to lock up behind her.

They were talking, but Paislee couldn't hear what was said.

Isla's mum flung her arms about as though upset and climbed into the front seat of the patrol car.

"Nothin' there she wanted," Grandpa observed.

"Including her daughter."

Grandpa scratched his beard, his eyes hard. "Some women arenae meant tae be mothers. You are like your gran, and dinnae see it that way, but trust me, lass, not every woman has the maternal gene."

Paislee flushed at the compliment of being like her grandmother, the woman she loved most in the world. "You forget about me own mum. She moved off tae America and never calls. After a while, I gave up trying. Last I heard, she has a whole new batch of bairns with her new husband."

"Ach. I hadnae realized she'd left and that yer on your own."

"I manage well enough," she said, shoulders tight in defense of any unsolicited advice.

He chuckled. "I was just going tae say that yer doing a fine job, raising Brody Shaw."

"Thanks."

"What happened tae the father, if ye don't mind me askin'?"

"If you plan on being part of our lives, then you won't question me on that."

Paislee held the old man's gaze, knowing that she would drop him off at the train station if he decided to rock the boat on that issue. It was a line that nobody could cross.

"I hear ye," he said after a full minute. "Doesnae he ask?"

"He knows that he belongs to me, and only me."

She watched as her grandfather thought of many things he wanted to say, but he finally settled on, "I dinnae know ye well, but I trust ye have yer reasons. Guid enough." He swished his hands together like brushing off dirt from his palms and she knew that would be the end of it.

She bowed her shoulders briefly before calling, "Brody! Wallace! Time tae go."

They arrived home tired but cheerful after their afternoon at the harbor. The ocean was part of her soul and she, Brody, and Wallace often spent their Sunday Fundays on the sand, chasing waves. Now that she knew how to make a kite, maybe they could do that next Sunday. She had in mind one of Mrs. Martin's more complicated patterns.

As they neared the house, she noticed Detective Inspector Zeffer's SUV in the driveway.

"What could he want?" she asked. Maybe he'd found Isla's killer?

Grandpa pulled the rented white car up alongside the navy SUV and parked. Brody and Wallace scrambled from the back seat, the terrier barking. Paislee and Grandpa got out, exchanging a glance, and he took a place beside her, next to the porch stairs, his hands intertwined before him.

The detective exited, pocketing his keys. It was late afternoon and the sun shone on his russet hair, bare of a hat. "Paislee. I was just about tae leave a note on the door. Can you come tae the funeral home? Mrs. Campbell would like tae meet you."

She'd been on the fence about it, but it seemed fate, or the detective, had decided for her. Paislee remained still.

"Go ahead, lass," her grandfather urged, handing her the keys to the Sentra.

"I can drive," the detective offered, gesturing to his SUV.

"Naw. I'm fine." Paislee shook her mind clear. The last thing she wanted was to ride through town in a police vehicle. Tongues would wag, then. "I should change." She'd dressed for a day at the park in jeans and a lightweight top, her hair in a side braid that had come loose.

The detective shrugged. "I wouldnae take the time. I called

your mobile, but you didnae answer. I volunteered tae ask you, but be warned. The woman is . . . emotional. She's *offended* two other officers already."

She pulled her phone free and saw that she had a missed call; she'd put it on silent when she'd snuck up on Roderick, and then he'd caught *her* checking out his car. "I saw her at Isla's flat. She didnae stay long." Paislee couldn't blame the poor woman for being upset—her daughter was dead.

"Listen, Charla Campbell knows what her daughter was doing tae people, and that you were her only real friend."

"I'll go." The last time she'd been at the funeral home had been for Gran.

Detective Inspector Zeffer scrubbed at his chin. "I'll be tae the side tae give you privacy, but just say the word when you're ready tae leave. I want tae talk tae you afterward."

Paislee gave a deep sigh and got into the Sentra, driving the five minutes to the funeral home next to the church. The detective drove behind, slowing to a crawl around the traffic circles. Was he trying to prove his merits as a safe driver? She flipped on the radio, not wanting to think about what had been so difficult that they'd sent the detective to bring her.

She parked at the funeral parlor. The single-story stone building was wide, with a deep basement where they kept the bodies ready for burial. Three stone steps led up to the front door, painted a subdued gray.

Detective Inspector Zeffer hesitated with his hand on the knob, as if ready to offer advice or caution, but in the end, he said nothing.

They entered the dim interior, the low lighting a comfort in sorrowful times. A section of couches was to their left, an empty desk to the right. To her relief, Father Dixon was speaking with Isla's mum on one of the couches.

"Hello," Paislee said.

The priest rose swiftly and hugged Paislee, saying he would prepare a mass for Isla, who was to be buried in their churchyard. "And this is Charla Campbell," Father Dixon said. The detective stayed by the empty desk.

The woman was forty, just, and had smooth skin and Isla's blue eyes. Hers were hard, and her mouth stern, and Paislee got a glimpse of what Isla would have looked like in twenty years—had she lived.

Father Dixon introduced Paislee, and gave her hand an extra squeeze before departing in a whir of black on black.

"Thank ye for coming." The woman extended her hand, not rising from her place on the soft fabric couch, also in a somber gray. Paislee had sat on that couch herself, crying tears of grief.

There was no sign of Isla, or a coffin, though that would be in the private viewing room the day of the burial.

"I'm so sairy for your loss." Paislee sat opposite her on a matching gray sofa.

The woman's face scrunched in anger. "Och, I know all about ye, Ms. Goody-Two-Shoes. Church on Sunday. A swear jar."

Paislee gasped and brought her hand to her rapidly beating heart. What exactly had Isla told her mother about her?

"Son with excellent marks in school. An entr—" Charla searched for the word, couldn't find it, and said sourly, "Ye own yer own business and aren't even thirty. Pretty, too." Charla squinted at Paislee as if searching for flaws.

Paislee had no idea what to say and folded her hands over her knee to keep her leg from trembling. She felt under attack. "Aye, Isla worked at Cashmere Crush."

"I heard, I heard. Isla looked up tae ye, then off she went tae Inverness, and now she's dead." Charla dabbed at her nose with a crumpled tissue. "Me poor lass."

Paislee's first thought was to offer a hug of comfort, but

Charla's bristling body was like a porcupine baring poisoned quills. Yet she'd just lost her only child. Paislee softened and patted the woman's knee. "I cared for her."

"She stole from me. From the moment she was born, she stole."

Paislee was certain she'd heard wrong. "Sairy?"

Charla's garish smile revealed yellowed teeth. "She ruined me." Tears streaked down her cheeks in black mascara streaks. "I lost my womb for a sickly babe that did nought but scream. When she left home, she had my diamond ring."

Paislee relied on her bravado to face the surly woman. What an awful way for Isla to grow up, as if owing for her very breath. "You wanted tae see me?"

Charla dotted tissue to the corner of her eye, staring down at the thin gray carpet. "I dinnae know where I'm going tae be in the future, and I certainly don't belong tae no church, so Isla should be at rest here. It's peaceful; I'll give ye that."

"Nairn is quiet," Paislee agreed.

Charla bowed her head, and when she looked up again, her mood had grown even darker. "Isla had nothing at her flat—nice place like that and she didnae have any jewelry, or cash?" She jerked her head toward the detective by the desk. "I think his blokes stole it."

Oh. That explained a lot.

She suddenly understood the gestures Charla had made outside Isla's apartment and matched them with the words. A bit of greed? An instinct to look out for herself in the bitter world? If she'd accused the police of theft, no wonder they were "offended."

Detective Inspector Zeffer had an elephant hide, she'd bet, letting nothing through.

"I hadnae heard from Isla since she and Billy moved away—only the email she sent, what, maybe two weeks ago, now, that she wanted her job back." She wiped her hand across her damp forehead. Was it hot in here? No, she just didn't care for Charla Campbell, or the truth about Isla.

"You were only one line in the water." Charla sneered and lost whatever prettiness she'd had, giving Detective Inspector Zeffer a sideways glance. "Billy, getting back with that tramp Tabitha. Aye, I know all aboot it. Me daughter was an emotional mess when Billy caught her in bed with her boss, and left her high and dry. Then Vierra had the gall tae fire my girl? I told her tae charge that bastard or rat him out tae his wife."

So that was how Isla had come up with the blackmailing scheme—her own mother. Paislee exchanged a brief look with the detective, who only gave away his thoughts by the muscle jumping at his tight jaw.

"I ken, that isnae how *you* would do things, but this isnae aboot you, Ms. Prim and Proper." Charla smoothed a blond lock of hair behind her ear. Cheap pearl earrings dangled from her lobes.

The joke of that was enough to make Paislee scoff. She kept her calm somehow and said, "I'm here right now because of Isla. You said ye wanted tae meet me? Well, we've met. I'll be going."

Charla sniffed, her eyes brightening. "Arenae you the cool cat? I wonder if Isla had found out secrets about you."

Paislee froze.

Charla waved her hand. "Yer diary would be hardly worth the peek."

Her cheeks flamed. Detective Inspector Zeffer pushed himself off the desk and entered the fray. "Mrs. Campbell. You wanted tae invite Paislee tae your daughter's service, and grant her authority for Isla's affairs within the church?"

Charla exhaled, suddenly looking eighty. "Aye."

"What authority?" Paislee asked the detective. "She's passed on."

"Just as a contact number, in case Charla cannae be reached," the detective explained.

Paislee quickly read between the lines. This woman would disappear in one fashion or the next. Paislee was being asked to take responsibility for Isla in her death. She only wished she'd been able to better protect her in life.

"I will." She would visit Isla when she visited Gran, and say a prayer for both their souls.

The detective nodded, as if he'd known this would be her answer.

The woman burst into real tears. "Thank ye. Now, leave me with me grief."

Detective Inspector Zeffer led Paislee from the funeral home and out again to the parking lot. She wrapped her sweater around her against the chill as the spring sun lowered. They stood by the front end of his Police Scotland SUV.

"Thanks for coming," he said. "She insisted on wanting you involved, but after how she treated the other officers I wasnae going tae leave you alone. She's a viper."

Paislee covered a smile with her fingers and then dropped her hand to her cardigan pocket and the keys to her rental. "I'm glad I can be here for Isla in some small way."

He wore another blue suit and she wondered if he had a closet full of them in different shades and styles.

Maybe it was time to update her wardrobe or risk being left in the last decade. "I should've asked when the funeral was. . . ." She eyed the door leading to Charla Campbell but couldn't bear the idea of going back inside.

"Father Dixon will know," he said, as if reading her mind.

"I'll call tomorrow."

"Will you be awright driving home?" He rested his hip against the SUV. "You look knackered."

"Och, thanks." She swallowed and rubbed her throat,

grateful to have gone all day without the soft brace. "Have ye had a day off since you've moved here?"

"No. I'll take one after Isla's murderer is found."

She nodded, appreciating his work ethic if not his manner. "What did you want tae talk with me about?"

"How'd you know that Isla was murdered?"

She would not give up Amelia. "*You* told me when you brought in the yarn from Isla's flat."

His pale green eyes narrowed and made her think of sea glass tumbled onto the surf. Full of mystery. "We have a leak in the department."

"How can I help with that?" She shifted toward the church next to the funeral parlor. "I thought maybe you'd want tae discuss Billy, or Gerald."

"Gerald called in, right before I pulled up tae your house, accusing you of harassment." He held up a hand. "But refused tae actually fill out paperwork."

She rolled her shoulders, wanting her couch and a cup of tea. "I promise not tae bother him again."

"What were you doing there?"

"I was actually across the street at the pier with my family. Grandpa is teaching Brody tae fish." She shrugged. "I saw Roderick taking boxes out of Isla's flat, and thought tae capture him in the act of stealing."

The detective slapped his hand to his thigh. "You didnae."

"Aye. He informed me that he owned the place." But she'd gotten a look at the front of his Audi.

"What were you going tae do?"

"I was taking pictures tae send tae you, for *proof* that he was breaking the law."

They stared at each other and his mouth lifted the tiniest bit, but he didn't smile. Since she'd already made a fool of herself, she didn't bother sharing what she'd learned about Billy getting sick off bad cod at the pub.

Which fired her temper. They were in this parking lot because somebody had killed Isla. "Tabitha and Isla were room-
mates and she knew about the digoxin she was taking because
of her heart condition."

"I'll read over Tabitha's interview, but from what I recall,
she had an alibi—she was at work."

"If Isla died in the morning, maybe Tabitha did it before
heading tae work at the flower shop? Ritchie said she'd been a
mess, crying."

"Ritchie?"

"Her manager at the florist."

He leaned back, crossing his arms, shutting her out.

Paislee pressed her point. "What if Billy and Isla had hooked
up again, and Tabitha, emotional about her ex and her ex best
friend, lost her mind?"

"I understand yer reason for wanting tae find Isla's killer—
you have tae let me do my job, ye ken?" He searched her face
in the twilight. "I dinnae want the person who drove you off
the road tae take it tae the next step."

"Are you saying that you believe me now?"

His mouth thinned.

"It wouldnae look good in the Nairn police books?" Her
attempt at levity fell flat.

"I'd never forgive myself if something happened tae you.
This is my town now and I take my duties very seriously." He
took his keys from his pocket. "I thought it had to be a gag
from the police department when you and yer grandfather
were the ones tae report Isla's death. It wasnae funny when I
got there, but odd, seeing ye both again, you must admit."

"It's been a strange week." She rubbed her hands as the
cold dusk pitched into evening. "I should go."

He watched her with a hooded gaze that felt like admon-
ishment.

"I'll go straight home tae eat fish and chips," she said defensively. "Drop Brody off at school in the morning and be at Cashmere Crush at nine thirty." She lifted her hand toward the detective and with the other grabbed her keys. "I will open at ten, and pick Brody up from school at three thirty. Dull as dishwater, I tell you."

Detective Inspector Zeffer finally broke down and smiled. "So why is it that I'm worried aboot you?"

Chapter 31

Monday morning, Paislee could move her right shoulder without it being sore.

"Up and at 'em!" she called to Brody, in a cheery mood after the first good night's sleep she'd had in a week.

Brody groaned but Wallace woofed, so she knew dog and boy would soon be up for breakfast.

Paislee paired her newest jeans with a fitted turquoise flannel that showed she had a waist, something that Lydia constantly accused her of hiding, and flats, and added a turquoise tie to her braid.

Dare she apply shadow to her eyes?

With a light step, she skipped downstairs where Grandpa had tea ready. He whistled appreciatively.

"And good mornin' tae ye," he said.

She patted her warm cheeks. "Amazing what a full night's rest can do for a lass. I didnae have a single bad dream."

"Weel, Isla's been settled, now." Grandpa sat at the table.

"Almost. There's still a killer on the loose."

He arched a silver brow and didn't argue. What could he say to that?

She took her mug of Brodies Scottish Breakfast to the

table and sat, pouring Weetabix into a bowl and adding berries. "What's your plan for the day, Grandpa?"

"Ye dinnae need me at the shop? Tae help drive?"

"Well, I'm fine for today." She wasn't used to having assistance. "But I'll make sure tae add you tae the pickup list at Fordythe, in case of emergencies."

"Ye should take advantage of me help while I'm here," he said somewhat defensively. "Once we find Craigh . . ."

"I know. You'll be gone." Her shoulders hiked. What was his rush? Maybe he wanted more hours at the shop? "Come in at noon, if ye want."

"I'm just tryin' tae help."

"Fine."

"Fine."

He glared at her, and she glared back. They each looked away when Brody joined them at the table.

"What?" Brody said, his gaze traveling from her to his great-grandfather.

"Nothing," they said in unison.

Paislee offered Brody the cereal. "Let's make sure we keep our good standing this week with the headmaster, aye?"

Wallace stayed home with Grandpa, and she and Brody made it out the front door at quarter till nine. They were at Fordythe with seven minutes to spare.

"Thanks, Mum!" Brody slid out of the car, his backpack over his shoulder, and ran inside the building with the wave of other schoolchildren. She recognized the blond shag of Edwyn as he greeted Brody and then the two disappeared.

No sign of Hamish McCall—not that she was looking.

She deep-sighed and headed toward work. Being early would allow her to get further on her fisherman's sweater and have it in the mail by the end of next week.

Paislee, humming under her breath, parked the rental in

the back of Cashmere Crush, and entered her cozy shop. The shop she loved. And had to leave. How had she forgotten that she was supposed to look at three new places this afternoon with Lydia?

Her good mood evaporated. She tucked her purse beneath the register and stocked the till with money from her safe. Then she logged onto her store laptop to check for orders. Two sweaters had come in! Two hundred pounds. She would gladly take it.

She turned the radio on for background noise and worked on the sweater for an hour. By eleven she was getting a crick in her neck, so she put the knitting down and stretched, discovering to her dismay that the yarn from Flora that Grandpa had priced hadn't been stocked on the shelves.

This was the sage that she always sold out of, and she knew she could have sold it on Saturday in the shop.

The front door opened, and Mary Beth entered with her customary smile, her hand to her ample chest.

"How was the christening party?" Paislee asked.

"The blanket and booties were a hit. This little girl will be a princess." Mary Beth sank down in one of the larger chairs, her blue eyes sparkling, her dark brown hair in waves around her face. "As she should be."

In for a chat, then. Paislee placed the box of sage yarn out of sight to put on the shelf later.

"It was so kind of you and Arran tae help Flora and Donnan at the festival. Not that it's any of my business, but I didnae realize you were such good friends."

Mary Beth pulled a square of yellow she'd started from her bag at her feet. "We used tae have dinner together a few times a year. The girls love Flora—it's a shame her and Donnan never had children."

Paislee brought out the Oxford Blue yarn, so she could knit while they chatted. The sweater wouldn't finish itself.

Mary Beth leaned close to Paislee. "Donnan never wanted

them, and we both know he ruled their roost. My heart goes out tae Flora, shouldering everything now."

"She said she wished she had some extra hands, and joked that she'd take Grandpa for me."

"She did more than her share of the work before," Mary Beth said ominously. "We both know it."

That was as close as they would get to discussing how Donnan, after a few drinks, used to treat Flora.

"Aye." Paislee finished a row.

"He and Arran would play eighteen holes of golf, and stay for the nineteenth until the bar closed." Mary Beth looped yellow over her finger, her tone deepening. "I dinnae mind picking them up so they don't drive, but men will be men, and think they can manage." Her pretty brows furrowed and rosy color speckled her chest.

What was she saying?

Did this have anything to do with what she'd said Friday night about drinking and driving statistics being up in Nairn? And why she hadn't been drinking that night?

Paislee's first thought was that perhaps Mary Beth had gotten a DUI.

Not Mary Beth. She couldn't see it—even when she did drink on Thursday nights it was only one or two.

Arran, then.

Paislee knit the next row of Oxford Blue, her mind searching for what her friend might mean. Finally, she just asked. "Mary Beth, what happened? You know you can tell me and I willnae say a word tae a soul."

Mary Beth burst into tears and dropped the yellow square. "I know yer going tae hear aboot it—Arran's arrest will be in the paper. It's awful—I'm so embarrassed. He might lose his job."

"Oh no! I'm so sairy." She laid the partially completed sweater aside and knelt down beside Mary Beth to give her a hug.

"That's not all."

Paislee settled back on her heels. What could be worse? She briefly closed her eyes as she realized that Arran might have been one of the "fish" Isla'd had on the line. Arran made an excellent living, and he would be keen to protect his reputation at the law firm. An arrest for driving intoxicated would cost him his position in the community.

A perfect mark for a girl digging up secrets in Nairn. "Blackmail?"

Mary Beth's expression darkened with disgust. "Isla contacted me. . . . I couldnae believe her nerve—you see, Arran was trying tae hide it from me. It happened last week, and he paid off someone tae keep it quiet, but somehow Isla found out." She shook her head and met Paislee's gaze.

The heartache in her blue eyes hurt Paislee to see.

"I didnae know. Me own husband! I thought he'd bought me the new van because he was being generous, not because he was covering for totaling his car."

"Totaled?"

Mary Beth sniffed. "Aye."

Paislee patted Mary Beth's arm, feeling sick. "Was anyone else hurt?"

"No, thank God in heaven," Mary Beth prayed fervently.

Paislee got to her feet. "When did Isla call you?"

"Not a phone call," Mary Beth corrected. "She sent a letter saying she wanted five thousand pounds or she would release the news that this wasn't Arran's first DUI." Mary Beth leaned forward, gripping her knees hard, her breaths quick in succession. "Somehow she found out about one from college, and she wrote that if I didnae pay, she would send the information tae his partners at the firm."

Oh. How awful.

Paislee darted a look at Mary Beth's bag. Mary Beth always

had shortbread cookies—she claimed they were her weakness. And she loved her tea as well as the next Scotswoman. Her stomach clenched. Five thousand pounds? That was a lot more than a hundred pounds. "Och, Mary Beth, what did you do?"

"I collected the money tae pay her. I told Arran, and we agreed it needed tae be kept quiet. But she died before I heard from her again," Mary Beth wailed, tears falling on the backs of her hands. "Do ye think I should tell the detective?"

Detective Inspector Zeffer was desperate to find Isla's killer. How could she send her friend to the wolf? Isla's cause of death wasn't public knowledge. "You swear you didnae contact her?"

"I was going tae pay. I have the money in me bag." She glanced down at her purse.

Paislee straightened. "Aye, I think you should tell him that Isla was trying tae blackmail you. Make it clear that you were planning tae pay her."

"What if he thinks I had something tae do with her death?" Mary Beth cried harder. "Or Arran? I didnae see her once she moved away."

"Do you want me tae go tae the station with you?"

Mary Beth sniffed and swiped her cheeks with her palms. "Naw. I'll do it. I have the letter she sent with me, too."

"He has Isla's laptop, so if there's anything that might incriminate Arran or you, you should be forthright."

"We are just trying tae protect Arran's job." Mary Beth's tears slowed to a trickle. "This has been a nightmare. Isla was bold as brass in her demand. She dropped the letter in the mailbox tae hide her tracks—no stamp. She was working with someone in Nairn, she had tae be, tae find out these things."

Billy had said that Isla wanted him to dig up secrets, but he wasn't going to do it. What if he'd lied to Paislee and he was mining for dirt on the folks in Nairn? The detective had also mentioned a leak.

"Are you sure you dinnae want me tae go with you? Do you have an alibi for Monday morning?"

"Alibi?" Mary Beth's voice rose and her brow crinkled. "We had breakfast together with the girls, and then I dropped them at school. Arran was with me because he didnae have a car. Tae be sure, we exchanged pleasantries with the headmaster."

"Maybe start with that."

Mary Beth stood, her chin quivering. "I'm so sairy tae dump all of this on you."

"That's what friends are for." She gave her one last hug and then helped stuff her yarn back in her knitting bag.

Mary Beth not drinking Friday night made more sense now. Also, she had a new minivan . . . in silver. It made Paislee feel terrible, but she forced herself to think back to what the van had looked like behind her that day in the car queue at Fordythe.

The van would have been taller than she remembered the vehicle behind her being. Och, this was Mary Beth!

"Thanks again, Paislee." Mary Beth left, ambling down the cracked sidewalk to the police station as if hobbling to the hangman.

Paislee paced the front of her shop and phoned the detective. The call went to voicemail, so she left a message for him to call her back.

Next, she called Amelia.

"Nairn Police Station," Amelia said.

"It's Paislee—is the detective in? I'd like tae talk tae him."

"Paislee—no, he's at a crime scene on Dartmouth. Billy Connal, Isla's ex?" Amelia's voice lowered. "Dead."

Paislee gasped and clutched her stomach. She'd known it—

hadn't she? That something was wrong. "What about Tabitha Drake?"

"She's in custody," Amelia said.

"Thank heaven. Please have the detective call me right away, Amelia."

"I will. Oh, Mary Beth's here."

"She needs a friend," Paislee said, and ended the call.

Chapter 32

Paislee peered out her front window of Cashmere Crush, the view blurred by the frosted glass, though she could make out the red from her geraniums, and the dark yellow of her marigolds in the flower boxes.

Maybe her vision was blurred due to tears of sadness combined with relief. Billy Connal dead, Tabitha behind bars, and Isla to be at rest.

Drawing in a deep breath and exhaling it, she released all of the pent-up energy she'd been carrying for the past week.

With a lighter step, she returned to her counter by the register and perched on a stool, streaming music on her laptop. Knitting the fisherman's sweater, she sang along with Calvin Harris, letting her fingers fly. For the first time since she'd started this project, she connected with it—the clack of her wooden needles, the smooth texture of the wool, the rib stitch pattern, all came together.

"Hey!"

Paislee's head swung up from her knitting, completely startled when her grandfather arrived via the back door. She smacked her hand to her chest in surprise. "Hiya!"

Grandpa spread his arms out to his sides. "Did ye forget I was comin'?"

"I was lost in this sweater," she admitted.

He'd rolled up the sleeves on a flannel shirt that he'd put over a plain gray T-shirt and his usual khakis, and didn't appear at all fatigued from the mile walk. Could it be he really was in better shape than her? She saw some changes in her future.

"Busy morning?" He ambled around the counter.

She shoved the project beneath the register on a shelf.

"Billy's dead," she said. She stood and stretched her back, then reached for the box of sage merino wool to stock the shelves.

"Dead?" Grandpa said loudly, then shook his head as if he'd heard wrong.

"Aye." She picked up two skeins, making sure they were priced, and filled the empty space. "I have a call in to the detective, but he's busy."

"How?" Grandpa shuffled toward her, his boot heels clomping on the polished cement of her floor.

"I dinnae ken—I talked to Amelia a couple hours ago." The only time the detective chatted her up was when he wanted something. "Tabitha's in jail."

"Tabitha?" Grandpa sank down on a hard-backed chair with a confused expression. "Can you be more specific, lass? A detail or two tae jog the memory?"

Right. She hadn't told Grandpa about her suspicions that Tabitha had murdered Isla, so she explained, ending with, "And Saturday after the festival, Lydia and I went tae Tabitha's flat—I'd called the detective and he wasnae concerned about Billy being drunk. Before we picked up our Chinese food?"

He scratched his silver beard.

Tears filled her eyes as it hit her that Billy had actually died and she swiped them away. She'd been right to worry for Billy despite being wrong about Gerald. "We shouldnae have left, but Tabitha showed up with a bag from the pharmacy, and Billy told me he'd had bad fish. And I'd been wrong about Gerald, so . . ." she sniffed.

Grandpa gave her arm an awkward pat. "Dinnae cry, now. You did what ye could. More than most, tae be sure."

"Aye." She wondered what had happened, and if her warning about Tabitha could have saved Billy, or if she'd already been too late. Paislee chose two more skeins from the box, checked for price tags, then slid them on the shelf.

"What's that?" Grandpa asked. "On yer hand?"

Thinking it might be a spider or something, she flapped her hand back and forth. "What?" She stopped but saw a fleck of sage green on her finger. *How odd!*

Picking up another skein, she brought it to the counter for a closer view. She flicked the yarn and a smudge came loose under her thumbnail.

What was going on?

"Is it s'posed tae do that?" Grandpa asked, off the stool to peer over her shoulders. His black glasses slid down his nose.

"Naw." Paislee lifted the entire box of yarn to the counter and dug through the twenty other skeins. They all flaked. "I cannae believe it." It wasn't like Flora at all to have poor quality. "This yarn hasnae been fixed."

"What does that mean?"

"I cannae sell them like this." She got the four she'd put on the shelf and tossed them in the box. "I'll have tae ask Flora what happened."

"I meant, what does *fixed* mean?"

"Dyes are set with a fixing agent, in order tae keep their color. While Jerry McFadden uses chemical dyes, Flora uses all-natural ingredients. She fixes them with minerals, copper or tin. But tae achieve colors like this, she'd have tae use chrome."

Grandpa leaned back, his elbow near the register. "That's the poison stuff you were telling me aboot earlier."

"Aye." She brushed loose sage flakes from her hand into the box. "Chrome is more toxic than the rest, but sometimes creates a better sheen. Usually she's so particular about her product." It was a good thing Paislee hadn't sold it after all.

Paislee took the scissors from her drawer and scraped at the wool with the flat side. Underneath was grayish beige, the same shade as what Baxter the dog had absconded with out of Isla's flat that morning.

How had Flora ended up with it?

"Oh no." She remembered the detective asking her if she'd bought stolen yarn.

"Ye have tae speak plainly, lass. I cannae read yer mind." Grandpa tapped his temple.

"I have tae see Flora and return this yarn." Isla had said that she had quality merino wool she would sell at a discount—yarn she'd stolen from Roderick Vierra.

Had Isla also contacted Flora to buy the yarn? Who knew who else?

Perhaps Flora was cutting corners because of Donnan's medical expenses since the stroke.

"Isnae it ruined? Ye should ask for yer money back."

"I'll talk to her and ask her to make the order again. I think she bought this from Isla's stolen stash."

Grandpa stepped back in surprise. "Ah. You can tell?"

"This yarn was never treated, and that would change how the dye reacts to each strand." She hated to be right about this, but she knew her yarn. "I feel bad for her, I really do, but this yarn isnae the place tae cut corners."

"Not when *your* reputation is on the line," Grandpa agreed. "Want company?"

"I can handle this, Grandpa. She only lives ten minutes

away. I'll be back shortly." She clicked her tongue behind her teeth. "I wish she would have talked tae me first!"

"She probably saw that it was quality wool, as ye say, and thought she was gettin' a bargain. Nothing wrong with that."

She scooped up the yarn and dropped it in the box. "There is if I cannae sell it."

Grandpa grunted. "Ye have a point."

"Let me check the yellow she brought in that day, too—"

"Let me help ye." Grandpa retrieved the ladder and opened it so she could reach the taller shelves.

"I've never had a problem before." Paislee examined the other six colors she carried of Flora's yarn—only the sage was flaking. She climbed down the ladder. Maybe the yarn had needed more time to dry?

"That's manageable then," Grandpa said.

"It had to be the batch she got from Isla." She recalled all the yarn Flora had sold on Saturday and truly felt awful for the poor woman. There would be complaints.

"I'll be back in an hour." Paislee grabbed her purse and the box, loading it in the back of the Sentra. She missed her Juke, which had more room. She'd get it back sometime this week, if all went well.

She started the car and texted Lydia about Billy's death. Her friend called back, but Paislee didn't answer. She was already on the road and the Sentra's hands-free hadn't been set up.

Paislee, after driving through a few older neighborhoods, reached a more rural area where the houses were on bigger lots and not packed so tightly together. No fences, just open fields of wildflowers between homes.

Taking a right down a long dirt driveway, she approached Flora and Donnan's brown bungalow with an attached garage. She'd only been here once, years before Donnan's stroke, when she'd been invited to see Flora's yarn-dying operation in her industrial-sized kitchen, where she created her large pots of dyes and mordants.

There were neighbors on either side—but the lots were large and backed up against a park, making the place relatively private.

She parked behind Flora's white Volvo and got out. She suddenly felt like she should have called ahead. It could be between them, and nobody else needed to know—so long as Flora didn't use the stolen yarn. Did Donnan even know?

Paislee loaded her purse on top of the box and stepped past the Volvo.

She recalled the relief on Flora's face the night Paislee'd handed her the check. There was no shame in that. She'd been flat broke a few times herself.

Paislee climbed the four wooden steps to the porch, rested the box on her hip, and knocked. Something metal rattled inside the house. Flora peeked out the curtain.

Paislee waved, shifting the box to the other hip as she admired the flowers in the front garden.

Her heart froze in her chest.

There, not ten feet away, below the windshield's early afternoon glare from the sunshade on Flora's white Volvo, bright silver with a long eyehole on the driver's side, was a smashed front bumper. Silver flashed in the white. The Juke's silver paint?

Chapter 33

The door opened and Flora's welcoming smile faded as she noticed Paislee eyeing the crumpled bumper of her car.

Paislee took half a step back, but Flora ushered her and the box inside the large living room of the house. Earth-toned furniture was grouped together before a fireplace and framed nature scenes on the walls. Afghans in many colors had been tossed everywhere, providing a homey atmosphere.

Flora wore an apron over a sleeveless floral tunic top and brown leggings—obviously at work.

"Am I interrupting?" Apprehension buzzed a warning.

"Och, arnae we always busy? I'm glad to see ye, lass." Flora tilted her head toward the box full of sage-green yarn.

Paislee prayed that her friend would have a good explanation for everything. She wanted to be fair. Flora had given her dried comfrey leaves for the aches—but only after sending her to the hospital. She couldn't comprehend it.

"Flora." Her voice sounded strained and she cleared her throat. "I . . ." She searched the room for a place to set the box down.

"Anywhere," Flora said tightly. Her long hair was in a

braid, a yellow Scots broom blossom above her ear. "Do ye have a problem with the yarn?"

Paislee set the box on the sofa, took her purse, and handed a skein to Flora. "I think you didnae add the mordant to this before you dyed it?"

Flora started to deny it but couldn't after she saw the flaking strands. "Heavens, Paislee, I'm sairy." She brought her hand to her forehead. "I've been under so much pressure that—I cannae believe it. I'll fix it, of course. You should have called. You didnae have tae drive out."

A commotion sounded from the kitchen, where Flora created her large pots of dyes and mordants. Flora took a step toward the racket but then stopped, contemplating Paislee.

A gruff voice sounded. *Donnan?* He shouted something unintelligible.

"What was that?" Paislee glanced to the kitchen and then to the unlocked front door. Should she make a run for it?

Flora shook her head, mute as a second noise clamored.

Paislee's belly tightened. "He sounds hurt."

"He's fine." Flora peered at the front door, her brown eyes hard. Instead of checking on Donnan, she stood by Paislee, and squeezed Paislee's upper arm as if to keep her from going anywhere.

Another crash echoed.

"What's going on?" She shook loose and ran toward the kitchen. Flora darted in front of Paislee.

"Stay back!" Flora blocked the doorway with her arm. Her eyes were wild; her mouth quivered. Green dye stained the tips of her fingernails. A harsh metallic scent filled the air. She remembered that vaguely from when she'd been here before— tin, or copper? And honeysuckle.

Paislee pushed at the woman, but Flora remained firm.

"Mind yer own business, lass."

Over Flora's shoulder, she saw the industrial-sized cooker and sink. Two tall iron pots of liquid with wide handles boiled atop the burners. Paislee fought her way past, and the woman grabbed her by the waist, heaving Paislee to the kitchen floor. She fell onto her back, her purse sliding out of sight. Flora hovered over her, her face brick red with fury.

To her left, Donnan groaned, his skin tone yellow and jaundiced. He was tied to a dining room chair, his cheeks sunken. A strip of silver duct tape stuck across his mouth. His eyes flashed with bewilderment.

Paislee scrambled to her feet, thinking to untie him.

"Stop!" Flora had retreated to the cooker beside him, where an enormous vat boiled. She partially lifted it, as though she'd pour it over her husband. Her pale arms shook at the weight.

Paislee froze. "Have ye gone mental?"

Donnan's next yell ended on a weeping wail that went directly to Paislee's heart. He kicked at the leg of his chair, trying to get loose.

"Chrome mordant!" Flora shouted. "Not one more step."

"How could ye do this tae him? He's helpless!"

Hysterical, Flora sobbed but didn't lower the vat. "I've been giving him Scots broom since his stroke. And I havenae once missed me Friday night beatin's, now, have I?"

"You know we care about ye, Flora—all the ladies at the Knit and Sip."

"Doesnae matter if ye do or don't." She raised the wet handle slightly. "Isla tricked me into buyin' that stolen yarn. I thought it'd been already treated at the factory. Then the demon-child figured out that I was dosing Donnan and demanded more money than I've seen in years. I couldnae pay!" Her brown eyes narrowed, and her mouth turned down. "She had tae be sent on her way!"

Sent on her way? Was that how she referred to murder?

"You mean the way you tried tae send *me* on my way, by running me off the road?"

Donnan stopped crying and looked pleadingly at Paislee.

Flora sniffed, then clanked the pot down—exchanging it for a silver knife from a butcher's rack on the counter.

Paislee stepped back.

"You were stirring up trouble. Paying a visit to Billy, *and* Roderick Vierra? I could tell you were getting tae the bottom of things and needed a warning." For an instant, her expression warmed and Paislee shivered at the madness in Flora's eyes. "I wasnae trying tae hurt ye none, just send a warning is all."

"You sent me tae the hospital. I could have been killed!"

"Fer that I'm truly sairy." Flora wiped her runny nose with the back of her hand, the blade close to her face.

"Flora . . ."

Flora pointed the blade at her whimpering husband. "This one says he loves me, then gives me his fists? Enough, I say."

"Flora!" Paislee stifled a cough as the pots continued to boil, sending wafts of toxic steam into the air. Donnan's head swung low against his chest, as he lost the fight against the vapors and who knew what else. "He needs help."

"Ha! We all need help." She brought the knife dangerously close to her husband's neck as Paislee half-stepped forward. "When I saw that Isla took digoxin, I knew that a spot of foxglove in her tea would do the trick. Looked like an overdose—until that detective wasn't satisfied."

Donnan was unconscious and she feared him dead unless she acted fast. "Please, I'm going tae call an ambulance for Donnan." She scanned the floor for her purse, and saw it by the table leg. "No one has tae know what happened tae him. We'll say it was an accident."

Flora pressed the knife against his throat. "I will see him dead this instant, if ye move another hair's breadth."

Paislee, by the threshold, stayed still but searched the kitchen for a possible way to defend herself and Donnan. A cluster of pots and pans hung on a rack nearby. "Did you also send Billy 'on his way'?"

Flora's eyes glittered with madness and she gave a shrill laugh. "He's dead? Guid. Can you believe the nerve? With Isla out of the way, he and Tabitha planned on steppin' in, having me make payment tae them." She cackled. "Over my dead body, that's what I told Tabitha. Ye were right not tae trust her, Paislee."

Paislee shuffled another half step, and Flora jumped for her—stabbing at her chest. Paislee fell back, grabbing an iron skillet.

Flora stabbed again.

The blade sank deep into Paislee's left shoulder as they struck the floor, Flora's muscular weight landing on her. The madwoman grinned down at her, twisting the blade as Paislee let the skillet fly. She swung it up with all her might, striking the side of the woman's head.

Dazed, Flora collapsed to the side.

Paislee screamed at the pain shooting through her shoulder.

Donnan roused, alive, thank heaven, and struggled against his ties. His chair tipped, and he toppled. Something cracked, and she winced, hoping it was wood and not bone.

A crimson stain gathered from the knife wound at her shoulder. Pain radiated. Coming to, Flora lifted her head, gazing at Paislee like a wild animal. Terrified, Paislee whacked the woman once more, as hard as she could. Flora crumpled, her legs sprawled on the kitchen floor.

Over the sound of the pots bubbling on the burners, Donnan whimpered. Managing to stand, Paislee withdrew the blade with a torturous gasp. Kneeling, she untied the man.

She studied him but couldn't tell whether anything was broken. "Thank ye." Donnan sobbed, sitting up and glaring daggers at his unconscious wife.

Paislee propped herself against the wall, grabbing an oven mitt to press firmly against her bleeding wound.

How awful. Her head swam.

Donnan had beaten Flora their entire marriage, and she'd slowly poisoned him for it.

Far off, Paislee heard the welcome sound of sirens getting closer.

She shouted when she heard the knock, and Detective Inspector Zeffer was first into the kitchen. His perusal of her from head to toe made her feel as if things would be set right. Drawing the medics' attention to her shoulder, he looked down, and she too noticed the steady trickle of blood catching at the cuff at her wrist.

Paislee blinked as the room tilted. It was good to be sitting against the wall. The medics administered assistance to Flora and Donnan. Paislee explained her ordeal to the detective. How Flora had been poisoning her husband with Scots broom. Flora had a wide knowledge of herbs and flowers.

"How'd you know?"

Zeffer peered down at her, his arms crossed. "Your grandfather said you were headed here when I returned your call. I dialed the shop when you didn't pick up your mobile. Amelia mentioned she'd told you that Tabitha was in custody."

"Tabitha didnae—"

"I know. During her interview, she told me how she and Billy had planned tae blackmail Flora about Donnan."

A medic in green trousers and shirt sterilized and dressed Paislee's wound with gauze. "This should be stitched," the medic said. The pain was fierce. Her shirt and jeans were covered with her blood.

The paramedics lifted Flora's unconscious body onto a stretcher and wheeled her out of the kitchen, headed for the waiting ambulance outside. Another pressed against Donnan's arms, legs, and torso, checking for injuries.

All the while, a crime team took pictures and asked questions.

Detective Inspector Zeffer oversaw things as he conversed with her. "Tabitha told us Flora had apologized tae them that evening at the pub, the one where you'd mentioned Billy'd gotten sick. She'd bought them a round, agreeing tae meet with them later tae discuss terms. Billy drank the beer, which is why he's dead. It seems Tabitha prefers stronger spirits, which was a good thing for her."

Paislee arched her brow at him—everything else hurt to move.

"Aye. I should've done more than just called Billy's mobile." He crushed the lapel of his blue suit. "Also, Tabitha said Billy gave her the scarf. Isla had left it behind when she'd moved from Billy's tae Roderick's flat."

Another question answered. Paislee glanced up at him, her bangs sliding back from her forehead. "Flora said that she'd slipped foxglove, which acts like digoxin, into Isla's tea."

He nodded. "I'll tell the coroner tae look for that with Billy, too." Detective Inspector Zeffer pointed at the gauze on her shoulder. "I think you should go tae the hospital."

"Naw. I'm fine."

His mouth thinned. "Why were you here? Did you know that it was Flora? That was a very idiotic thing tae do, if ye did—"

She cut him off. "Hold up! I'd realized that Flora had bought the stolen yarn from Vierra's and wanted tae let her make it right. I didnae know she was the one tae run me off the road until I got here and saw her car. I had you looking for silver cars, but I guess white looks silver when you're half-blind from glare and worried for your life."

"Ah." He bowed his head—was that a smile he was hiding? Medics strapped Donnan to a stretcher. A yellow oxygen mask covered his nose and mouth.

This situation wasn't at all amusing. "I had tae hit Flora over the head with a pot. She was going tae kill Donnan."

Zeffer scratched the back of his neck. "You'd told me that you saw Flora at Dr. Whyte's for allergies, but she was actually taking antidepressants that werenae helping. The doctor had warned her that the herbal remedies she was using might interfere with the medication and prevent it from working."

"*Natural* doesn't mean safe," Paislee said softly. "It can be deadly."

"The doctor was about tae make a call tae Social Services. They hadn't seen Donnan since his stroke and they were getting worried by Flora's erratic behavior."

"She was abused for many years by Donnan. She just wanted peace." Paislee reached for her purse by the table leg and retrieved her phone. Sure enough, five missed calls: the detective, Amelia, Grandpa, and two from Lydia.

"Why didn't they just get divorced?" the detective asked in all seriousness.

Just as seriously, Paislee said, "Nairn is an ancient fishing port. They were married at Saint Ninian's fourteen years ago— yesterday was their anniversary—for better or worse. Divorce isnae an option."

Detective Inspector Zeffer shook his head in bafflement.

Paislee texted Lydia the address of where she was at, and asked for a ride home.

Lydia must have tested the gas pedal on her little red Mercedes, because she was at Flora's house in no time, arriving just as the ambulances carrying Flora and Donnan sped away. Two patrol cars with flashing lights were parked near the flower beds, and the detective's SUV blocked the Volvo.

Detective Inspector Zeffer walked out with Paislee to meet Lydia.

Paislee's bestie stepped out of the Mercedes looking like a

femme fatale in a black and white skintight pantsuit with stilettos.

The detective greeted Lydia with his typical cool demeanor, unfazed.

"Paislee needs medical attention," he said. "Do you know where Town and County is?"

Lydia gasped, zeroing in on the blood-soaked gauze at Paislee's arm. "What happened? Ye said ye needed a ride home!"

"Stabbed," Paislee said, her world tilting slightly.

"Why didnae ye take the ambulance?" Lydia took her by the good arm, leading her to the red sports car.

"It was full," Paislee half-joked.

"She wouldn't be going at all if we weren't making her," said the detective.

Paislee glared at him.

Lydia's black brow lifted. "Let's go to the hospital, love."

Paislee tossed the detective a reluctant smile as they reversed out of Flora's driveway. He hadn't believed her about Billy, but he had shown up just now. She gingerly touched her shoulder as she shared with her friend all that'd happened.

Detective Inspector Zeffer strode back inside Flora's brown bungalow. The normal façade had hidden a poisonous marriage, poisoning Flora, who in turn had poisoned others.

Chapter 34

Lydia drove to Town and County Hospital's urgent care, nabbing a spot close to the door where she parked. The ambulances carrying Flora and Donnan Robertson unloaded on the other side; a police car had followed. *What a nightmare.*

Paislee's shoulder throbbed with an inferno of pain.

"Hang on." Lydia quickly ran around the car to open the door, as Paislee couldn't manage the inside passenger handle.

Tears filled her eyes. "Thanks, Lyd."

Lydia held her hands before her, not knowing where to touch Paislee. "Should I get a wheelchair?"

"No." Her shoulder hurt. Her arm hurt. Even her neck. But blast it, she could walk on her own two feet. "I'm fine."

She hobbled into Urgent Care, and Lydia signed her in, taking care of the paperwork. There were only two other patients waiting in the all-white lobby. Even the chairs were hard white plastic, with metal legs.

"Scots are stubborn," Lydia remarked. "It takes something major tae admit tae pain or sickness. The detective might be new, but he was smart enough tae make sure I'd get ye here; otherwise ye'd have gone home and tried tae bandage yer own arm."

"Ye don't have tae twist the screws, Lydia. I'm here. I want that nice shot Dr. Raj gave me before."

"Yer a junkie now?"

Paislee tried to laugh but couldn't.

Nurse Scott, tall, thin, and memorable with his wild carrot-top hair, entered the waiting room. "Paislee Shaw. Did ye miss me?"

She stiffly rose to her feet and Lydia assisted with a light touch near Paislee's elbow. "I wish this was a friendly visit, but no, I have a wee cut."

Lydia snorted.

"You've been having a run of bad luck." Scott led them into a back room where he removed the gauze and inspected the wound. "Guid ye came tae see us. That looks deep." He handed her a gown. "Want tae shimmy oot of that shirt?"

Her newest pair of jeans and turquoise shirt had been ruined by bloodstains.

"I think we need tae take ye shoppin' when this is over," Lydia said.

Scott excused himself to find the doctor.

"I need tae be able tae knit my sweaters, Lydia; that's more important than clothes. Besides, I hate shopping." She hated it because she was always on a budget and didn't have the time to shop for sales.

Lydia helped her into the gown, tying the paper ties in the back. "Shopping. My treat. Which means I get tae pick out things that show your figure, Paislee Ann."

"You cannae be mad at me. I'm wounded." She sat back on the exam bed and checked out her shoulder.

"I dinnae think that I will be able to be friends with Flora after this," Lydia declared. "She should be uninvited tae Knit and Sip nights."

"She'll be in jail for *murder*; that's harsh enough."

Lydia's gray eyes turned wide with shock. "I guess I still cannae believe it. Flora Robertson. I fed her Gruyère."

At that, Paislee chuckled.

A light knock sounded and then Scott and Dr. Raj entered.

"Paislee," Dr. Raj greeted her with a clucking of his tongue as he saw her bloody shoulder.

She quickly gave him the watered-down version of what had happened.

"That's quite a tale. What's your pain level?"

She thought of saying five, but it had to be an eight, maybe nine. All she wanted to do was curl up and cry. "Six?"

"Liar," Lydia said. "She wants the good stuff, Doc. She helped catch a murderer, and I'm driving her home. She should be feeling no pain at all."

Scott hid a smile behind his clipboard.

Paislee heard what Lydia said. She'd helped catch Isla's killer. Billy's killer. A wave of pain traveled through her, and she swayed on the edge of the table.

Dr. Raj steadied her. "It's all right, now. Let's get you stitched up. You will have to take tomorrow off."

Paislee felt so terrible that the idea of staying in bed all day sounded like heaven. "I will."

"Now I know yer hurtin'." Lydia got up and offered her hand for Paislee to squeeze. "I'm here. Where's that shot, Doctor?"

By Tuesday evening, Paislee was well enough to get out of bed and eat dinner.

Lydia had hung up a sign on the door of Cashmere Crush saying that Paislee would return to work on Thursday, possibly Friday. They'd had a bit of an argument, but when Lydia brought her the fisherman's sweater to work on at home Paislee let it go and decided she could rest for another day.

Detective Inspector Zeffer had dropped by, but she'd been upstairs sleeping, so he'd left a card wishing her well.

Flora's arrest for Isla's murder was all over the news—Donnan was in the hospital under a doctor's care, and he was expected to slowly recover.

Mary Beth's husband's DUI was at the back of the paper, buried under the splash on Flora, Billy, and Isla. She'd received a flurry of texts she'd deal with later. Amelia'd sent a very long message, sharing that Norma had been meeting Isla for tea and conversation, without realizing that Isla was mining for blackmail tips. Detective Inspector Zeffer had put the poor woman on probation, but she was lucky to keep her job.

For now, Paislee, Brody, Grandpa, and Wallace sat around the kitchen table taking the final bites of their raspberry scones.

"Isla's funeral is tomorrow," Paislee said. "At seven. I think I'd like tae go."

Brody's protective instincts had been fired up over the stitches in Paislee's shoulder and the brace she was wearing again for the next few days after wrenching her sore muscles in the tussle with Flora. He didn't like for her to be out of his sight for too long.

"Why, Mum? She wasnae a nice person." Brody snuck a piece of scone to Wallace.

She'd thought long and hard about this, wrestling with this issue within herself. "Isla didnae have anybody in her corner, Brody. She'd had a bad hand dealt to her, but she also made poor choices. I dinnae condone her actions. Blackmailing people for money was wrong."

"I know!" Brody kicked his heel back against the chair leg once, then twice.

"Stop it," she said. "Otherwise, you'll be polishing the furniture."

Grandpa Angus chuckled. "Yer sounding more like your gran every day."

She met his gaze. "I asked myself what Gran would do in this situation. She was always compassionate toward her fellow man."

"Except fer me." Her grandpa scraped a wrinkled hand through his silver hair.

Someday Paislee would discover the truth behind their story, but for now she kept the topic on Isla, and right versus wrong.

"Granny said it was for God tae judge, not her. She taught me tae think the same, and that is why I am going tae be at Isla's funeral." She'd thought she'd seen herself in Isla, but in reality, she'd seen her worst fears personified.

"If she hadn't died, would you still be her friend?" Brody's quick glance made her realize that there was something else going on in her son's head.

"You mean, is it right tae be someone's friend even if you know they are doing something wrong?"

Brody's face paled beneath the freckles he'd gotten on Sunday.

Her grandfather scratched his silver beard, looking from her to Brody. "Hmm. Is it illegal, lad?"

Paislee shot her grandpa a look. "He's only ten!"

"Stealing," Brody said. "Crisps from the lunchroom."

"Ach." Grandpa Angus waved his hand dismissively. "That's— Ouch!"

Paislee kicked him again for good measure even though it pained her.

"That's wrong, no matter what," Grandpa amended.

"We don't steal." Paislee made sure that Brody was looking her in the eye when she said this.

"I dinnae do it," Brody said. "But I ken someone . . ." He hesitated. "If I say somethin', then they willnae be my friend anymore."

Paislee considered his dilemma. How best to answer so that it was helpful and he wouldn't be ostracized at school? She took a sip of tea and thought back honestly to what she would have done about Isla.

"If I had known that Isla was blackmailing people, I would not have hired her tae work for me at Cashmere Crush."

Brody scooted his chair back and helped Wallace onto his lap. The dog bared his belly for a good scratch, and Brody obliged.

Sensing that he needed a bit more explanation, she added, "I would have been forced tae see that she was not the person that I thought she was—and couldnac be a true friend tae me."

He rubbed Wallace's belly and the dog's tail wagged like crazy. Brody giggled but then exhaled as he looked up at her with understanding. "I dinnae want tae steal crisps in order tae be his friend. But I don't want to be a clipe, either. That's lame."

"Ye can't grass up on yer mates," Grandpa said.

"I agree," Paislee said. Brody'd been mature enough in bringing the problem to her—she wouldn't make him regret it. "How about I drop a word in with the headmaster?"

His face turned red and Wallace hopped down with a bark of alarm. "Ye can't do that, Mum!"

"Awright." She took another sip of tea. "What about an anonymous message?"

"What does that mean?"

"A note with no signature, dropped on the receptionist's desk."

"Why can't we ignore it?" He crossed his arms.

"Because it's wrong tae steal." Which he knew already, and why they were having this discussion in the first place.

"Can I tell them not tae do it anymore, and then we don't have to get them into trouble?" He pushed his empty dessert plate toward the center of the round table.

"First off, 'we' are not getting anybody into trouble. They are the ones doing the thieving." She was careful not to sound too harsh.

"I wish I didnae know about it."

"But you do. And because you do, ye cannae ignore it."

He stared gloomily at the tabletop for a few seconds. "I'll tell them not tae do it anymore or else I dinnae want tae be their friend."

It was her injured shoulder closest to him, so when she reached to ruffle his hair, she winced. He got off his chair and gave her a careful hug.

"I love you more than life itself, Brody." She looked into his eyes until he nodded. "You can always come tae me, and we'll figure things out." His announcement would, she hoped, stop the thievery, but she'd be sure to check back later. Good enough for now.

Brody's mood flashed bright again. "Can I be excused?"

"Aye."

He raced into the living room and turned on the telly.

She drank the last of her tea. "He's growing up so fast."

Her grandfather put the electric kettle on for more hot water. "Ye're doing just fine, lass. Just fine. I know your gran would be proud."

Paislee could feel Granny's warmth in this room around them. "I know she would be. I miss her, so much. And I think she would be okay that you're here now, too."

"Just until Craigh—"

"I know, I know. Just until we find out what happened tae your son. I promised tae help you, and I will."

The doorbell rang and Brody raced to answer it.

"Ask who it is first!" she yelled, following him down the hall from the kitchen. "Ye want someone tae nab you?"

Brody flung open the door, just missing her nose. "Sorry, Mum."

"I have half a mind, Brody, to—" She looked up into Hamish McCall's clean-shaven face and dark brown eyes.

"Is now a bad time?" he asked, looking at her brace and the bandage on her shoulder visible beneath her shirt. "I heard that you were involved in another accident, and I was just driving by, and . . ."

Driving by, was he?

Paislee waited at the door, very conscious of her neck brace and her mum jeans—but she'd ruined her best pair.

Brody held up his hands in surrender. "I swear I didnae steal the crisps."

Paislee opened the door wider, smiling at the confusion on the poor man's face. "You'd better come in. It's a long story. Can I get you a cup of tea?"

Connect with U s

Visit us online at
KensingtonBooks.com
to read more from your favorite authors, see books
by series, view reading group guides, and more.

 Join us on social media

for sneak peeks, chances to win books and prize packs,
and to share your thoughts with other readers.

facebook.com/kensingtonpublishing
twitter.com/kensingtonbooks

Tell us what you think!

To share your thoughts, submit a review,
or sign up for our eNewsletters, please visit:
KensingtonBooks.com/TellUs.